MY
HUSBAND'S
SECRET

BOOKS BY L.G. DAVIS

Liar Liar

Perfect Parents

The Stolen Breath

Don't Blink

The Midnight Wife

The Janitor's Wife

MY HUSBAND'S SECRET

L.G. DAVIS

bookouture

Published by Bookouture in 2022

An imprint of Storyfire Ltd.
Carmelite House
50 Victoria Embankment
London EC4Y 0DZ

www.bookouture.com

ISBN: 978-1-80314-673-7
eBook ISBN: 978-1-80314-672-0

This book is a work of fiction. Names, characters, businesses, organizations, places and events other than those clearly in the public domain, are either the product of the author's imagination or are used fictitiously. Any resemblance to actual persons, living or dead, events or locales is entirely coincidental.

Rhianna, my heart tells me this book is for you. Who am I to disagree?

CHAPTER 1

AVERY

After pulling off the white sheet from the massage table, I wipe my hands on it, removing every trace of oil from my palms. Almond, coconut, and lemongrass combine in the air to give it a calming scent. Although the massage session was only a few minutes long, I can still smell the musky perfume from my client's skin.

Celeste pokes her head through the door, her long-lashed, nut-brown eyes squinting. "That was a short one," she says with a wry smile on her face, as her tight brown curls bounce. "Didn't she like the massage?"

"Apparently she doesn't like being touched by strangers." I stifle a smile as I line the massage oils up next to each other in the glass cabinet.

Celeste crosses her arms, amused. "I don't get it. Why did she book a massage if she doesn't like to be touched?"

"She didn't." I sweep the white sheet to the side. "It was a birthday gift from her husband, and she didn't want to tell him how she felt."

"Well, I hope she at least enjoyed the calm ambience. You're so skilled at setting up this place. One step inside and people instantly relax." She tips her head back and sniffs the air. "This is how I imagine paradise smells, and it's so nice and cool in here. It's scorching outside."

"That's late June in Minnesota for you. But I don't care how hot it gets, I'll always choose summer over winter."

I smile as I take in my surroundings. The hanging plants, the potted flowers, and all of the other space-filling flora make the room feel like a tropical forest, far away from city life. Candles in glass jars scattered over the tables and shelves provide a sense of coziness and luxury amid the shadows. Sometimes when I'm stressed, I come to the parlor and sit in one of the rooms with my eyes closed. Little do I know that later, when I look back on this time, I'll see it as a brief moment of quiet before a storm hits. A storm that is already coming for me; one that will change everything forever.

"I cannot believe it's been a year already," I say. "Time sure flies."

"A year of being the best massage parlor in Willow Gate. We're still celebrating tonight, right?" Celeste's eyes twinkle. "Dinner at the Lobster Roll?"

"Absolutely. I look forward to it."

After a year of working our tails off to get Opal Touch on its feet, we do deserve a night out.

Celeste and I have been best friends since high school. We had an instant connection, because we both had parents who were largely absent from our lives.

While my parents have their own issues that prevented them from being fully present, Celeste's mother is a wealthy, narcissistic woman who was more concerned with her social standing than spending time with her daughter, and she bought expensive gifts to make up for her absence, particularly after Celeste's father died when she was ten. I had Ruth, my parents' neighbor and close friend, to help take care of me, but Celeste was raised by nannies.

So it's understandable that, other than the occasional text and email, Celeste does not have a close relationship with her mother, who lives in New York. But the huge checks continue to come every month, and Celeste gives most of the money to an orphanage and to charities geared toward helping children. She's vowed to be a better mother than her own, and seeing how loving and caring she is with my daughter, I have no doubt she will be.

As kids, we were so close, and we only separated when I left town to study marketing at the University of Minnesota while also taking a massage therapy course on the side. At the same time, Celeste left the country to study in France, where her late father originally came from.

My decision to study massage therapy was an easy one. A week before I turned fifteen, my parents and I had a huge argument that left me angry and frustrated. Ruth overheard it, and she gifted me a full body massage as an early birthday gift to help relieve me of some of the stress I was carrying. Lying on a massage table for the first time, listening to soft music and inhaling the soothing scents while the masseuse massaged away the tension in my shoulders and back, I felt almost like a weight had been lifted off me. And by the end of the session, I knew this was what I wanted to do for a living: help people break free of their stress and pain, even if just for an hour.

To our mutual delight, Celeste and I reconnected when we moved back to Willow Gate, four years later.

After offering French language classes to the locals and finding there was not enough demand, Celeste tried a few odd jobs before I infected her with my passion for massage and she signed up for an eight-month therapy course.

Meanwhile, I worked as a massage therapist at a local hotel while dreaming of having the money to start my own business.

By the time Celeste was done, she not only loaned me the money to start my business, she also offered to be my first employee.

I asked her to be a partner, but she declined, saying that she wanted to be able to go off chasing other dreams if she chose to do so.

Celeste grins at me. "I can't wait. We haven't gone out in a while. So, what are your plans for the rest of the day?"

I glance at my watch. "I have two more massages to give today, and then I have some interviews scheduled for the new masseuses."

"It's finally happening." Celeste holds up her hands and wriggles her fingers. "These babies are finally getting a much-needed break."

With only two massage tables and a lot of hope, Celeste and I started Opal as the only employees. Over the course of six months, we gave massages, manned the reception desk, and cleaned the rooms ourselves. Our receptionist Justine, who was once employed by the Sandbar Hotel across the street, joined our team four months ago. She often came in for lunchtime massages and was one of our most loyal clients.

Then, during one of her appointments on her days off, she asked if we needed a receptionist. Although we were not hiring, she made her offer on our busiest day and jumped right in, demonstrating what she was capable of. She was hired that day, and the following morning, she handed in her notice at the Sandbar. It was such a relief to have someone handle the phone and schedule appointments while Celeste and I focused on what we both loved most.

Justine enters the room now with her hair up in a loose bun, and in a hot pink blazer over a black dress; she looks lovely.

"Avery, I'm sorry for bothering you, but Mia's school is on the phone. It sounds urgent. They tried calling your cell, but they couldn't get through."

When she hands me the phone, I rush out of the room and into another massage room, closing the door behind me. My husband, Keith, should have already picked up Mia. Could he have been late? He works from home on Fridays, so he can't be at the office.

"Hello?" I say into the mouthpiece.

"Mrs. Watkins?"

"Yes, this is Avery."

"This is Principal Jordan. Sorry to bother you, but Mia still hasn't been picked up and we were unable to reach you or your husband on your cell phones."

"I'm so sorry. My husband was supposed to pick her up today. I don't understand."

There's one thing I know for sure about Keith, that he hates being late for anything. I was fifteen minutes late on our wedding day, nine years ago, and by the time I got there, he was a mess, as he had convinced himself that I had gotten cold feet and wouldn't attend.

"I'm afraid your husband didn't show up. We thought he might be running late, but it's been forty minutes."

A heavy feeling of anxiety begins to churn through me. "All right, I'll... I'll be there in twenty minutes."

I hang up and run back to the reception, and Celeste interrupts her conversation with a client. "Avery? Is everything all right?"

"I'm not sure. Mia's school called. Keith didn't pick her up." I grab my purse from the office and head for the door. "I have to go, I'll call you." I turn to Justine. "Please cancel my appointments for the day."

Minutes later, I drive out of the parlor's back parking lot and merge with the other cars on Willow Gate Boulevard.

Despite having a population of only fifteen thousand, the place can get quite busy, and when I reach a red traffic light, I pick up my phone, which was on silent. I missed two calls from Keith, two from my mother, and three from Mia's school. On speakerphone, I listen to the last message Keith left.

"Hey babe, please call me back. I need to talk to you about something. It's important."

My phone rings before I can call him, and it's my mother.

"Hey, Mom, I can't talk right now. I'm—"

"Is Mia with you?" she asks. Her voice sounds nervous, as if she's been crying, but that's not unusual. "Her school called to say she hadn't been picked up."

"I know. I'm on my way there now. Keith was supposed to pick her up. I'm not sure what happened." The light turns green, and I accelerate. "Mom, I need to go. I want to try calling Keith."

"You must be so busy with work. Are you sure I shouldn't ask Ruth to go instead?"

"It's okay, Mom. I'm closer to the school and can get there before her."

Ruth is Mia's godmother and very much like my second mother, always ready to drop everything to be there for me. I know she wouldn't hesitate to jump in to help, but then Mia would have to wait too long as Ruth and my parents live forty minutes away from the school. My parents were very often late picking me up from school, so I always try to be there on time for my daughter.

I'm thirty-five now, but not much has changed with my parents. My father, Harry, still drinks as if someone pays him to do it, and my mother, Jodie, is still too terrified of having a panic attack behind the wheel. It made it quite difficult for them to hold down jobs in the past.

When her head is clear, my mother makes quilts and sells them in her spare time, and when my father is sober, he helps her with the accounting. They had a small amount of family inheritance that kept them going all these years, and they keep their costs low. But I know they've been struggling often, and Keith and I have had to help them out on more than one occasion.

I hang up and dial Keith's number, but he doesn't pick up. When I arrive at the school, he still hasn't returned my call, but I don't have time to wonder about where he is. Exiting my car, I rush into Willow Gate Elementary School, a white-washed building that has been there since the town was established. Besides an old oak tree in the middle of the school yard, it has a small playground with a swing set, a jungle gym, and a metal slide. Most kids have already been picked up, and my daughter is sitting on the school doorstep next to her class teacher, Miss Simmons.

I run up to the two of them, kneeling in front of Mia. "I'm sorry you waited so long, sweetheart. Are you okay?" I brush fine flyaway strands of her black hair from her face and gaze into her wide hazel eyes. Now seven years old, she's starting to look more and more like her father.

Nodding, she replies, "Miss Simmons was keeping me company."

"I'm so sorry." I look up at my daughter's teacher. "I thought my husband was going to be here. Something must have come up."

"That's all right." The petite woman with ringlets of golden hair and doe-like eyes gets to her feet and smiles at me. "It's never happened before."

I turn to Mia and put my arm around her shoulders. "Let's go. We'll stop by the store and get you some caramel cheesecake. How does that sound?"

"Yay! That sounds too good." She jumps off the step and runs toward my parked car as I thank Miss Simmons again.

With Mia clutching a white box full of cheesecake, we turn into our street. And then all at once, I know everything has changed.

I don't know how—I don't want to think about how—but as soon as I see the squad car parked up front, I know deep in my soul that the very earth I'm standing on has changed, forever.

A heavy-set policeman with dark shades and a baseball cap opens the cruiser's door. "Mrs. Watkins?"

"Yes," I say, my voice high and strange. "Avery Watkins."

He nods and looks down at Mia, who's gazing up at him with her big eyes. "Do you mind if I have a quick chat with your mother?"

"About what?" Mia asks, and I shake my head at her discreetly.

"Officer, please come in," I say, my voice shaking.

As I try to open the door, my hands tremble so much that the officer takes the keys from me and unlocks the door himself. While Mia runs to her room to change out of her school clothes, the man asks me to take a seat in my own sitting room.

"Mrs. Watkins, I'm so sorry to tell you this, but your husband was involved in a terrible accident."

As the man's words ricochet around my mind, nausea rises in my stomach and I stare into his eyes, waiting for him to say it's all a joke. A sick, twisted joke. Anything but what he just said. But he does not.

"I'm sorry," he says instead.

My stomach clenches and I hear myself taking a deep breath in. The air feels thick and my ears are ringing. The officer continues to speak to me, but I can't make out the words. It's as if he's speaking another language, one I can't translate.

"What happened to my husband?" I manage to ask finally, the words like sandpaper in my throat.

He leans back and exhales loudly. "I'm very sorry to tell you this, but he was hit by a car."

CHAPTER 2

I cannot take Mia to the hospital until I know the extent of Keith's injuries, so I drop her off at the parlor on the way there, where Celeste takes her away from me.

"I don't know how long I'll be," I say, choking over my words. "In case it takes too long, you can drop her off at my parents' or at Ruth's."

"You don't need to worry, Avery. Do what you have to do." She pulls Mia close to her body as my little girl looks up at me with questions pooling in her eyes. "If she needs to spend the night, so be it. We'll have a fun pajama party together, won't we, Mia?"

Mia doesn't respond; she knows something is wrong. Just a few minutes ago she asked why I was crying, and I tried to explain but couldn't get the words out. I don't know what I'm going to do.

"I'll see you later, baby." I kiss her on the forehead and get back into the car.

At Willow Gate Memorial Hospital, a doctor takes me aside and tells me that Keith is in surgery and his condition is critical.

He may not survive his injuries. The very words I dreaded most.

Catching my breath in the waiting room, I see another police officer seated in one of the chairs. He has dark hair with dirt-colored curls that fall softly on his forehead, and his nose has a faint scar running down its middle. Often filled with humor, his deep brown eyes now glisten with emotion.

"Liam?" I say, and he stands up to pull me into a hug as tears well up in my eyes.

"I'm so sorry, Avery. I'm so sorry."

Liam Wright is one of Willow Gate's police officers and Keith's closest friend. With his wife, Lucy, and their two sons, we've gone on several family excursions together, and they've come to our house for birthday parties and barbecues over the years.

"I don't understand," I say weakly. "I don't understand what happened. The other police officer said he was on his bike when a car hit him."

We both have cars, but Keith prefers to cycle everywhere, especially when it's hot and humid. The hottest month in Willow Gate is July. On the last Friday in June, the temperatures have already started climbing and there's nothing Keith hates more than feeling trapped in a car when he could be out enjoying the fresh air. Who would have thought that while riding his beloved bike on a beautiful summer day, he'd be hit by a car and end up in the intensive care unit?

Liam nods in agreement. "Yeah, that's what happened. I don't want you to be hurt more than you already are, but it was a hit-and-run."

I'm filled with rage, instant and burning. Why would anyone do such a thing? Who would hurt an innocent man and leave him to die on the street?

"Oh my God," I say, my voice quivering as the pit of my stomach turns cold and hard. "Are there any witnesses?"

Liam's face wrinkles in pain. "Not really," he says. "Keith was found lying on the side of the road by the man who called in the accident. The driver who hit him was already gone."

"He didn't see the car, then?"

"Unfortunately, no." Liam reaches for my hand. "We will track down the person responsible for this, Avery, and they will pay for what they did."

I nod slowly, mechanically, in response. "Liam... I'm scared. What if Keith doesn't make it?"

"You know as well as I do that Keith hates losing." He chuckles despite the pain. "He won't give up on life easily."

Although I manage a small smile, I have difficulty believing him.

"The doctors are doing everything they can," Liam continues.

"Do you know if he was still conscious when he was brought to the hospital?"

"No." He shakes his head. "I don't know."

After sitting in silence for another forty minutes, Liam tells me he has to get back to work.

"I'll just go take care of some things. I'll be back later. Please call me when you know more."

I nod and squeeze his hand. "Thanks, Liam."

A sad smile spreads across his face. "I hate that you're alone. Maybe you should call one of your friends to be here with you."

"I will," I promise him.

He leaves and I sit and stare at the clock on the wall. I feel the need to do something, anything, but I don't know what.

Then it occurs to me that Keith's family, two cousins, and his uncle Norman in South Dakota, have not been notified. Keith has had a strained relationship with his uncle for years. They used to be close when he was growing up, but then Keith's father died and left his business, Oak Tree Landscapers, and everything he owned to him instead of Norman, who wanted it all for himself.

The only time I saw Norman was at our wedding nine years ago. To my knowledge, it's also the last time Keith saw him. When Mia was born, we called to let him know and invited him to come and see her, but he never showed up. But he's still Keith's family, and he deserves to know. I pick up my phone and dial his number.

Despite the tragic news, he doesn't seem particularly upset, and it breaks my heart when, after a long silence, he asks, "So, what do you want from me, Avery?"

"Are you serious?" I ask in a low, tight voice. "Your nephew is in the hospital, and you're asking me what I want from you?"

"You heard me right," he says mockingly. "If it's money you want for his medical care, I don't have it since everything my brother owned, he left to Keith."

I clench my fist tight around my phone, fighting and failing to keep my anger at bay. "You know what, Norman? I'm sorry I called. I thought that maybe you had a heart. I guess I was wrong." I cut the phone because right now, I wouldn't want the man's toxic energy around Keith when all he needs is support.

I do feel better after calling Keith's cousin, Silas, who, unlike his father, promises to come and see Keith as soon as possible in the next few days.

"Julius won't be able to make it. He moved to Italy two years ago. But I'll share the news with him."

"Thank you, Silas. I'll keep you updated."

My body and mind are numb. I shove my head between my knees and try not to think about my husband's broken body lying in the middle of the road.

Keith is in surgery for two more hours without me receiving an encouraging word from anyone. I don't call my parents or Ruth because I don't know what to tell them. As exhaustion falls over me, I lean my head against the wall, closing my eyes.

I'm trying to rest, I know I need to, but my mind refuses to shut off. Minutes later, I'm startled by a warm hand on my shoulder, and a red-headed nurse tells me Keith made it through surgery and is now on the third floor.

"May I see him?" I ask, pushing to my feet.

"I'm sorry, but he's heavily sedated and out of it completely. I can take you to him, but I worry he won't be able to communicate with you."

"It's fine. My husband needs me right now, and I need to be with him."

She nods. "Come along with me."

We walk silently to the third floor, passing rooms and corridors filled with people moaning in pain, murmured conversations, doctors walking purposefully around.

The nurse points to the end of the long hallway. "He's in the last room on the right. He will remain in the ICU for at least the next twenty-four hours."

"Thank you," I whisper and walk away.

Keith's room is sterile white, the linoleum floor hard under my feet. The walls are naked, there are no pictures or paintings, and the lighting is cold and harsh. Beeps and whirrs fill the room, stealing the sounds of the laughter we've shared over the years. He's hooked up to a bunch of life-support equipment, and his face is bruised and swollen. As I rush to his side, I feel a weight on my chest, so heavy it threatens to crush me. I hold on to the bed rails for support as I lean in close. Under my hands, the metal feels hard and cold. The sheets are soft and smooth, but the hospital bed is stiff and cheap.

I stare at the face of the man I love, the man who was supposed to spend the rest of his life with me. His eyes are closed, and his head and left hand are a mass of bandages and gauze. Only the lower part of his face isn't bandaged, and as I take in the bruises covering his forehead, cheeks, and chin, I struggle to hold it together. His eyelids are caked with dried blood, and his lips are cracked. Before he was pumped with medication, he must have been in a great deal of pain.

Although I want to touch him, I'm afraid of causing him more pain, so I hold on to his right hand. It's still warm and soft, and tears well up in my eyes as soon as I feel his skin on mine, a sharp ache spreading through my chest. Before I know it, I'm sobbing uncontrollably.

There are many things I would like to say to Keith right now, but I'm not sure how to begin. As I feel an overwhelming sense of helplessness, rage soon overtakes me. I want to punch and scream at something, to do anything to relieve this feeling of impotence I have. The burden of my weakness is overwhelming me, and I am close to breaking down completely.

Keith has always been the stronger one, and I feel like I'm just not able to handle this situation on my own. Right now, I feel incapable of doing anything but cry.

In an effort to get closer, I rest my head gently on his chest. My head rises and falls with his breath as I remain in that position for a little while, and my eyes only open when I hear a broken whisper. As I glance up, I see his eyes flutter open.

"Ave..."

Holding my breath, I cup his face in my hands. "Yes, sweetheart. I'm here for you. Fight for us, okay?" I kiss his cheek and run my fingers through his hair.

His lips part, close, and part again. He's trying to tell me something but can't find the strength.

"Baby, you don't need to speak," I say through my tears. "You're okay. You're going to be okay, you hear me?"

His fingers encircle my hand. He has an unusually firm grip for a man in critical condition.

"I..." he murmurs. Clearly struggling to breathe, his voice trails off.

I take a deep breath to collect myself before I lean closer to him.

"I took..." His breath is ragged, and I have to strain to hear him. "I took a life."

Trying to conceal the fear and confusion in my voice, I say, "Keith, no, that's not true. The medication is making you confused." I want to believe that I misheard, but the words he just spoke were clear and their meaning sends a sudden jolt of terror through me. I feel as if my entire body is going numb and my hands feel suddenly cold.

Keith tries to shake his head, but he's too weak and the effort is futile. "True," he murmurs and a tear rolls down his cheek.

Dread grips my body and I shake my head. "Oh my God, baby, you're so confused. You didn't hurt anyone. It's you that got hurt." I'm trying to convince myself as much as him.

It has to be the medication clouding his judgment, and once it wears off, he will tell me it was all a mistake.

So why is my stomach knotting up with fear?

Keith is trying to speak to me again, but he has trouble getting the words out. Then, suddenly, a calmness falls over his features and he closes his eyes.

CHAPTER 3

As I'm walking back to the waiting room, my legs stumbling one in front of the other, I hold the phone close to my ear. I know I should call my mother first, but I don't. Instead, I call Ruth, who answers immediately.

"Keith is in the hospital," I croak. "He was hit by a car."

"Oh my God," she whispers down the line. "That's just awful. How is he?"

"He came out of surgery a while ago, but he's still in critical condition. I don't know what to do, Ruth." I swipe at the fresh tears threatening to spill out of my eyes. "The doctors don't know if he will make it. I don't…" The words get stuck in my throat.

"Oh, Avery. I'm so sorry, my dear girl. Do you want me to drive up to the hospital?"

I shake my head. "No… I don't know. No, it's fine." I can't think straight enough to make even simple decisions right now. Even if she comes, what can she do? She can't take away the pain or the fear raging through me.

"Okay, I'll keep my phone close if you need to talk, darling. Have you told your parents?"

"Not yet," I say. "Please don't say anything. I'll call them now." I wouldn't want my parents to find out that I had called their neighbor first, even if they have long accepted her as my third parent. I hang up and call my mom, but before long she's sobbing so hard that my dad takes the phone from her. His words slur together as he also offers to drive up, but we both know that he's not fit to drive. My father's addiction, which I have witnessed for as long as I can remember, is so unwavering that we've had to accept it as part of our lives and work around it.

"Oh no, Avery," Celeste says when I call her after ending the call with my parents. "Are you okay? I'm so sorry, sweetie."

"Thank you," I say, a sob escaping me. "I just can't believe this... that this is happening. I feel like I'm stuck in a nightmare." I don't tell her that my husband is not only in a grave condition but he also just confessed to killing someone. How can I possibly make sense of that? How can this be my reality?

"You should let me take care of Mia the next few days," Celeste says, her voice trembling.

"No, you don't need to do that," I say, feeling misty and out of touch, as if I'm floating on a sea of nothingness. "I'll be fine. At least, I'll try to be."

"But you will need help looking after her while Keith is in the hospital..." Her voice trails off. "I'll take good care of her."

"I know you will." I let out a quivering breath. "But, Celeste... I don't want to trouble you."

"Trouble? Avery, I want to do this for you. Please let me help. You're going through a lot, so you won't be fully present for Mia. She will need someone to make her feel comfortable and safe. You can't be taking her to the hospital with you; it might upset her to see Keith hurt."

"That's true." I wipe tears from my eyes. "I can't thank you enough for offering. And you're already helping a lot by keeping her tonight. I might need you tomorrow evening when you've finished work, but I'll confirm with you later when I'm able to think straight."

"Sure, no problem at all. It's my pleasure to be there for you and Mia."

"I'm so grateful for you," I whisper, the lump in my throat making it hard for me to speak. It's good to know that Mia is in safe hands for at least one night.

I hang up the phone and take a deep breath to try and slow my heartbeat, before calling Liam to update him on Keith's condition. As I speak to him, I try to control my panic, but my mind is whirling and my body feels stiff and heavy.

The last person I call is Drake, Keith's right-hand man at his landscaping company. Drake will need to deal with the business for a while when Keith is unable to do so.

"This is so painful to hear, Avery," Drake says with a quavering voice. "Please do not worry about the business. I'll take care of it all. Just focus on Keith, yourself, and Mia. If you need anything else, please call. I'll drop by the hospital tomorrow to see Keith."

My eyes well up with tears as I thank Drake for being willing to step in. "I can't thank you enough for your help."

Finally done with the calls, I sink into a plastic chair in the waiting room, next to a woman with a young girl about Mia's age. The little girl is wearing a purple princess dress and is watching cartoons on the woman's phone while the woman flips through a magazine. As I watch them, I wonder if she's the mother, and if she's raising her daughter on her own. I cannot bear to imagine my life without Keith.

I need to stop doing this to myself. I can't allow myself to think like that.

On the other side of the room, a woman with blue hair is reading a dog-eared health magazine, her legs crossed at the ankles. Despite the sounds from the other people in the waiting room, it's eerily quiet, a bit like a church. People come and go, but no one updates me on Keith's status.

I pick up a local newspaper and flip through the pages, hoping it will distract me. It doesn't work; no matter how hard I try, I can't forget the image of Keith lying helpless in that hospital bed, and I can't forget the words he said to me. I have to believe it was the medication talking. I need to believe that.

I drop the newspaper again, gaze out the window, and watch people passing by, hurrying along in the evening rush. Over the city, ominous dark clouds have formed and the first raindrops hit the glass as thunder rumbles in the distance.

The hours pass slowly until finally a doctor with a trim mustache and thick glasses approaches and gestures to me. I walk over to him, my legs leaden.

"Mrs. Watkins, I'm very sorry to tell you that your husband is in a coma," he says gently. "He suffered a hemorrhage in his brain."

He proceeds to explain to me exactly how his head and brain were impacted, but all the medical jargon is beyond me and I only need to know one thing. "Will he wake up? Is he going to be okay?"

"I'm afraid I cannot tell you that just yet. We'll have to wait and see. But I can assure you that we're doing everything we can for him. We'll run several more tests and monitor his progress. I'll update you in the morning."

I drop my face into my hands and let a few sobs escape before I look back up at the doctor. "Can I spend the night here?"

"I wouldn't recommend it. You should go home and get some rest, and we'll call you if there are any changes in his condition."

"Okay," I whisper. "Thank you."

The doctor gives me a sympathetic smile before he turns and walks away.

I don't want to leave my husband, but I have to think about Mia. She still doesn't know what happened to her father. I feel torn, caught between the desire to be with my daughter, to hug and kiss her, to read her a bedtime story, and my burning need to stay with Keith. With a heavy heart, I pick up my phone and call Celeste to tell her I'm on my way to pick up Mia. I can't withhold the news from her any longer.

An hour later, Mia and I open the door to our house, and I sit her down on my lap.

"Honeybee, there's something I need to tell you. It's about Daddy."

As I explain what happened to Keith in simple words that a child can understand, her eyes grow wide and fill with tears.

"But he'll come home?" she asks, putting her head on my chest as she sobs.

"Not tonight, baby. He needs to stay at the hospital to rest before he comes back home."

She rubs her eyes with her fists and looks up at me. "But Mommy, it was his turn to read me a goodnight story."

"I know, baby," I say, stroking her hair and trying hard to keep my dam of tears from breaking. "But he can't come home tonight. He's in a coma."

"What's a coma?" she asks, her face crumpled with worry.

I immediately regret telling her that. How does one explain a coma to a seven-year-old?

"It's like sleeping, honeybee," I say. "He needs to rest for a few days, and when he wakes up, he'll come home to us."

Still staring at me, she tries to piece what I've said together and stares at me like she's figuring out whether I'm telling her the truth or not. Then she takes a deep breath, her shoulders rising and falling softly. "But he will wake up, right, Mommy?"

"I don't know... I mean, I hope so." I give myself an inward kick. I shouldn't have said that.

Her brow furrows. "You mean Daddy might not wake up?"

That's a horrible question to answer, so I take the easy way out. "He will wake up. We just have to pray for him."

"Will he die and go to heaven?"

"No, he won't," I say too quickly, not wanting the thought to sink into her little head. "He's staying right here with us on earth. The doctors will take very good care of him, and he'll be well soon."

Mia sighs and cranes her neck to look at me. "Is Daddy going to wake up tomorrow?"

"Yes, honeybee, he'll wake up tomorrow," I say, hoping that by putting the words out there, they will come true.

I feel myself breaking inside, but I have to stay strong for my daughter. She needs me now more than ever. But how will I be able to be there fully for her when I can barely stop myself from falling apart?

"Okay." Mia wipes her tears with the back of her hand and wraps her little arms around me. "Don't be sad, mommybee."

"As long as you're here with me, I won't be," I say, clearing my throat. "How about we do something fun tonight?"

I glance up at the clock above the flatscreen TV, and it's already 7 p.m.

"Like what?" she asks, then her eyes light up. "Can we play with your makeup?"

"It's a little too late for that, sweetie." I pull her in closer to me. "But since you couldn't have a pajama party with Celeste today, how about you have it with me instead? We'll eat pizza for dinner, ice cream with sprinkles for dessert, and read a really long princess bedtime story."

"I like that idea, mommybee."

"Good. Go on and put your jammies on then."

Squealing, she bounces off my lap and runs to her room,

and I take a deep breath, blinking back my tears. No matter how hard it is, right now my job is to make sure my daughter doesn't know how terrified I am. We eat the ice cream and pizza together, then after she begs me to, I paint her nails a clear color and let her put on an avocado mask and cool cucumber eye pads. Playing dress-up and trying out my things is one of Mia's favorite things to do, particularly when I do her hair and makeup and we have a fashion show. Sometimes she likes to pretend I'm the child and she's the mom. Since so much of my own childhood is a blur, I always make an effort to create happy, positive memories for my daughter. I think that, what with my father's drinking and my mother's illness, I have blocked out a lot of unpleasant memories along with the happy ones.

I *do* feel guilty for planning a fun night when Keith is in the hospital, but I tell myself if my prayers are not answered and he doesn't wake up, soon I will have to break my daughter's heart. I want to treasure this happy moment with her before her life changes forever. But I still pray that day will never come.

Finally, we settle into her bed, and I read a story about a princess who rides a unicorn. Mia is asleep when I reach the part where the unicorn flies, and after closing the book, I set it down on the nightstand and watch her sleep. Her lips are slightly parted, and she's breathing evenly. With her soft strands of dark hair framing her face, she looks like an angel. It's hard to believe that she will turn eight in just a couple of months.

She was a very easy-going baby, and at this moment I wish she still was. Then I wouldn't have to tell her why her daddy is in the hospital, that it's possible he won't live to celebrate her next birthday. I kiss her cheek, switch the light off and tiptoe out of the room. I know I won't be able to sleep myself, so I go to the kitchen to put the leftovers of our pizza dinner in the fridge and throw away the empty ice cream containers. But it doesn't stop there. Suddenly, I'm on a cleaning spree, washing the dishes, scrubbing the already clean kitchen counter and floor, tidying up the living room and putting away toys, and throwing in a load of laundry.

When there's nothing left to do, I slouch down next to the couch and deep, heavy sobs burst from me. There's no point in trying to hold them back. All of it comes spilling out, the anger I feel toward the person who ran over my husband, the unbearable pain that has filled my chest since I received the news, the aching fear of losing him. I feel crippled, and I'd like nothing more than to escape this nightmare. But there's no way out.

Two hours later, when I lie in my bed, I feel like I'm sinking into a pit of despair. Without thinking, and out of habit, I pick up my phone and speed dial Keith's number, and it's only when his voicemail picks up that I remember. He's in a coma and can't speak to me. He can't comfort me like he usually would, not when we're on two opposite sides of consciousness.

I toss my phone on the side table, and burrow my face into the pillow. Just as I fall into a slumber, I remember Keith's words.

"I took a life."

I'm positive that he was not aware of what he was saying, but despite my longing for him to wake up and return to us, part of me is scared that he will repeat those words.

What secrets could my husband be hiding?

CHAPTER 4

The doorbell rings, and I sit up in bed. My head is pounding, and I feel completely exhausted. I *did* sleep, but my body still feels like a wrung-out rag. I go to the door, pushing my hair out of my face, then I take a deep breath and unlock it.

Ruth is standing in front of me looking pale and wan, with her green eyes dimmer than usual and the faint lines around them deeper somehow. She's wearing a moss-green, shapeless dress with a white lace collar.

Before I can speak, she grabs me and pulls me close to her. She smells like vanilla lotion and the hairspray that always works overtime to keep her gray-streaked, mousy-brown hair—that's currently styled in a 1960s bouffant hairdo—in place.

In the comfort of her arms, I can't stop myself from bursting into tears. I'm still finding it hard to believe that Keith is in a coma, hit by someone who doesn't give a damn about anyone except themselves.

"Hush now, my dear Avery. Everything will be all right, you'll see." Her hands run up and down my back, soothing and consoling me as she did when I was a kid.

After what seems like an hour, she leads me to the couch, and hands me a tissue.

"I'm sorry. I'm a mess," I say, and she shakes her head.

"Don't apologize. You're going through a lot."

I nod and press the tissue to my sore eyes to soak up the tears. "Ruth, you didn't have to drive all this way."

She waves her hand in the air, dismissing my words. "Nonsense, child. I wanted to see for myself how you're holding up. I didn't mind the drive." She brings a hand to my cheek. "I did want to bring your mother along, but she took one of her pills last night and could not get out of bed. Poor Jodie. The news hit her pretty hard."

I stare at my hands, my eyes and throat burning. "At least you're here."

"You know I'll always come running when you need me."

"I know. Thank you so much. I have to go to the hospital soon to check on Keith. Do you think you can stay with Mia? She's still sleeping."

Ruth claps her hands together. "I'd be delighted to, as always. She's my godchild. But you seem like you're in dire need of a cup of coffee, my dear."

"I think I am," I admit, "but I don't have the energy to make one."

I'm so relieved that Ruth is here and I don't have to take Mia to the hospital with me.

Like a battery-operated toy, Ruth jumps up from the couch. "I'll make us both a cuppa. Leave everything to me. You take a shower and prepare yourself to go to the hospital."

Even in her early sixties, Ruth is as energetic as ever and I'm very glad she came to use some of her energy on me because I've run out, frankly.

"Go on, child," she pushes. "Do what you have to do." Her voice is as chirpy as always, but it doesn't cheer me up this time.

In the bathroom, I stare at myself in the mirror. I look like a wreck, almost unrecognizable. My long, black hair is tangled, my face pale and haggard, and my brown eyes are small red balls with dark circles underneath them. In an attempt to feel alive again, I step into the shower and turn it on almost to the hottest setting. The water feels wonderful on my skin, and I tilt my head back and allow it to hit my face and soak into my hair before it falls onto my back and shoulders. Though the heat soothes my muscles, it doesn't empty my mind and I can't stop thinking about Keith. Will I ever hear his voice again, his laughter? How can I live without him?

I stand under the water spray until my skin is flushed, my head pounding from my tears. As I step out of the shower, a cool breeze caresses my skin and I dry myself off with a towel, putting on a pair of jeans and a white sleeveless shirt that I tuck in at my waist.

Somehow, I'm still going through the motions even though all I really want to do is curl up in that bed with Keith and never leave his side.

I find Ruth sitting at the kitchen table, sipping her coffee and reading the paper. The air smells of pancakes, coffee, and her hairspray.

"There you are, dear. This is for you." She hands me a cup of fragrant coffee and sits down next to me.

"Thank you, Ruth. I'm so glad you're here."

She smiles and reaches for a plate with pancakes stacked on it. "Eat something. You'll probably be at the hospital for hours, and hospital cafeteria food doesn't have a taste. I remember living on it when Elijah was near the end."

Elijah was Ruth's late husband, and he died years ago. She would be all alone, but she's become like family to us.

I take a sip from the cup and swallow the scalding liquid. "I'm afraid I'm not that hungry." I feel like crying again, but I'm too tired to shed more tears.

"Nonsense. It's just pancakes. You don't need to be hungry to enjoy comfort food." She narrows her eyes, the wrinkles deepening in her cheeks, then she gives me a sad smile. "I know this is a hard time for you, dear. But you're a strong girl. You'll get through it." She pushes the plate toward me until the aroma drifts into my nostrils. "Go ahead, take a bite."

Since she's made such an effort, I pick one up and take a bite of the pancake. It tastes wonderful, but I only manage a few bites and swallow them down with coffee. Then I push my chair back, steeling myself for the day ahead.

"I need to go. I'm not sure how long I'll be."

She squeezes my hand with both of hers and looks into my eyes. "Stay as long as you need to. Mia and I will be just fine."

For a second, I remember how I used to wish she were really my mother as a child. As always, she's here for me now when I need her most, filling the role my mother never could.

"Thank you," I whisper again.

"No need for that." She pauses. "Do you mind if I take her home with me for the day? I know your mother would be happy to see her. I could also keep her for the night, if you like. She hasn't slept over in a while."

"I know, but I think I want to spend the evening with her. But you can definitely spend the day together. I'll pick her up in the late afternoon."

I suddenly feel the driving urge to sleep under the same roof as my daughter tonight—in our home—to hold her tight when she falls asleep, to comfort her as much as she comforts me.

I make a mental note to call Celeste on the way to the hospital to let her know she's off the hook as well, for today at least.

"All right then," Ruth says. "But if you change your mind, just call. Now you better get on your way."

"What would I do without you, Ruth?" I wrap my arms around her, and she hugs me back before pulling away.

"You'd be just fine. Go on and see your husband, and let's pray good news awaits you." She shoos me out of the kitchen.

Before I leave, I go and kiss Mia. Since she went to bed later than usual, she's still sleeping, wrapped around a giant giraffe Keith won for her at the Willow Gate annual fair. I press my lips to her forehead and stay like that for a few seconds until she stirs.

"Honeybee, Mommy's going to see Daddy. Be a good girl for Ruth, okay?" She murmurs something unintelligible in her sleep, and I kiss her again and whisper, "I love you."

I walk out of her room and quietly shut the door behind me. Ruth's in the living room, tidying an already tidy place.

"I'll see you later, Ruth. Thanks again."

"Stop thanking me. It's the least I can do."

Grabbing my purse, I smile weakly and step out the door. The hospital is not too far from my place, but I still have to drive for twenty minutes before I arrive. I'm dreading seeing Keith hooked up to machines. But more than that, I'm dreading walking into his room to find that he is not miraculously awake, like I dreamed last night.

In my dream, he was sitting up in bed, gray-skinned and shaken, but healthy and waiting for me to take him home. Since his mother died from stomach cancer when he was sixteen, he's had a solid aversion to hospitals because he spent so many unhappy hours there as a teenager. I know that he would want to leave here as soon as he could.

Inside the ward, I head over to speak to one of the nurses.

"Hi, I'm Avery Watkins. I'm here to see Keith Watkins. He's my husband."

The nurse checks her computer and nods. "He's just been moved to room twenty-six."

"How is he? Can I see him?"

My heart drops as she tells me that he's still in a coma, but I can see him.

As I reach room twenty-six, I stop in front of the door and take a deep breath.

Inside, an ER nurse is checking Keith's vitals, and she looks up and smiles at me. "Hello there, are you his wife?"

I swallow hard and nod.

She glances at his chart and then looks at me with concern. "Mrs. Watkins, I'm so sorry this has happened. Your husband sustained serious head trauma, but he's lucky to be alive. The good news is that he's stable." She pats my shoulder. "I'll leave you alone now. If you need anything, just call. I'll be right outside."

I take a seat and gaze at Keith.

"Hey, baby. I'm back." I touch his hand. "I don't know if you can hear me. Can you let me know if you can, please, somehow?"

I focus my gaze on his face and wait for a flicker of his eyelashes or a slight movement in his fingers. But his eyes are still, closed and puffy, and there's no sign at all that he can hear me. After a while, the same doctor from yesterday comes in to tell me that if Keith doesn't wake up today, he might be in a coma for a while longer.

"It's a good thing. The brain needs lots of rest during healing." He smiles at me. "We'll keep an eye on him."

I nod, unable to speak as I hold back tears, afraid that if I start crying I might never stop. While the doctor is talking, I stare at the ventilator, the only thing keeping my husband alive.

A few hours later I leave the hospital, and there's still no change in Keith's condition. Even though I hate the idea, I'll have to bring Mia to see him.

Liam calls me when I'm in the car. "I'm so sorry, Avery. We still haven't found the person who ran Keith down," he says and when I end the call I finally break down, my tears turning the steering wheel into a blur.

Stopping the car at the side of the road, I bang my head against the wheel in rage and despair. I don't know what to do, I feel so lost and alone. I love Keith with every fiber of my being. He is the person I trust most in the whole world. How will I survive if he doesn't make it?

CHAPTER 5

THE WATCHER

Almost every day I watch them, sometimes in broad daylight and sometimes at night, keeping my distance, but never too far away. It's Saturday evening, and Avery brought her daughter Mia to the hospital today to visit her father, a day after his accident. I don't approve of the visit; it would obviously be traumatizing for any child.

After watching them walking toward the hospital doors, I'm now waiting outside, dreading what Mia must be going through right now. I want to go in there to tell Avery to get the child out, that she's doing more damage than good by bringing her to a place where people are dying and in pain.

But all I can do is watch from the shadows. I can't interfere, not yet. No one can know I'm watching.

After a long time they're back outside the hospital in the car park where I can see them, and I manage to get close enough to hear their conversation.

"Is Daddy going to die?" Mia asks, but Avery doesn't answer; tears are running down her cheeks.

Mia can't take it anymore and starts to cry too. My heart

goes out to the child. She must feel so lost and abandoned, caught between her father's fight against death and her mother's grief. Instead of watching her father dying, she should be playing, happy and laughing somewhere, protected from this pain.

Avery just stands there shaking her head, her face filled with guilt.

"Daddy will be all right," Avery finally says, trying to reassure Mia, stroking her hair away from her face. "The doctors are doing everything they can to make him better."

She keeps talking to Mia in an attempt to calm her down, but the little girl doesn't respond. It's unbearably painful watching helplessly from here, unable to go over and comfort Mia. Minutes pass, but they seem like hours before Avery eventually succeeds in making Mia stop crying, and the two of them get into their car.

I follow them home.

As the sun begins to set in the shadows, spreading golden fingers across the horizon, I continue watching Mia through their windows, when I can see her. While her mother is crying in the kitchen, the girl is watching TV and playing with her toys, all alone. I realize more and more as I watch her that nothing is okay. Her behavior isn't normal for a healthy, happy child. There's no life in her eyes, no spark in her soul. To make her mother happy, she's just going through the motions, pretending.

I'm furious that she's going through this. Her mother has the power to stop her child's suffering, but, instead, she continues to ignore her, focusing on her own pain, too lost in her misery to see that her daughter needs her. Parents' needs should never come before the children's, and Avery seems to have forgotten that.

I watch as shadows grow around the house and darkness creeps in, and I wait all night for Avery's bedroom light to go out. I hope Mia is dreaming peacefully, finding some relief at least in sleep. I'm determined to make sure she is protected from the cruelties of the world while she's an innocent child, to make sure no one ever hurts her.

I think of myself like her guardian angel, there to watch and protect. I will never be far away.

CHAPTER 6

AVERY

A child is screaming, a high-pitched screech that startles me awake, but I'm so wrapped up in sleep that it takes me a few minutes to realize that it's Mia. I jump out of bed and, in a sleepy haze, I stumble across the hall to her room. When I switch on the light, I see her sitting up in her bed, crying, her fists bunched up at her sides, her eyes wide, her face red and sweaty. She doesn't even seem to notice me. I rush to the bed and pull her into my arms, holding her tightly against my chest, but she continues to cry, her body shaking with each sob.

"Daddy," she keeps repeating along with something else I can't make out.

"Shh, honey, it was just a bad dream," I whisper.

She opens her wet eyes and looks into mine. "I saw Daddy." Her voice is hoarse from crying. "He was in the dark. He wanted to come home." Another wave of tears crashes over her. "I'm scared, Mommy. I want my daddy to come home. I miss him."

I bury my face in her hair and inhale her scent of strawberry shampoo. "Oh, baby, I'm so sorry. I wish Daddy was here too.

He will come home when he gets better. We just have to be patient."

I took her to see Keith yesterday evening, and now I'm thinking that maybe it wasn't such a good idea. Before we left for the hospital, Mia took a book with her, planning to read to him like he used to read to her. I told her that he might hear her talking to him even in a coma. Unfortunately, things didn't go as planned. She ended up refusing to read and kept asking when her father would wake up. I couldn't tell her what she wanted to hear, and that destroyed me. I had to hide my face, so she didn't see me cry.

Now this.

When Mia starts crying again, it takes both me and her imaginary friend, Mr. Waddles, to calm her down. One thing I do remember from my childhood is that I also had an imaginary friend who I spoke to when I felt sad and alone. I can't recall her name or appearance, but she was always there for me when I needed her. I hope that, in the next days and weeks, Mr. Waddles will help Mia through this tough time, especially when I'm too broken to be everything she needs.

The weekend has sped by and yet also dragged on. It's Monday morning, and I'm driving Mia to school. I was concerned about whether or not to take her after what happened on Friday, but, in the end, I decided it would be good for her to be surrounded by other children. I can't let her see me crying all the time. I grip the wheel tight, wondering how I'll make it through the day. Celeste asked me to stay home and not go to work, but I feel guilty leaving her alone with so many clients booked.

As we approach the school, I turn to Mia and force a smile. "Have a good day, honeybee," I say. "I'll see you in the afternoon."

"Don't be late," my daughter warns me, and I wince,

thinking of her waiting for Keith to pick her up from school
while he lay broken in the middle of a road.

"I won't be. I promise." I take a deep breath and try to smile
at her. "Do you mind if I walk in with you?"

Two weeks ago, Mia decided she was a big girl now, and
told us that she no longer wanted to be escorted to her class,
only to the front door. But I need to have a word with her
teacher to fill her in on what is going on in our lives.

"Okay," she says after a brief moment of silence. "But it's an
excapation, Mommy."

"The word is exception, baby," I say, laughing in spite of
myself.

I get out of the car and follow her into the school, but when
the bell rings, she runs off to her class, ignoring me to merge
with the crowd of students hurrying inside. When I arrive at her
classroom, she's already sitting at her desk, calmly rummaging
through her bag to get out her homework. The room is a huge
contrast to that hospital room where Keith is being kept alive by
all kinds of beeping and whirring machines. It's decorated in
cheerful and bright colors with drawings the children have
made during the week on the walls and the bulletin board. The
windows have colorful designs painted on them and are wide
open so the air can carry the scent of vibrant summer flowers
into the room while making the yellow curtains flutter like flags.

The children are whispering and giggling as they get ready
for the first lesson, and when Miss Simmons sees me, she gets
up from her desk and walks over to the door where I'm standing. I'm at least two heads taller than her, but she has a powerful
presence around her; she always seems so confident and authoritative.

"Oh, hi, Mia's mom," the teacher says. "I'm surprised Mia
allowed you to walk her to the classroom today."

"I asked politely," I say to her, smiling. "I'm sorry to disturb you, but I need to have a quick word. Do you mind if we step out into the hall for a minute?"

"Is there a problem? I hope it's not about Friday. If you came to apologize again, you don't need to. I didn't mind waiting with Mia."

I shake my head. "No, not that. I just need to update you on something that happened that day."

"Well, of course." She glances back into her classroom. "Kids, I need to step out for a moment. Be good."

In the busy hallway, I stand opposite her as she shuts the door behind her. Laughing and yelling, kids with swinging backpacks zip past us on their way to their classrooms while their parents are walking purposefully in the opposite direction, holding keys in their hands.

"I'm afraid I have some bad news," I say heavily.

Miss Simmons dips her head to the side as she studies my face. "Is it about Mia?"

"No. She's fine, I think." I take a deep breath and press myself against the wall for support. "I'm not sure how to say this," I start, twisting my wedding ring around my finger. "Mia's father was hit by a car on Friday. That's why he couldn't pick her up from school."

"Goodness gracious!" Miss Simmons says, her small hand fanning against her breastbone. "I'm so sorry to hear that. Is he all right?"

I swallow the lump in my throat. "He's in a coma."

"Oh my God." Her eyes widen. "That's terrible."

"It was quite a shock," I murmur and blink away the tears. I don't plan on breaking down in a hallway full of kids.

Miss Simmons puts a hand on my arm. "I'm so terribly sorry."

"Thank you." I tilt my head upward to send the tears back where they came from. "I just wanted you to know in case Mia gets upset. So far, she's handling it better than I am, but that could change."

"Okay," Miss Simmons says and takes a deep breath. "We'll keep an eye on her. I'll be undergoing back surgery soon, so I'll be on medical leave for a while, but I'll make sure the teachers who will be substituting during my absence know what's going on. They will do everything they can to make sure Mia is okay."

I get to my feet and push my hands into my jeans pockets. "That would be great. I better get going. I wish you a quick recovery after your surgery."

I also stop by Principal Jordan's office to let her know. She is a tall, lean woman with fluffy brown hair and a sharp nose, who is fond of yellow. Tapping on her open door, I see her sitting on the edge of her desk, working on her computer. Her outfit today consists of a white blouse, a canary yellow scarf, and yellow sneakers. It always amazes me that she doesn't tire of the color.

After hearing what I have to say, she expresses her sympathies and assures me that Mia will be taken care of.

"Is there anything else I can do?" she asks in a nasal voice.

I shake my head. "I just needed to let you know."

"I'm glad you did. If you need anything, feel free to stop by the office any time."

"I will, thank you," I say and head out the door.

Back in the hallway, most children have disappeared into their classes, and on my way out, I walk past a tall blonde woman with bone-straight hair and amber eyes. She's stunningly beautiful, and I've never seen her in the school before. I know most teachers by now; she must be a new parent. I turn to look behind me when I reach the door, but she's gone.

Fifteen minutes later, I arrive at the Willow Gate police station because Liam asked me to stop by.

The station is a modern building made of steel, glass, and concrete and it's slightly taller than the houses in the neighborhood. I park my car in the visitors' parking lot, a graveled area to the right of the main entrance. Inside the building, wooden benches are bolted to the floor, which is covered with white, cheap industrial tiles. The air smells of floor wax and fresh coffee.

The receptionist at the desk asks me to sign the visitor's book, then I walk down a hallway lined with glass walls with offices on either side and nameplates on their doors. As I round a corner and make my way to the end of the hall, I see two officers in a conference room. Their voices are muffled, but their tense body language makes it clear they are arguing.

The walls are covered with posters of missing people, both young and old, and I wonder how many of them have been found. Liam's office is at the end of the hall, so I take a deep breath before knocking on the door. When I enter the room, he gives me a warm hug and asks how I'm doing. "I hope it wasn't inconvenient for you to come in today."

"No, not at all," I say and glance at his desk.

On it is a pink and white box of chocolate chip cookies from Lucy Bakes, his wife's bakery. He offers me one, but I shake my head and sit, looking around me at the small office. The white walls are decorated with pictures of him, Lucy, and the kids. In the largest photo, one of his sons is dressed as a panda bear, and the other as Spiderman. Liam smiles at the camera in almost all the photos, except for the one where his wife must have just given birth to the newborn in her arms, where he looks slightly dazed.

"Do you have any news on the accident?" I ask him, hoping that's why he called me in.

He sighs with frustration. "I'm sorry, Avery, but I don't have any good news. We're still investigating, but we don't have anything so far. We've questioned everyone around the scene of the accident, but none of them saw it happen and we don't have any CCTV footage to work with." He sinks into his seat and takes a gulp of coffee. He looks like he hasn't slept for days.

"Are you okay, Liam?" I ask, putting my own problems aside for a moment. "You look troubled."

He rubs his temples. "My best friend is in a coma. I'm dealing with a nasty domestic abuse case as well, and innocent kids are affected. Social services are involved, and the court will likely take them away and place them in a foster home. But at least that's better than leaving them with people who don't care about their well-being. Some people are just not worthy of being parents," he says, his voice hard and low. "We have a few cases like this every few months, and it sickens me."

I nod. "I'm sorry to hear that. I hope the kids will be okay."

"I hope so as well. They deserve better than to be caught up in a mess like this." Liam takes a deep breath. "I'm sorry, Avery. I didn't mean to vent to you about my work problems. You have so much more going on. It pains me that I don't have good news to share with you."

I reach out to squeeze his arm. "That's all right." I pause. "I just thought that maybe the reason you wanted to see me is—"

"Honestly, I wanted to see how you're doing."

"It's been hard, Liam. I'm not sure how I'll make it through the next few days."

He rubs the scar on his nose. "I wish there was something we could do for you."

"I know." I rake a hand through my hair and sigh. "I think the only thing that might help is if the person who hurt Keith is found. I can't bear the thought of them being out there, after what they did."

"As soon as I know something new, I'll let you know. I want the same thing as you, believe me." I watch his hand curl into a fist. "There's nothing I want more than to see the son of a bitch behind bars."

I wipe my eyes roughly, and he reaches across his desk to offer me a tissue.

"Thanks." I shake it out and blow my nose.

Liam leans forward on his desk. "I *did* want to ask you something, though."

I curl my fingers around the tissue. "Yeah, okay."

"Do you know of anyone who might have wanted to hurt Keith? Maybe one of his employees at Oak Tree?"

My stomach tumbles as I stare at Liam. "Of course not. Are you saying that someone meant to hurt him, that it wasn't just a random accident?"

"I don't know. I just have this feeling in my gut that there's more to this than meets the eye." Liam leans back in his seat and gazes up at the ceiling before looking back at me. "I'm sorry to think that, but I'm looking at every possibility. I just needed to ask. Do any names come to your mind?"

"No," I say with conviction. "I can't imagine anyone wanting to hurt Keith."

"Okay." He taps his fingers on his desk. "What about the woman he fired a month ago? She was handling the money, I think."

"Yeah, I know about Doreen, the accountant. She was stealing from the business, but I don't think it was her. As far as I know, she's currently out of town."

"I see." Liam pinches the bridge of his nose and blows out a breath. "You know what, maybe you're right. It could have been a random person. I just wish I could talk to Keith. There may have been something going on, something he didn't feel he could talk to either of us about."

I took a life.

The words sneak into my mind, and my shoulders tense up as a sickening realization crystalizes in my head.

What if Keith really *did* hurt someone and a person close to them took revenge?

Surely that's not possible. Keith wouldn't hurt a fly; he's the gentlest man I know. But those were his last words to me.

Unless they were caused by the medication addling his mind, they must have meant something.

"Liam," I say. "I need to go to the hospital. I'll let you know if I think of anyone."

I rise to my feet, but before I reach the door, he calls me and I turn to find him holding out the box of cookies toward me. "Take these to Mia. She might like them."

"Thanks, Liam." I take the box and stumble out of the office to my car.

On my way to the hospital, I call Ruth, who suggests that I should move back home for a while so they can all help out with Mia. But going back home would mean I'm accepting that it will be a while before things get back to normal, that Keith won't wake up any time soon. It would be too much like giving up, and the thought fills me with dread.

I can't think about Ruth's suggestion right now. I can only focus on getting to Keith, to try and talk him out of his coma. I'm desperate to see him, to get the answers only he might be able to give me. I need to know what he meant by those words.

CHAPTER 7

It's been two days since I went to see Liam, and I can't stop thinking about what he said: that maybe Keith was hiding something from us. Those strange final words keep replaying over and over again in my mind.

I don't want to believe that my husband would hurt anyone. I *can't* believe it. He's a good man who volunteers at homeless shelters and donates money to charitable causes. In his spare time, he likes to watch videos online about people performing random acts of kindness, cute little videos about dogs being reunited with their soldier owners. He has a heart of gold, and it's what I've always loved most about him. Just last month, he surprised a stranger by paying for her groceries at a local store, and there have been times when I've even worried that someone could take advantage of his kindness and generosity.

But what if there was something else going on, something dark and terrible, something he couldn't tell me? The thought tortured me all through last night, so much so that I only fell asleep at 5 a.m., two hours before I had to get up to take Mia to school.

Now I've been woken up by the sound of the toilet flushing,

and I glance at the time and jump out of bed. Mia was supposed to be at school ten minutes ago. For two days in a row, she'll be late and I'm to blame. I'm getting dressed at the speed of light when she walks in.

"Is it the weekend, Mommy?" she asks.

I freeze with my T-shirt in my hand and give her what I hope to be an apologetic look. "I'm sorry, baby. Mommy overslept."

We've always taught her that when someone does something wrong or makes a mistake, they should own up to it.

Is that what Keith was doing? Ignoring the ice in my stomach, I push the thought aside and pull the T-shirt over my head.

"Miss Simmons is not going to be happy," Mia says. "And everyone is going to stare at me."

"I know, baby." I give her a quick hug. "I'm really sorry. I'll tell her it's my fault."

When I let go, Mia pushes her curls from her face and looks up at me. "It *is* your fault, Mommy."

Ouch.

"You're right. Now please, let's get you dressed, so we're not even more late."

By the time we're both dressed and out the door, fifteen more minutes have gone by and I know the drive will be at least forty minutes long. Being over an hour late is inexcusable.

When I finally pull up in front of the building, Mia turns to me with a pout. "You forgot to give me breakfast."

My heart shrinks inside my chest. This has to stop. I need to pull myself together and be the mother Mia needs right now. I grab my purse and dig inside for anything she can eat. Then I remember the cookies Liam had given me for Mia at the station two days ago; I'd forgotten all about them until now.

"I have something for you to eat in the trunk," I say to her. "It's a little treat."

We both get out of the car, and I grab the box and hand her

two big cookies. I feel like a rotten mother for giving my child chocolate cookies for breakfast, but it's that or nothing.

Mia looks at one of the cookies for a heartbeat, then bites into it. "They're yummy."

"Yes, they are. They're from Lucy Bakes. Uncle Liam said I should give them to you."

Mia takes another big bite. "Can I have more after school?"

"Of course you can, but only after you eat lunch."

Before we reach the front door into the school, I urge her to finish the cookies. In a recent parent–teacher newsletter from Miss Simmons, she reminded us to always give our children a healthy breakfast and stay away from sugary foods because they make children hyperactive and unable to pay attention in class.

Thankfully, by the time we enter the building, the cookie is gone and Mia's licking the crumbs from her fingers. As soon as she enters, I apologize to Miss Simmons and she gives me a sympathetic smile.

"It *is* quite late," she says, "but don't worry about it. I understand."

I give her a smile of gratitude and walk back down the hall, where I bump into Principal Jordan. My stomach clenches when she waves me over, and, as I walk toward her, I feel like a schoolkid again, about to be scolded. But that's not why she wants to talk to me.

"I just wanted to find out how your husband is doing. Mia says he's still in the hospital."

I nod. "Sadly, yes. He's still in a coma. The doctors can't say how long it will be until he wakes up."

Every day I go to the hospital hoping to come back with good news, but every day starts and ends the same way, with nothing to give me hope.

"I'm sorry to hear that," she says. "We'll keep him in our good thoughts. And you don't have to worry about Mia. She has been a little more sensitive lately, but, given the circumstances, that's expected. Miss Simmons will be on medical leave from tomorrow, but we have a lovely new teaching assistant, Miss Campbell. She's assigned to Mia's class, starting today. She will be supporting Mr. Singer, the main substitute teacher. I filled them in on what happened, and they will keep a close eye on her."

"Thank you," I say. "I really appreciate your support of Mia during this difficult time."

She smiles at me. "It's our pleasure. But please do try to get her to school early. We wouldn't want her to miss the morning lessons."

Heat floods my face. "Yes, of course. I will."

As I walk toward the double doors, I wonder if the new assistant is the woman I saw a few days ago in the hallway. She looked just like the princesses in my daughter's favorite book, and she had kind eyes. I'm glad Mia will have some extra support.

Before heading home, I stop by the parlor to talk to Celeste, but Justine tells me she has a client. One more client is in the waiting area, but I don't have the mental or physical strength to massage her. Fortunately, things are about to get easier. Celeste has conducted the interviews on my behalf, and two new masseuses are scheduled to start soon.

"I'm really sorry about your husband, Avery," Justine says. "What a terrible thing to happen. Everyone in town is saying that he—"

"Thank you, Justy," I say, cutting her off when I see the waiting client lowering her magazine to listen to our conversation. Then I add quietly, "I'm doing okay, all things considered. I'm just hoping for good news soon."

"Fingers crossed." Justine holds up her right hand and crosses her pointing and middle fingers.

I give her a half-hearted smile and turn to leave when I

remember why I came in the first place. "Please tell Celeste to call me when she's free."

Five minutes after I leave the parlor, my phone rings and I put it on speaker. It's Celeste.

"I have a quick break before taking the next client. Are you okay, love?"

"I'm hanging in there," I say. "At least I'm trying."

Even though she's my best friend, I haven't told her what Keith said to me. I'm terrified of telling anyone, but keeping it in is also killing me.

"I'm worried about you," she says.

"I know. I'm also worried about me, if I'm honest. I feel like I'm failing Mia. I'm a terrible mother at the moment; I was late taking her to school again today."

I slow down at a pedestrian crossing and watch an older man with a walking stick take his time crossing it.

Celeste is silent for a few seconds, then she sighs. "Honey, I know it's really hard right now, but be careful with Mia. This must be a really difficult time for her too."

My blood goes cold. "Are you serious, Celeste? You of all people should know how hard I'm trying." I bite down on my lower lip, trying to remain calm as I speak. "You know I'm doing my best to keep Mia feel safe and well taken care of. I just... I just lost track of time."

With the crossing clear again, I step on the accelerator a little too hard. Even though I know that this is not about me, that after all these years Celeste is still reacting to the neglect she experienced as a child and her hurt bubbles up from time to time, I can't help but take it personally, especially since I already feel like I'm failing my daughter.

"You're right and I'm so sorry. That was crappy of me to say.

You *are* an amazing mother and you're handling this better than most people probably would."

"Thank you for saying that. It really does mean a lot. I just hope Keith wakes up soon."

But what if he wakes up and repeats what he told me before? What if he tells me something I can't bear to hear? I'm so caught up in my thoughts and distracted by the phone conversation that I almost run a red light, hitting the brake at the last second.

"He will, darling," Celeste says. "Let's just keep praying for him."

"Yep, that's all we can do at this point. In the meantime, I need to do what's right for Mia. I want to take a few weeks off."

"That's what I've been telling you to do. You have too much going on right now. You don't have to worry about the Opal. I've got you covered, and our new masseuses are starting soon anyway. You should take all the time you need for you and Mia."

"I will, but it will be really hard not to do anything. Maybe I can catch up on the paperwork while spending all those hours at the hospital." I rub my temples to relieve the tension building there. "I've also decided I'm going to move back in with my parents for a while."

"Really? Do you think that's a good idea?" The surprise in her voice is evident. She knows how desperate I was to leave after graduating from high school. "I mean, your parents are not exactly in a position to help you care for Mia."

"Celeste, I know you care a lot about Mia, but I think she needs all the support she can get right now, however little, especially since I have to be at the hospital so often. I know that half the time my mom and dad are checked out mentally, but Ruth is ready to help out. It was actually her idea."

Celeste lets out a sigh. "You know how much I love my tiny

apartment, but now I wish I lived in a larger place. Then I'd be able to house you and Mia."

Celeste grew up in an enormous lakeshore estate with seven bedrooms, which has now been sold. There were so many hallways and rooms that I often got lost when I visited. Even though with her mother's money she could afford somewhere expensive, now she lives in a small, cozy studio apartment that she furnishes with second-hand furniture and local artwork. She says she prefers this to the pompous and overpriced things her mother spent her life accumulating, and she'd rather give the money to children's charities.

"You are very sweet to say that." I manage a laugh. "But, honey, you don't have to worry. Mia and I will be fine."

"You're right, I know you will be." She laughs then pauses. "You know what? Maybe it's not such a bad idea for you to go back home. I'm sure Ruth will be excited to be able to see her goddaughter more often. I love that she has always been there for you."

"That's true, and she treats Mia the very same way she treated me as a child."

Celeste is silent for a moment, then she says, "But you know it will be a longer drive to get to Mia's school, right?"

I turn into our street and adjust the speed to the limit. "I know, but I think Mia will be happier there. If I have to drive longer to get her to school, so be it."

"I hope the extra help will make Mia feel more secure," Celeste says. "And if you ever need me to help with anything, you know what to do."

"Yes, I do. You're the best friend ever. Look, I'm almost home, I'll speak to you later."

After we hang up, relief sweeps through me. I've made the right decision for both me and Mia, and I know she will be excited when I tell her.

I only stay in the house long enough to take a shower before heading to the hospital again.

Since I was late dropping off Mia, I make it a point to be fifteen minutes early at pickup, and as soon as she walks out of the building, I'm already there. The moment she gets into the car, she starts talking non-stop about the new teaching assistant, Miss Campbell.

"That's her over there." She points to the entrance, where the blonde woman I had come across in the hallway is standing. I lift my hand and wave.

"You should say hello to her," Mia suggests. "She's really nice, Mommy. She gave me a special project. For one week, I will take care of the class pet frog."

"That sounds like fun." I start the car. "But I don't have time to greet her today, honeybee. We have things to do and places to go."

"Where? Are we going to Disneyland?"

A sharp pain plunges into my heart. Before Keith's accident, we'd planned to take Mia to Disneyland in a few weeks' time, and she's been so excited about it.

"Not Disneyland," I say, my voice strained. "But how about moving in with Grammy and Grampy?"

"For many days?" Her voice is high-pitched with excitement.

"Yes. While Daddy is in the hospital, they can keep us company."

"Yay! And can I also sleep at Ruth's house?"

"Sure. Sometimes. Now let's go and pack a few things."

"Okay. Can Mr. Waddles come with us?"

"Of course, we have to take Mr. Waddles with us. We wouldn't want to leave him all alone in the house!"

. . .

We arrive at my parents' just as the sun is about to set, and we find my mother standing outside waiting for us. My childhood home, which stands right next to the road, resembles a log cabin and has a large porch and a white swing hanging from the ceiling. However, like the people who inhabit it, the house is in disrepair. The paint is peeling in places, the porch is faded, and the grass in the front yard is overgrown and dying. Even the sky above it looks gray and ominous today.

My mother is standing on the front porch steps with a big smile on her face.

"I'm so happy you came back home," she says, her cheeks flushed, her eyes sparkling.

When she's in a happy place, you'd never guess that she goes through such serious bouts of depression and anxiety. She's a completely different person. Those were the days I lived for as a child. Sometimes they came once or twice a week; at other times, I went weeks without seeing my mother's smile. Good times could last anywhere from fifteen minutes to an entire weekend. Never longer than that. But on those days, life was better. My father drank less when his wife surfaced, and she cooked, baked, and sang lullabies I had never heard before. My mother has an angelic voice; it's a shame she keeps it locked away most of the time. I used to think that her illness was like the flu, a contagious disease that could infect us as well, making us all sad. In a way, it was.

"I'm happy to be home too, Mom," I say, hugging her tight. Today, instead of sweat and neglect, she smells of soap and something sweet and her long blonde hair has been washed and brushed. She clearly made an effort to clean herself up, to show me that she's feeling okay. But she still feels thin in my arms, her bones delicate under her skin. Just like a porcelain doll, I'm afraid I'll break her if I squeeze too hard.

She releases me and goes to hug Mia before ushering us

inside to eat the food she prepared: mashed potatoes, green beans, and roasted chicken.

"I hope you like it," she says nervously. "I haven't cooked in a while."

"It's excellent, Jodie," my father says, grinning from ear to ear as he scoops mashed potato into his mouth.

After dinner, my father does the washing-up, just as he used to do when I was a child on those rare happy days when my mother would cook, and he would clean up. While Mia is helping him dry the dishes, I decide to head next door to pay Ruth a quick visit, but my mother stops me before I step out.

"Where are you going, sweetheart?"

"I'm going over to see Ruth for a bit. I saw her car pull into her drive a few minutes ago."

My mother frowns. "But don't you think it's late to pay someone a visit? I'm sure Ruth would like to rest after her water aerobics class. You should wait until the morning."

"Mom, it's Ruth. She'd be happy to see me any time."

My mother's face falls and she folds her hands in front of her. "You're right. It's just that you have only been home for a short time and we missed you. I was thinking we could watch a movie after Mia goes to bed, just you and me... like in the old days."

I cringe inwardly because the few times we did that, my mother ended up crying. Every movie we watched was either too sad, or too happy, reminding her of the joy that was missing from her life. Each time, I ended up consoling her instead and it was exhausting.

"I'm sorry, Mom, I'm not really in the mood for a movie right now. Maybe another day—"

"Of course, I understand. You have a lot on your mind." She looks away, her eyes misty and I immediately start sensing her mood shifting.

Changing my mind about going to see Ruth, I close the door

and wrap my arms around her before she spirals downward again. "Mom, I'm sorry. I didn't mean to hurt your feelings. Instead of a movie, how about we just sit on the porch and have some tea? It's a nice evening out and we could use the fresh air. I'll visit Ruth tomorrow."

Her body relaxes and she hugs me back. "I'd like that."

Thirty minutes later, before joining my mother on the porch, I stand in the doorway of my childhood room listening to my father reading a bedtime story to Mia. Seeing him sober, even for a day, is such a welcome change, and I love that there are still moments when he can bond with his granddaughter. I know it's hard for him to stay sober, but he's trying, and I appreciate it.

A smile tugs at my lips as I watch them together. He's reading her the story of Cinderella, and Mia is transfixed even though she's heard it countless times. My father sets the book down on the bedside table and gently brushes Mia's hair out of her face before kissing her forehead.

"Goodnight, little one."

I turn and sneak into the hallway before either of them can see me, and a sigh of relief escapes my lips.

Later on, before he goes to bed, my father knocks on my door and comes in to sit with me on my bed.

"I'm sorry that you're going through a rough time, pumpkin." He pulls me into his arms and I hold on to him, wishing he could always be there to comfort me without alcohol coming between us.

"You'll make it through this," he says as he leaves the room.

Watching him go, I whisper the words I used to say as a child, pretending I'm answering him. "I love you too, Dad."

CHAPTER 8

THE WATCHER

I watch Avery get out of her car before Mia emerges. She did it again. It's Wednesday morning, and Avery is late again bringing her daughter to school.

As I watch her rushing the girl into the building, I feel a deep sadness stirring inside of me, sorrow for what could happen to the girl if her mother doesn't start taking her responsibilities seriously. Failed grades. Repeated years. Lost opportunities.

I turn my attention to Avery as she walks her daughter into the building. I saw her come out of the house in a rush, I saw that she did not give Mia breakfast. I saw her give the child cookies to make up for her forgetfulness.

Anger starts bubbling inside of me, but I resist the urge to go after Avery and give her a piece of my mind. I take a few deep breaths and calm myself down. I have to just keep quiet. For now.

Watching Avery walk back to her car, clearly exhausted and emotional, I start thinking maybe I'm too hard on her, too judgmental. Perhaps she does care about her daughter, and maybe she's doing her best and will get better with time.

But I change my mind when I remember where she'll be spending most of her day today. She may forget to take her daughter to school on time or to give her breakfast, but when it comes to visiting her husband, she never misses a day. Today, she will put him first again and put her daughter in second place. If something happens to Mia because of her neglect, I'll have to take action. I hate to think about it, but I might be left with no choice.

I want to follow her, but I can't because I have work to do. But when she picks up Mia, I will be right here, watching and waiting for her to step out of line.

CHAPTER 9

AVERY

Eighteen days after Keith slipped into a coma, I'm in the hospital waiting room poring over some business financial reports when I hear a familiar voice.

"Thought you'd be here," Celeste says, walking into the room. She's wearing a tight blue blouse, her curly hair straightened and glossy as it flows from a center part. Rose-brown highlights make the dark brown shade of her hair pop to life. It's been a while since I've seen her so done up.

I put the papers on the empty seat next to me and stand up to hug her. "Wow, you look stunning. What are you doing here?"

"Just stopping by to see you after my date. I miss my friend."

"Oooh! Don't tell me it's the blind date your client arranged for you."

She only shrugs, and I laugh.

A month ago, a woman had walked into the Opal and got on so well with Celeste that she told her all about her son, and how she thought they would make a good couple. She gave the man the parlor's phone number and, two days later, he called to ask Celeste out on a date.

"I thought you were not interested in being set up," I say, sitting down and removing the papers so Celeste can sit next to me. "You said you wanted to find your Prince Charming yourself."

"I wasn't interested, but I figured, what would it hurt? It's not as if I have men lined up at my door. I'm not far off thirty-five, and I can literally feel my eggs drying up."

"Come on. There's no rush." I nudge her in the side. "In this day and age, there are women who have babies in their forties, fifties, and even beyond."

"True, but if I don't have a baby by forty, I'm closing shop. I don't want to use the little energy I have left waking up in the middle of the night to change diapers."

I laugh and lean into her, warmth spreading through my chest like a balsam. "Thanks for coming. I missed you more."

"I brought you food." She produces a bag I hadn't seen she was holding and hands it to me.

"What's inside?" I ask, even though I don't have an appetite at all. Whatever she brought will be the first meal I'm eating today.

"Something from the Noodle Palace. It's a new restaurant on Laurel Drive. That's where Donnell and I had our date."

I give her a mischievous smile and wriggle my eyebrows. "Donnell, huh? So, tell me. How was it?"

"It was perfect, actually. He's a little shorter than me, but he has gorgeous green eyes and dimples to make up for it."

"So, you're planning on seeing him again?"

"Yeah, tomorrow night."

"Wow. That's really great, Celeste. It's been a while since you went on a second date."

"I know, right? It's also been a while since a man made me laugh as much as Donnell did." She reaches for my hand and clasps it in hers. "But let's talk about that later; I want to hear about you. Has anything changed with Keith's condition?"

"No," I say, my mood plummeting immediately. "I keep waiting and hoping for him to wake up, but nothing."

"Oh man, I'm so sorry. I hate that you have to go through this."

"Me too, but we can't choose our battles." I look at her and suddenly feel like I'm going to snap into two. "I don't know what I'll do if he doesn't wake up."

Celeste shakes her head and squeezes my hand tighter. "Don't talk like that. He will wake up, honey. You have to believe that."

"But what if... What if he doesn't? I feel like maybe I should prepare myself."

Celeste averts her gaze and says nothing. When she looks up, her eyes are as wet as mine. "I wish I could make all your pain go away," she says.

I smile and pull her close. "You being here and assisting with the business helps more than you can imagine."

"I just wish I could do more." She pulls away. "How is Mia? Is she doing better now that you're back at your parents'?"

"Yeah, and she loves all the attention she's getting from Ruth. There's also a new teaching assistant in her class, and she likes her a lot."

"That's good to hear. Mia needs all the love she can hold in her sweet little heart." Celeste puts the bag of food on the floor between her feet. "And how about you?"

"That's a different story."

"It's not going well with your parents?"

"Not really." I close my eyes and lean my head back against the wall. "I don't know. I feel uncomfortable somehow, like I don't belong there anymore."

"That's not a first. You never felt like you belonged, and I don't blame you."

"I know. But don't get me wrong; they are trying. My

mother is doing her best when she's feeling better and, when Dad is sober, he's a great grandfather and he's very protective of Mia, but"—I rub my forehead—"I just feel uneasy being there. Maybe it's just because I'm going through so much, but I can't do this anymore. I feel so lost."

Instead of responding, Celeste just holds me and, after a few minutes, I get myself together and wipe my tears. Then she fills me in on what's going on with the parlor.

"Maria and Lily are really hard workers, and so far the clients are so happy with their massaging skills. We got five new reviews online in the past week, so you can bet the business will pick up."

"That's great." I allow myself a moment to feel proud of what we've accomplished. "Is there anything I can help with from a distance?"

"You already have your hands full, and even though you should be on leave, you're still doing the financials. Thank God, because I'm hopeless at numbers."

Celeste stays with me for an hour, and when she leaves it's nearly eight, so I decide to go home as well.

Close to an hour later, I walk through the door and into my bedroom, ready to crash, but after undressing and climbing under the covers, I feel too restless and edgy to shut off. I turn on the small TV on the wall, and a news program comes on. The main story is about a woman in New York who was found dead in a parking garage.

Death is not something I want to think about right now, so I switch off the TV again and get out of bed to get something to drink. I find my mother wandering the dark hallway in her quilted bathrobe, with two long, blonde braids hanging down her back, murmuring something to herself that I can't hear. She doesn't notice me because she's so distracted by her thoughts. She seems to be looking for something, but only she knows what that is. It would be nice to see inside her mind sometimes, so that I could understand her better. She's so often lost in her own world and doesn't seem to want to be found.

"Mom?" I whisper.

She jumps back in fright. "Oh, my goodness, Avery. You scared me half to death."

"I'm sorry." I switch on the light. "Are you okay? What were you doing?"

"I... Ummm... I was praying."

I frown and walk toward her. "In the hallway?"

She did things like that when I was a child. Sometimes it would be late at night, and she would be walking around in the garden like a ghost. It used to freak me out. With a childhood like that, no wonder I feel a little uneasy being back home.

"I didn't want to wake your father," she says.

My father drinks almost every night before he goes to bed, and no amount of noise will wake him. Even as we stand in the hallway, I can hear him snoring from the living room couch where he sometimes spends the night when he's too drunk to climb up the stairs.

"What are you doing up?" Mom asks me, tucking her hands under her armpits, releasing the scent of an unwashed body. She can go days without showering, even weeks.

"I couldn't sleep, so I thought I'd get something to drink."

Mom takes a few steps and stands in front of me, and then she covers my cheeks on either side of my face. "You look thinner."

"You think so?" I ask and the familiar urge to pull away from her grows inside me, but I stay put.

"Yes. You've lost so much weight since Keith's accident."

"Well, it's hard to eat when my husband is in a coma. What if he doesn't wake up, Mom?"

She drops her hands from my face and rubs her arms as if she's suddenly cold. "You have to believe in a higher power, Avery. You have to believe that everything happens for a reason."

I look at her in shock. "How can you say that? I wouldn't want Keith to die. I don't care what reason there is for it. I want him to wake up so we can continue living our lives together."

Mom nods and presses her lips together in a tight line. "I'm sorry, love. You're right. We have to believe he will wake up."

There is an awkward pause. "I have to go to bed," I say, finally, changing my mind about the drink.

"Okay. Goodnight, sweetheart."

I force a smile and squeeze her arm. "Sleep well, Mom."

Before I disappear through the door, she asks me what my plans are for the next day, as she has been doing almost every day. She's been quite controlling lately, asking me where I'm going, what I'm doing, and when I'll be back, as if she has forgotten that I'm no longer a child. She also constantly complains that Mia and I visit Ruth too often.

Right now, it's difficult to keep myself from snapping at her, so I simply say, "I'm going to visit Keith. It's a long day tomorrow. I should get some sleep."

In my room, I lie on my bed, and stare at the white ceiling, thinking about the conversation I've just had with my mother, how she was there and not there at the same time. She has fleeting moments when I see her, but she goes through her days like a zombie most of the time. It's hard to remember the last time we had a normal conversation without her zoning out.

When I was thirteen and found out that she was seeing a therapist, I asked Dad to tell me if something happened to Mom in her childhood that made her struggle so much. He just laughed and said there was nothing wrong with her, that she's just eccentric.

Unable to sleep, I call Celeste, and we chat for a while

about the business. Immediately after I end the call, I hear a shuffle of feet padding across the hardwood floor outside my bedroom. The sound stops for a moment, then resumes as if someone is pacing back and forth in the hallway. I open the door in time to see my mother disappearing into their bedroom, her robe trailing behind her before the door closes and the hallway is quiet once more. She must have been listening in on my call, just like she used to when I was a child. I guess since I never felt close enough to her to share my private thoughts, she felt she had to get the information some other way.

Since I've been back home, I suspect she's also been going through my things when I'm not around. When I walked into my room yesterday, I saw that the contents of my nightstand drawer had been rummaged through. Despite my anger at the invasion of my privacy, I didn't say anything to her because I didn't want to start an argument with someone who's already so fragile.

As I stand in the hallway, I hear her crying behind her bedroom door. She's not loud, but distinctly audible. If I knock on the door to ask if she's okay, she will deny anything's wrong and pretend everything is fine, and we will continue tiptoeing around her.

Upon returning to my room and seeing the nightstand drawer she had been looking through, I open it to get a book to read. I can't help wondering if she had been looking for something in particular.

A while later, as I'm about to drift off to sleep, I hear the noise of a door shutting downstairs, and find myself out of the room again and descending the stairs. It's pitch black except for a thin strip of light emanating from under the basement door, and I gently push down on the door handle, but it's locked, so I lean my ear against the door to listen. I can hear both my parents' voices and they sound like they're arguing. My mother sounds like she's crying. I strain to hear more, but they stop talking and I suddenly hear footsteps climbing the stairs.

Not wanting to be caught eavesdropping, I retreat to my room, where I sit on the bed and wonder what my parents were arguing about, and why they would do it behind the locked basement door.

CHAPTER 10

Keith's eyes flutter open and, for a second, I think he sees me. I lean closer and brush his cheek with a fingertip. My touch seems to wake him a little more, and he smiles. It's the most amazing thing in the world. I missed his smile so much.

"I'm so happy you're back," I say, hugging him tight.

"Yeah, I figured I'd get a bit of a break from my boring life." He gives me a heart-melting grin.

"How can you say that? Our life's not boring. We've had some pretty exciting times."

"You're right about that. I was just kidding." As soon as the words leave his lips, a cloud crosses his features, and his eyes darken. "There's something I need to tell you."

Before he can say it, I sit up in bed, my heart pounding.

For two nights in a row, I've dreamt about him, and every time, he says he wants to tell me something. Before he says the words, I always know what he wants to say. I can't hear it again, not in person and not in a dream.

"Keith is not a killer," I whisper to myself. "He didn't take a life."

I've heard the words repeatedly in my head, and they still

leave me breathless as they did the first time. I wish I knew how to shut them off.

As much as it terrifies me, I need to talk to someone about it. Now. I throw back the damp comforter and get out of bed. Grabbing my warm dressing gown, I put it on haphazardly. If I don't do something, I will go mad.

I don't bother to look at the time when I throw open my bedroom door and head to the room that used to be mine when I was a kid. It now belongs to Mia while I sleep in the guest room. Maybe if I climb into bed with my daughter, I'll feel better and will no longer feel the need to tell anyone about what Keith said to me.

I quietly push open the door and stand in the doorway. The window is open, the moonlight drenching the room in soft light. It still looks the same as it did when I was a kid. The walls are painted light pink with the green glow from stars scattered across them, and a large picture of dolphins still hangs on the wall above the heart-shaped headboard of my bed. I was obsessed with dolphins as a child, always impressed by their beauty and intelligence.

Maybe it's just my imagination, but I feel like the room smells like the first perfume I bought for myself when I turned thirteen, a birthday present to me. It was fruity, a mix of vanilla and several kinds of berries. I admit I probably loved the bottle more than the scent, a crystal vial with a picture of a mermaid etched on it and a pink ribbon around the neck. It was my first grown-up perfume and I sprayed it on my pillowcases and sheets every night; it must have sunk into the very walls after a while. The scent made me happy during tough times, and maybe that's why I can still recall it, even though it has surely long since faded.

I lower my gaze to the bed, expecting to see my little girl curled up in it. But it's empty.

I smack my forehead. Of course it is. Mia is spending the

night at Ruth's house, like she does most Fridays. Ruth. Maybe I should talk to her about my worries; I've always confided in her. It's late, but she won't care. She'll be happy I came to her with my troubles and will do whatever she can to make me feel better. I certainly can't talk to my mother about it; it would just worry her.

Before I can change my mind, I tiptoe down the stairs and burst through the front door of the house and out into the cool night. I draw in a breath of fresh air, trying to calm my racing heart. I'll feel better soon, once I get everything off my chest.

The street is quiet and peaceful, and the air is still, but I feel uneasy. As if someone is watching me. The back of my neck prickles, and I shiver as I glance down both ends of the street. As I tighten my gown and hurry to the house next door, I keep my head down and don't look at the other houses' windows.

Ruth opens the door wearing a faded blue silk nightgown and large pink rollers in her hair, which she holds in place with a black hair net. The fact that her eyes are wide open and alert means she wasn't sleeping either, so I feel a little less guilty for coming to her house in the middle of the night.

"Avery, dear, whatever's the matter? You look as if you've seen a ghost."

I shake my head. I can't seem to find the words. Feeling overwhelmed, I throw myself into her arms, and burst into tears. She pats my back in a soothing manner, and I breathe in her familiar hairspray scent.

After a moment, she pulls away. "Come on in, child. Tell me what's wrong. Mia is fast asleep, so let's go to the kitchen."

Ruth's house hasn't changed much since I was a child. The kitchen is just as I remember, bright with pale-green walls and a white granite countertop. I stare at the old gas stove, which still stands proudly after years of use. I remember standing on a chair in front of it with Ruth next to me as we spooned pancake batter into the hot non-stick pan. The fridge is covered by Mia's drawings. If anyone didn't know better, they would think Ruth is my mother and Mia's grandmother.

It never fails to warm my heart to see the toddler table with two green chairs that match the kitchen walls tucked in one corner of the room. I used to sit there to draw or play with puzzles and games while Ruth cooked. The small drawer is still filled with coloring books, puzzle pieces, coloring pencils, and other things to keep a small child occupied. I'm grateful to Ruth for so much. Without her stepping in to calm the storms, my childhood would have been a mess. She certainly took the pressure off my mother. When her anxiety took over, she always told me to go next door to Ruth, who would receive me with open arms.

Before I can talk, Ruth makes me a mug of hot honey and cinnamon milk.

"This always soothed you as a child," she says, putting it in front of me. "Take a sip. You'll feel better."

I nod and blow over the hot liquid before taking a sip, and after a few minutes the sweet drink gives me the courage I need to speak up.

I look up at Ruth, who has taken a seat in the chair next to me.

"What's on your mind, dear? Talking always helps."

"I don't know where to begin."

"How about at the beginning?" She puts a gentle hand on my arm.

I nod and take another sip of my milk. "A few seconds before Keith slipped into a coma, he told me something."

A frown flits across Ruth's face, lines creasing between her eyes. "It must have been... something terrible, from the way you look."

"It was." I swallow hard. "He said he took a life."

Ruth's hand goes to her lips. "Dear God. Why would he say something like that?"

I shrug. "I don't know. He slipped into the coma before I could ask him to explain."

"Did he say who?"

I shake my head. "No. Just that he took a life."

"Well, listen to me, darling. Your husband is a good man, and so very kind." She gives me an encouraging smile. "I'm sure he didn't mean it, not like that."

I shake my head. "I know, but of all things to say, why would he say that?"

"I'm sure he was just rambling. It's not uncommon for people who are heavily medicated to say ridiculous things." She reaches for my hand. "I'm sure it's nothing to worry about."

Ruth smiles at me, but I can't force a smile in return.

"But what if it's true?" My voice cracks, and I rub my eyes with a shaky hand. "What if he really did kill someone?"

"Nonsense. He's not that kind of man, and there is no evidence that he did. Why would he? Don't break your pretty little head over it."

I nod, feeling a little reassured by her words.

"How are things at the house?" Ruth asks, changing the subject. "Is your mother managing okay? I saw her again in the garden in the middle of the night. I tried talking to her about it, but she insisted she was fine."

I sigh. "She's the same. But I guess we have to just accept her the way she is."

A moment of silence passes between us, both of us lost in our thoughts. Ruth speaks first.

"I've been thinking about it, dear."

"What?" I ask.

She shrugs. "You're going through a lot. If staying with your parents starts to stress you too much, you and Mia are welcome to move in with me for a while. I'm sure Jodie wouldn't mind; we're practically family. Remember when you used to stay with me during some holidays?"

I'm moved by her offer, but I shake my head. "That's kind of you, but I think we're all right. Knowing you're just a door away helps a lot."

She raises her eyebrows. "Are you sure? I don't mind at all."

"I'm sure. We're really okay."

As much as I feel uneasy about staying in my childhood home, they are still my parents, and even if my mother wouldn't mind, I'd feel guilty.

"If you change your mind, let me know." Ruth pats my hand.

She hugs me at the door, and as I make my way home I feel like someone is watching me again. When I look up at the upstairs bathroom window of our house, I see the curtains move.

It has to be my mother.

Once upstairs in my room, I fall onto the bed, closing my eyes. My chest feels like a heavy weight is pressing it down, and it's hard to breathe. Maybe the stress of everything has gotten to me. Perhaps I'm picking up my mother's anxieties.

One thing that often helped when I was feeling anxious was writing in my diary. It's a habit both Keith and I share. It's been a while since I did it, so I sit up in bed again and get the leather-bound journal.

I always leave the bookmark on the last page I wrote on, but now it's three pages back. I never read my past entries. Ever. As I run a hand over the slightly bent page, I know without a doubt that my mother was reading it.

CHAPTER 11

THE WATCHER

The living room is dark and quiet, and the muted TV is on, but there's nothing worth watching. These days, there's an abundance of depressing news. War, terrorist threats, violent crime, and children dying due to stupid decisions made by people who are supposed to look out for them.

Even so, I leave the TV on. In a way, the soft blue light is hypnotizing and comforting, and, likewise, the rain outside has a similar effect. Despite the tap tap on the windowsill, it's just a constant patter now; no thunder and lightning, no storm.

There are some people who enjoy storms, but I'm not one of them. They remind me of my father. To me, he was like a thunderstorm in that he sometimes could be loud, terrifying, and destructive. While I loved him and knew he loved me in his own way, he also scared the hell out of me. Ironically, when he died, his funeral was postponed by two days due to an angry storm that wouldn't let up, and as a child, I thought that the storm was my father refusing to be silenced forever.

Drowsiness is setting in now. My eyes are drooping, and I'm having trouble holding the remote control. My day was stressful, to say the least. I'm always on edge while I'm watching, always waiting for something to happen, always listening. There are times when I wish I could just switch off, but that's a risk I'm not willing to take.

I get up to head upstairs to bed, but my legs won't hold me. As a result of the drink I had not long ago, coupled with my body's sleep hormones, I feel unsteady on my feet, swaying with each step I take. In frustration, I collapse back on the couch and start flipping through channels. When I find a nature documentary, I turn up the volume and the sounds of animals in the wild relax me and finally lull me to sleep.

After only half an hour, I wake up again feeling restless and unable to sleep any longer. The rain has stopped, and everything is quiet and still. I flick the TV off and turn on the lamp beside the couch. Though my eyes are fatigued and unfocused, I'm sure reading will put me to sleep. I pull out a two-day-old newspaper from underneath the couch, and scan the headlines —the same topics as on the TV news.

The face of a woman whose story I remember all too well stops me in my tracks.

Six months ago, she had black hair, china-blue eyes, and a plump face which made her look younger than her actual age, but in the article she's shown with short spiky black hair and a thin, hardened expression. Having followed her case in such an intense manner—from her arrest to her conviction—it almost feels like I know her personally. As I read the article, my throat is closing up, and my lungs are choking on something heavy and black inside of me.

> In a shocking turn of events, Amanda Lawson, 34, who murdered her two-year-old daughter and hid her body in a safe, has been found dead by her cellmate, who is also serving a life sentence for murder.

I toss the newspaper aside and shut my eyes. There may have been some people who wished Amanda Lawson dead, but not me. If anything, I am enraged by her death. It is not enough; I wanted her to live with the knowledge of what she did, to suffer for the rest of her life. Death eliminates pain. Lifelong suffering behind bars would have been more suitable. It would have been more just. No one who harms a child should be allowed to rest.

Although, sometimes, death may be the only answer.

Mia's innocent face suddenly comes to mind. It is a comfort to know that the little girl's life will never be cut short, because I will always be here to watch over her, just at the edge of sight, ever vigilant, ever on guard.

CHAPTER 12

AVERY

Having decided to introduce myself to Miss Campbell, I'm a little early to pick Mia up from school. Mia still won't stop talking about her, and I want to thank her for taking care of my daughter. She's just finishing her conversation with another parent in front of the school when I catch sight of her, and her amber eyes light up as she sees me. "You must be Mia's mother."

"I am." I extend my hand to shake hers. "I'm sorry we haven't met up close yet. I'm glad to finally meet the woman who has been paying so much attention to my daughter. I'm sorry it's been weeks and I didn't make time for—"

"You don't have to worry about it. You have bigger issues to deal with. I was told about what happened to her dad. I'm so sorry."

Wrapping my arms around my body, I nod. "She's going through a lot."

"So are you." She puts her hand on my forearm gently. "Mia is in good hands." She leans closer and winks. "She's one of my favorites."

"She knows it too, I'm sure," I say. "Thank you for everything."

"That's all right." She smiles and I get a peek of her dimples. "She's a wonderful child and I love watching out for her." She beams at me. "And I'm happy I can be there for her at this time."

"It really means a lot. Thank you."

In the midst of our exchange, Mia rushes out of the school doors and leaps into my arms. Her little arms wrap around my neck and squeeze me tightly.

"Mommy, I missed you," she says, then she looks at her teacher. "Miss Campbell, this is my mommy."

"I just met her," Miss Campbell says, lifting then dropping one of Mia's pigtails. "And she's every bit as pretty as you said she was."

Mia's face lights up, then she giggles. "See. I told you."

Mia hugs Miss Campbell in a way that tells me she's very fond of her, and I smile before she finally takes my hand and tugs me toward the parking lot.

"It was very nice to meet you," I call out to Miss Campbell.

She waves at us. "It was lovely to meet you too, Mia's Mom. Maybe next time we can have a longer chat."

"That would be nice," I say and we leave her standing there until we get into the car.

I decide to treat Mia to ice cream to brighten up her day even more, and I pick out the flavors with her assistance before we sit in the back next to a big window. The sunshine warms my skin and Mia chatters about her school day. After a few minutes, she puts her elbows on the table, resting her chin on her fists, just as Keith likes to do. My mind immediately goes to him and the dream I had last night, right before I confided in Ruth.

"Mommy," Mia says, digging her spoon into the caramelized vanilla ice cream.

"Yes, baby?" I pick up a big spoonful of chocolate syrup, drizzling it on top of my own ice cream.

"You look sad." Mia shovels ice cream into her mouth and winces at the cold.

"I do? I'm sorry. I was thinking about Daddy."

"Mommy, Miss Campbell told me that if we think happy thoughts, miracles will happen. So we have to think good thoughts about Daddy, and he will wake up from the deep sleep." Her eyes light up, and I know she has thought of something exciting. "Maybe if you kiss him, he will wake up like Sleeping Beauty."

I laugh out loud. It's impossible not to be drawn in by her innocence. "I like that idea a lot. I'll try it when I visit him this evening."

Mia's joy is contagious as she dances in her seat. "I hope he wakes up. I want to tell him about Miss Campbell."

"Me too." I press my lips to her cheek. "If it doesn't work the first time, I'll just keep kissing him every day."

She brings her hands together in a happy clap. "That's a good idea, mommybee."

As I spoon chocolate chip ice cream into my mouth, I nod. We eat in silence, then I say, "Tell me more about your school day."

Like a little princess, she dabs the corners of her lips with a napkin then rests her chin back on her fist. "Really good. Miss Campbell gave me another special project."

"Wow, you are one busy girl. What project is that, sweetheart?"

"She gave me a book, and I have to write about the things that make me happy every day."

"Miss Campbell seems to have so many great ideas. That's a good one."

Journaling helps me and many people cope with difficult emotions. I should have thought of that for Mia.

We're just about done with our ice creams when through the window I catch a glimpse of a familiar figure walking along the street, a woman with dark-brown curls. She turns around and glances in our direction. It's Celeste, and as soon as she sees us she smiles and waves. She taps on the window and points to the door, signaling that she will come in.

"Look, Mommy, it's Celeste." Mia jumps out of her seat and runs to the door just as Celeste enters.

She reaches for Mia and pulls her into her arms. "Hi there, sweetheart. I'm sorry to disturb the ice cream party." She helps Mia into her chair before pulling out one for herself. "I was just driving by when I saw your car out in the parking lot and wondered if you girls were in here eating ice cream without me."

"There's no need to apologize," I say with a smile. "You're a little late though; we're just finishing up."

"We can order more if you want," Mia says, looking up at Celeste with adoring eyes.

"No, young lady." I wag a finger at her. "You've had enough ice cream today."

Celeste leans closer to Mia. "You know what, Miss Mia? If your mommy lets you come and sleep over soon, we can make our own ice cream. I used to do it all the time as a child."

Mia turns to me, her eyes bulging. "Can I please, Mommy?"

"Of course you can. I'll arrange the perfect day with Celeste."

As we're walking to the car and Mia is running in front of us, I turn to Celeste. "You don't have to worry about Mia, you know. Ruth is there too and she's a great help."

Celeste links her arm with mine. "I know, and it's not as if you're not there as well. I just can't stop worrying sometimes. I think about your childhood and how unhappy you were around your parents."

"But this has more to do with you, doesn't it?" I ask, squeezing her hand. "I know both our parents kind of neglected us in different ways, but Mia's life isn't like that. You know that, right? She has two parents who love her very much. And once Keith comes back to us, life will be great again."

"Of course I know that. Ignore me. I'm just silly sometimes." She pulls me into a hug. "My break is over; I better get back to work."

"Okay. It was so nice bumping into you." I pause. "By the way, how are the new masseuses getting on?"

"They're fantastic. Would I be out here enjoying fresh air and freedom if they weren't doing a great job? You know me, I'd be watching them like a hawk." She gives me a gentle warning look. "You shouldn't think too much about work, remember?"

"I know. It's just that... I miss it sometimes."

"No." She places her hands on my shoulders and looks me directly in the eyes. "You need to take some time off from work and focus on Mia... and Keith. You're doing enough already from home."

"Okay, I will." I give her a quick hug. "Have a great weekend."

Celeste hugs Mia again and reminds her of the promise to make ice cream together. Then she walks back to her own car, a white Honda CR-V, and drives off.

Half an hour after we arrive home, I take a shower then head to the hospital, where I spend the remainder of the day waiting for good news, talking to Keith, and working on my laptop to distract myself. It's 7 p.m. when I step out the doors again into the night.

I'm halfway home when I turn the car around suddenly. Keith kept a diary too, and I think I have to read it. Although it feels like I'm betraying him, it might be the only chance I have to understand those last words he said to me. I call home on my way to our house, and my father's slurred voice comes on the line.

"Dad, it's me. Is everything okay with you?"

"I'm fine," he says. "Just watching TV. The game is on."

"Okay. Well, I just wanted to let you guys know that I'll be late home tonight. Please let Mom know."

"What time is it?" he asks, even though he could look at the living-room clock.

"Seven-fifteen," I say.

"Are you at the hospital?" he asks. "I will come and see Keith one of these days."

My parents have not visited Keith once since the accident. Ruth, however, has stopped by twice. My father said it would only upset my mother and, despite his repeated promises to stop by, he never does.

"Yes," I lie. "I'm at the hospital."

"Okay, I see. Your mother is in bed, and I just fed Mia and we played a round of UNO. She was waiting for you to read her a story." He coughs, then clears his throat loudly. "Avery, I understand you have to be there for Keith, but you need to remember that Mia needs you too."

"I know, Dad," I say through gritted teeth. "And I'm doing the best I can. You might not hear me come in tonight, so I'll see you all in the morning."

"Yup," he replies, his tone tinged with disapproval.

Why he thinks he can tell me how to parent my child when he's drunk half the time is beyond me. If he's not at the bar or passed out drunk on the couch, he plays with Mia, takes her fishing at the river, and even helps her with her homework, but that's only half the time when he's sober.

I drive through the dark streets toward the house that had felt like home before Keith's accident, but is now so quiet and full of memories that remind me of the good times Keith and I might never experience together again.

My stomach is in knots as I get closer to our street. I've never intruded on Keith's privacy before; I always trusted him. Would he understand what I'm about to do?

Upon arriving in our neighborhood, I turn off my car and

stare up at the white-washed house. Keith and I did not fall in love with our house at first sight like some people do. Rather, we fell in love with the concept of turning it into our dream home. It was run-down and in disarray when we bought it, and that excited us. A love of interior decorating is one of the things we have in common. From the white marble tiles on the bathroom floors to the silver doorknobs on the doors, from every plank of oak wood on the living room floor to the paintings on the walls, we renovated the house top to bottom. It has now been converted into a beautiful three-bedroom home with an open floor plan, a large kitchen with a breakfast nook, a deck over-looking a man-made lake, and a greenhouse in the backyard.

As I get out of the car and approach the house, I feel like a stranger, and looking at my home makes me feel sick in the stomach. It's as if someone smashed our dream onto the ground and now everything is broken and the shards of glass are too many to pick up.

The night is quiet and still, with the only sound coming from the crickets in the backyard. After unlocking the front door, I rush to our bedroom, where I head to Keith's side of the bed, and I pull out the bedside table drawer hoping to find the brown leather diary I gave him for Christmas last year. But it's nowhere to be found.

It was here; I'm certain of that. Several days after the acci-dent, when I came to pack Keith's hospital bag, I saw it. And Keith is very organized and obsessed with putting things back where they belong.

Knowing that it's gone, along with whatever he might have written inside it, is like a punch to my gut. I race to the bath-room and barely avoid tripping over a pair of my shoes. Inside, my back rests against the shower stall as I sink to the floor. With my knees pressed against my chest, I sob out loud until my eyes are dry.

I feel sick whenever I think of those words. *I took a life.* It seems insane, completely impossible, but I can't help myself. My mind keeps returning to that sentence repeatedly, until it feels as if my brain will explode.

I have to do something, anything.

I get up from the floor, blow my nose, and wipe away the tears, before I continue to search every inch of the house. But the diary is nowhere in sight.

CHAPTER 13

Like a blade, the teenage cashier's voice cuts through the silence. "Sorry, this card is declined again," she says. "Have you got another one?"

My chest pulses as I gaze down at the piece of plastic in my hand, then at the groceries on the belt. "I don't understand. This shouldn't happen."

The cashier pops her gum loudly and shakes her head. "It might be time for you to call your bank, lady," she says in a bored tone. "Or check your balance."

"You think I'm not aware of my own account balance?" I snap at her and immediately feel embarrassed by my outburst. The last time I checked the balance on this card was maybe a week before Keith's accident—and in three days, he'll have been in a coma for a month. I don't use the card often, but I didn't think there was anything to worry about. There should certainly be enough money in the account to pay for more than just groceries.

The girl shrugs her shoulders and bats her fake eyelashes at me. "It's a suggestion, that's all."

Behind me, another customer, a man with greasy black hair

and a spotted face, snorts at me. It would be so satisfying to turn around and tell him off, but my attention is focused on the cashier.

"I only have this card with me, and I know there is money in my account. There must be something wrong with your machine."

"Whatever." She doesn't look interested as she twirls a lock of blonde hair around her finger while chewing gum with her mouth open, giving me a peek of a yellowed tooth.

All eyes are on me, and I feel humiliated. As much as I want to continue defending myself, the words die on my tongue, and with a sigh, I slip my card back into my wallet. "I'm sorry for the inconvenience. I don't have cash on me, so I guess I'll have to come back," I say in a defeated voice.

The grocery store parking lot is crowded with cars and people, and I keep my eyes trained on the ground as if it could shield me from the world.

Once I reach the safety of my car and unlock the door, someone calls my name. "Mrs. Watkins, stop! Here are your groceries." It's a familiar voice.

Behind me, Miss Campbell is holding two grocery bags. "Thank God I caught up with you. I paid for your groceries. Here." She holds out one of the bags for me to take.

I don't know what to say; I am completely taken aback by her gesture.

"Thank you," I mumble. "But I can't accept this. I'll just get some cash and come back." Having my daughter's teacher pay for my groceries is inappropriate, to say the least.

Miss Campbell waves me off. "Nonsense. You're not going to convince me otherwise. It's my pleasure to help you." She hands me the bag. "I can't take these back inside."

Tears form in my eyes at her kindness, and my hand trembles as I take the bag from her, my throat tight. "But I'll have to pay you back."

"No. Don't worry about it. It's nothing, really. I'm just glad I was there to help."

I look down at the bag in my hand. "I... I don't know what to say."

"You don't have to say anything at all."

"Well, thank you so much." I raise my gaze up to meet hers. "I'm surprised to see you around here. Do you live nearby?" I'm desperate to change the subject and to get back to feeling comfortable.

"Yes, I do. This is my closest grocery store; I live ten minutes away from here. How about you?"

"What a coincidence. Mia and I are staying with my family, who live close by on Riverside Drive. I guess we both have to drive a long way to school, then."

Now I feel even more ashamed of getting to the school late when Miss Campbell travels the same distance to get there, yet always arrives on time.

"I see... your parents?"

"Yes, we moved in with them shortly after my husband's accident. I needed help with Mia."

"Okay, well, I'd better run, I'm cooking lunch for friends. See you around, Avery." She gives a little wave and walks away.

Confused, I stare after her. I can't recall telling her my first name. I guess Mia must have told her, or she saw it on the school's documentation.

Around me, people walk out of the grocery store laden with bags, and a boy of about thirteen carrying two giant boxes of cereal stares at me as he passes. With my keyless remote, I unlock my car and place the bag on the passenger seat. Once I'm seated behind the wheel, I reach for my phone and access the joint bank account Keith and I share.

My mouth falls open.

We have a negative balance of ten thousand dollars. The transactions show a significant withdrawal from the day before

Keith's accident, followed by a payment to Seeds & Buds, a local florist. There's a possibility Keith bought me flowers from there before, but I haven't received any in a while. My mother would have told me if he had bought some for her. Florals always get her excited.

I would have driven straight to the flower shop, if it weren't for the fact that it's 4 p.m. and they close at 2 p.m. on Saturdays.

How will I be able to make it through the weekend without knowing what's going on?

After driving around, trying to process both what I saw on my phone and my embarrassing moment at the store, I get home at nearly five o'clock. For the first time in a while, my father is as sober as iced tea and he has cleaned himself up. He's wearing a black button-down shirt and black slacks with his gray thinning hair neatly combed back. But he doesn't look happy.

"What's going on, Dad?" I ask, setting the groceries on the kitchen counter.

He narrows his eyes and says, "I was worried about you. Where were you?"

"Dad, you know I went to the hospital. I also had lunch with Drake. He wanted to update me on Keith's business."

"I know that, sunshine, but you are neglecting your responsibilities. Your daughter kept asking for you all day."

"Not again, Dad." I put the milk in the refrigerator and turn to him. "You know I need to go to the hospital. Keith may be in a coma, but the doctors say he might still be aware of my presence." I try to sound calm and rational, but my temper is rising. Almost every conversation I have with my father lately is focused on my parenting abilities, and it's starting to get to me.

"And your daughter needs you right now!" he says firmly, his voice rising. "Mia can't have both her parents gone." He inhales a breath. "She might look like she's coping, but that little girl is hurting. Sometimes she only pretends to be happy so you won't be upset."

"I'm aware of that, Dad." My head drops to my chest.

He clasps my shoulders and makes me look into his eyes, which still have a faint red tint to them. "You need to spend more time with her. Let her know you still love her."

"What about you?" I ask, my eyes welling up with tears. "Do you love me?"

"How can you ask me that?" He drops his hands and his face crumples. "I'm your father. Of course I love you."

"It's just that I haven't heard you say it in a while."

Clearing his throat, he parts his lips, but doesn't say more. I can count on my fingers how many times my father has told me that he loves me. Most often, it has been on my birthday.

"You know I love you," he says, looking embarrassed. "But this isn't about us. It's about Mia."

Stepping away from him, I turn back to the grocery bag.

"I'll spend more time with her this weekend."

"I know you will." He smiles. "You're a good mother, it's just that you're preoccupied. I know how much you love Keith. But there is no one more important than your child, especially one so young."

He leaves the kitchen, and I finish putting away the groceries with a heavy weight on my chest. Being made to feel like a bad mother at the most trying time in my life is too much for me. When I am spending time with my daughter, it's getting more and more difficult to maintain the charade that everything is fine when I feel as if it's all falling apart.

Calling out to Mia, I climb the stairs. "Honeybee? Mommy's home."

When I open my daughter's door, I find her curled up on the couch with her nose in a copy of *The Simple Princess*, a book that Miss Campbell gave her recently. Her hair is tied in one braided ponytail with two red ribbons, and she's wearing a black dress with pink and white polka dots.

"Hello, Mommy," she says, setting the book aside. "I was

waiting for you the whole day. Grandpa took me fishing, but I wanted to go to the zoo with you. You promised."

I sit down next to her on the couch and hug her. "How about we do something different tomorrow?" I ask. "How about we go to the playground and have a picnic?"

Mia's eyes sparkle with excitement and she kisses my cheek. "Thank you, Mommy," she says. "It will be so much fun."

When she wraps her arms around my neck, I remember her as the baby girl with chubby cheeks and eyes that stared into mine so intently when I breastfed her. I used to feel like I was the most important person in her life.

I spend the rest of the evening with her, listening to her telling me about the things she did with my dad, then, for the second time in ages, we all have dinner together as a family, instead of me eating hospital sandwiches washed down with coffee.

After dinner, I tuck Mia into bed and go to the kitchen to watch my father load the dishwasher. I decide to have another conversation with him while my mother is having a bath.

"Dad," I say, "do you need help?"

Turning around, he smiles. "No, it's okay. Why don't you have a seat? I could use some company."

We don't talk for a few minutes as I listen to the china clinking, and after a while, I decide to break the silence.

"It's nice that you're back, Dad. That you're, you know, here."

He turns his back to me and starts scrubbing a pot. "I've always been here."

"Not really," I reply cautiously.

Turning away from the sink, he wipes his hands on a white kitchen towel, and then he goes to the fridge, opens it, and takes out a bottle of beer. Leaning against the counter, he opens the bottle and takes a sip. My heart sinks. I should have known he wouldn't last a day.

"I know I sound like a hypocrite right now, telling you how to be a parent to your child when I failed at the job." He drops his gaze. "I'm not saying I was perfect, far from it. I had... have problems, and I will not pretend they don't exist. I failed a lot as a father and I'll live with the guilt for the rest of my life. I can't help my addiction and I can't change the past, but I know only too well how flawed parents can be and the consequences." He closes his eyes briefly. "I just... I want to make sure you don't make the same mistakes I did. You have the opportunity to do a better job."

As I rise from my seat, I take a deep breath. "I'm trying my best, Dad. I really am."

He raises his beer in a toast. "That's all I'm asking for, darling."

CHAPTER 14

THE WATCHER

I'm in Rodeo Park, surrounded by happy children running around and laughing while the sun is shining down on them. Clean and refreshing air carries the scent of grass trampled by little feet, causing it to release its perfume. I briefly tilt my head back and watch the sun glisten through the leaves of the tree I'm sitting under. Although today's weather forecast predicted rain, the sky is a bright blue. Several adults are sitting on the sidelines watching the children play.

I'm one of them.

I sit on a bench a safe distance away and watch the kids for a few minutes before removing a ham sandwich wrapped in plastic from a bag on my lap. I bite into it, then return it to the bag.

As I watch a boy of about five or six years old sitting off to the side crying, my heart sinks and my eyes scan the area, trying to locate the boy's parents without success. The only people present are other children playing, and their parents, who are seated on benches, are eating, reading, or staring at their mobile phones.

In response to the boy's crying, my hands curl at my sides,

and the weight grows heavier in my chest. It was not that child's choice to be born into this world. His parents once wanted him, and even if they didn't, he's here now, so they have to face up to their responsibilities.

I can see his mother now. She's walking toward him, but her face does not show concern, and her arms are not open to pull her son into a hug. Instead, she grabs his arm, yanks him up, and drags him toward the small gate. The wind carries the sound of her angry voice to me. She's scolding the boy even though he's already in pain. Why would she want to hurt him more?

Looking away from the sickening sight, I take several deep breaths to regroup.

My gaze soon finds Avery, my reason for being here. On a patch of grass beneath a tree, she and Mia are sitting with a picnic feast laid out on a blanket between them. Mia is speaking, but Avery is staring into space and doesn't seem to hear her.

As I watch Avery pretend her daughter is not there, I feel my chest ache, burning with frustration, but pity replaces my anger when I look at Mia and see how sad she looks.

As my fingers go numb from gripping the bench too tight, I let out a shaky breath, forcing myself to calm down. Mia needs me to stay in control. The girl needs comforting, her mother needs scolding, and this madness needs to end. I want to fix things.

Three boys on bicycles are riding around in circles. After watching them for a few seconds, I turn back to Avery, who's still engrossed in her own thoughts. It is not long before Mia is fed up with being ignored and gets up. I can feel her sadness as she walks to the swings and swings herself back and forth, her eyes downcast. With her feet, she pushes off the ground, her little hands holding onto the chains. Her composure is slipping, but she's fighting to keep it together. Even from a distance, I can sense she's doing her best to push back the sadness, trying not to cry.

Should I venture out a little closer? Maybe there is something I can do to make her realize how special she is. My first instinct is to swoop her into my arms, protect her from rejection, and take care of her.

But not yet. Not today.

Avery finally remembers she's a mother and glances over in Mia's direction, then she stands.

"Mia," she calls out as she approaches the swings, but the girl doesn't respond. As she continues to push herself back and forth, she ignores Avery, just like she was ignored earlier.

Avery steps in front of Mia and reaches out to touch her cheek until she looks up. Because children are quick to forgive, Mia believes whatever lies her mother is telling her and is now throwing herself into her arms. It won't be long before the little girl's heart is broken again, but for now, I can relax and breathe easy knowing that she's safe.

Tossing the barely eaten sandwich into the trash can, I get up from the bench and walk back to where I parked my car. After walking a short distance, I stop and look back at the park. Avery is now chasing the girl around the swings. Giggling and squealing with delight, Mia appears to have forgotten the pain her mother had just caused her.

Just as I'm about to get back in my car, I spot the mother who had dragged her crying son away earlier. They are both getting out of a car parked a few feet away from mine. With his head hung low, the boy walks in front of his mother. I can't see his face to determine if he is crying. I'm getting the feeling that his mother punished him in the privacy of the car, where no one was watching.

The boy quickens his pace whenever the mother gets closer, and when she falls back, he glances over his shoulder to prepare for whatever is coming next. He's clearly afraid of her. It's easy for me to recognize an abused child by their posture: hunched back, slumped shoulders, and dragging feet.

The boy lifts his hand and sweeps it across his eyes, which confirms my suspicions. He's wiping away tears.

A parent should never hurt their child.

After they have both returned to the park, I pick up the biggest stone I can find before approaching the parked car, a red Toyota Corolla. I crouch down on one side of the car where no one can see me, wedged between the vehicle and the bushes. Then I completely shut out the world as I slam the stone into the body of the metal until a dent appears, and I smile as it gets deeper and deeper.

I expected the car alarm to go off, but it's my lucky day. The only sound I hear is the crunching of metal. I'm out of breath and my shoulders are burning, but I keep going. In my mind's eye, I imagine that I'm inflicting pain on the abusive mother, the kind she inflicted on her son. After the damage has been done and my head is clearer, I get out the small notebook and pen I usually carry around with me, and I scribble a few words on the paper.

Don't you dare hurt that boy again. I'll be watching you.

I place the note on the ground next to the car and secure it down with a smaller rock. Then I walk away.

Inside my car, my hands are still trembling and I shake them out, then turn on the radio. As I drive home, I feel my anger draining from my body, leaving me tired. My body feels weak, and I'm having trouble focusing on the road, so I pull up to the curb and turn off the engine.

What I really need is a strong drink, something to take the edge off.

CHAPTER 15

AVERY

I walk out of the bank, feeling dejected. I've been anxious all weekend, but the banker has not been able to put my mind at ease. It was not a mistake; our joint account does have a negative balance. And Keith was the one who walked into the bank a day before his accident and withdrew ten thousand dollars.

Getting back into the car, I drive down the street with my head spinning from so many questions. What did Keith do with the money? What did he buy? We have an agreement that if either of us wants to spend more than a hundred dollars, we must consult each other first. However, he did not consult me this time. Could it be that he didn't want me to know? Is it possible that he had intended to replace the money but was hindered by the accident?

I guess I'll only know that answer once he wakes up. But there's another question I might be able to get an answer to. The flowers. Who did he buy them for? I need to know.

A few minutes later, I pull up in front of the Seeds & Buds flower shop and rush inside. As soon as I enter the store, I sneeze due to the overpowering fragrance of so many flowers and all the pollen in the air. There's a rush of people crowding into the shop and queueing up at the counter, laden with summer blooms.

I look around for a member of staff, but everyone seems busy, and I browse around the place like a customer, hoping that will attract their attention and they will hurry to assist me.

On display are many vibrant flowers in an array of colors, shapes, and sizes. There are also leafy plants, ferns with exotic fronds, and a collection of succulents ranging in size from tiny to large enough to fill up a small room.

"Can I help you with something?" a cheerful voice asks.

I turn around and see a smiling older woman with two long braids standing in front of me. Her name tag reads "Caroline."

"Oh, hi. I was just looking," I say, pretending to be interested in the plants around me.

She clasps her hands under her chin. "Is there anything in particular you were looking for?"

"Well, actually, I have a question about an order you recently received."

"Is that so? Did you order something for yourself or someone else?"

I shake my head. "No, my husband placed the order, but it wasn't delivered."

She wrinkles her brow in confusion. "It never arrived?"

"Something like that." I take the bank statement out of my purse for proof of payment.

She glances down at the date and then looks up. "June twenty-fifth. That's a month and two days ago. Come with me," she says and leads me to a back office filled with flower-arranging supplies, such as floral foam, buckets of water, and floral supply boxes.

She motions for me to sit at a corner table.

"I'm Caroline, by the way," she says, pointing to her name tag.

"Hello, Caroline." I smile, but my heart is pounding wildly. "I'm Avery Watkins."

"Thanks for coming by, Avery. I'm glad to meet you."

Another woman walks into the room. The woman looks younger than Caroline, who must be somewhere in her late fifties. Her hair is up in a ponytail, and she's dressed like someone who has just come from a yoga class.

Caroline puts a hand on the woman's shoulder. "Avery, meet Bree, one of our floral consultants."

"Nice to meet you, Bree," I say. I'm desperate for the introductions to be over so I can get the answers I need.

"Bree, Avery's husband ordered from us on June twenty-fifth," Caroline explains. "Unfortunately, the order was never received."

"Oh, no, I'm so sorry," Bree says as she pulls a binder from a shelf. "This binder contains all of our successfully delivered orders. If it is here, it has been signed for by the receiver. What was the date again?"

"June twenty-fifth," Caroline says as I wait with bated breath.

Someone in the store calls for Caroline, and she excuses herself and leaves the room, her long skirt swishing around her.

Bree stops turning the pages and taps a finger on the one in front of her. "Yes, it is here. The flowers were delivered and signed for the day after the order was placed."

On the day of the accident.

"Does it say who it was delivered to?" I ask. "It could have been delivered to the wrong address."

Bree shakes her head as she closes the folder. "It was the same address the customer provided."

I rise to my feet, pull out my phone, and open the notes app. "Can you tell me the address?"

"I'm sorry, but we do not share addresses with anyone."

My phone slips from my hand as I go to rub my forehead, my eyes closing in dismay.

"I'm really sorry," Bree says as she picks up the phone and hands it to me. "I wish I could share the information with you, but it's against company policy."

"It's not your fault." I put my phone back in my bag and nod. "I understand. Thank you for your time, anyway."

Bree continues, "I'm sure your husband will tell you who he ordered the bouquet for. We have the best customer service in town, and our customers love our flowers and plants. I hope he will do business with us again."

I leave the floral shop with more questions than before, my mind churning. Just how many secrets was my husband keeping from me?

When I get to our house and exit the car, someone calls my name.

It's my neighbor, Mallory Bolder. She's standing on her front porch, dressed in faded blue jeans and a tight T-shirt. It seems like almost every month she wears a new hairstyle, and this month, she dyed her hair blonde and cut it in a shag. In her hand is her dog Peanut's leash.

"Hi, Mallory," I say, a bit taken aback. Right now, I'm not in the mood to talk to anyone.

"Avery, it's good to see you. I heard about Keith. Is he doing all right?"

"He's still in the hospital, but he's doing better," I lie, because I can't handle anyone's pity at this moment, or more questions. Mallory is also a fan of neighborhood gossip.

"I am so glad to hear that. We have all been worried since we haven't seen you around much recently."

"I've been at the hospital almost every day, and we've been staying with my parents," I say, stepping toward the door.

She bends to scoop Peanut into her arms. With her fine hair and button eyes, the Maltese puppy looks like a toy. "How's Mia doing?"

"She's fine. She's at school right now."

"You need to bring her over to play with Jane some time; it's been a while since the two girls played together."

"I will," I say, eager to get inside.

Yipping, Peanut tries to wriggle free from Mallory's grip, which is so tight that the dog can barely move. When Mallory finally lets go, the dog charges toward the backyard, barking at something only she can see.

"Bye," I say and hurry inside before anyone else in the neighborhood shows up.

I don't have time to speak with anyone. I need to figure out who Keith ordered the flowers for and why.

Keith's wallet was found in the pocket of the jeans he was wearing when the accident happened, and I put it in the kitchen drawer. It's made of old, worn leather, a gift Liam gave him for his birthday. When I open it, my heart races in anticipation of finding a name, phone number, or address written on a note or card.

I find his credit cards, driver's license, and several business cards belonging to vendors he works with to run his landscaping business, and nothing that gives me the information I need. Just as I'm about to close it, I decide to dig deeper into his wallet's back pocket.

There's a folded piece of paper. My heart speeds up, my palms slick with sweat as I unfold it. Bingo.

The receipt is from Seeds & Buds, for a bouquet of flowers that cost fifty dollars.

He must have sent the flowers to someone who meant something to him.

I stare at the piece of paper for a few minutes, hoping that I can make out a name or something that would help, but there is nothing. Just the date, the amount, and the words, "Thank you for your business. Seeds & Buds."

In a moment of frustration, I'm tempted to return to the floral shop and ask for the information again, but Bree made it clear that none will be shared. The paper goes into the pocket of my jeans and the wallet goes back to its rightful place in the drawer.

I sink into the chair at the island. It pains me to think about it, but a seed of doubt has been planted in my mind.

What if my husband was having an affair?

CHAPTER 16

A red sedan honks at me and I jolt, my heart racing. My mind was so entangled in my thoughts that I did not notice it pull up next to me. When we stop at a red traffic light, the Afro-haired driver gestures for me to roll down the window and, with a gulp, I do it. I have no idea what I did wrong, though it could simply be that he wants to point out something to do with my car.

The man leans across and says, "Ma'am, you were about to drive off the road. Are you okay?" His voice is thick and deep, as if he's smoked for many years. "Keep your eyes open. You were practically in the opposite lane."

"I'm sorry," I say, smiling in gratitude to the kind stranger who woke me up before I caused an accident. Thank goodness he isn't a cop.

I try to calm myself down by taking a deep breath. I need to be more cautious. I won't allow my daughter to end up with both parents in the hospital or worse.

I'm still finding it hard to believe that my husband could have been hiding things from me. When we celebrated our last wedding anniversary, I remember thinking how happy I was, how wonderful it was for us to still be deeply in love after nine years of marriage.

The light turns green, and I roll up the window and put my foot on the accelerator. According to the dashboard, it is 2:55 p.m. so I need to be at Mia's school in five minutes. I'll be late, but not by much.

I pull up in front of the school and Mia is already waiting for me outside by the steps. When she sees me, she waves and heads for the car.

"Hello, Mommy," she says, climbing onto her car seat and fastening her seatbelt just as I'm about to do it for her.

As I kiss her on the forehead, I notice that she's clutching a gray stuffed rabbit toy. The ears and fur of the animal are worn out and tattered. There's something about it that makes me wonder if I've seen it before, and it clearly isn't new, but I know for a fact that it doesn't belong to Mia.

"Where did you get that, sweetheart?"

Mia's eyes light up as she hugs the toy. "It was in my gym bag."

I look at the rabbit again, carefully inspecting it. "Did someone put it there by mistake?" I ask. "Maybe it was put into the wrong bag."

"No, Mommy. It was a surprise, and the letter said it's mine. I showed it to Miss Campbell and we read it together."

"Mia, what letter? Can I have a look at it?"

She hesitates for a second, looking confused, and says, "I forgot it in my gym bag."

Mia loves gym class so much that I'm not surprised she forgot about whatever letter she's talking about. She's holding on so tight to the rabbit that I'm not sure she'll ever let me take it away from her.

"Well, maybe you can remember what was written in the letter?" I suggest.

Mia tightens her arms even more around the toy. "It said this is a magic rabbit and her name is Holly."

I frown as I look back at the rabbit, and I'm suddenly filled with the oddest feeling that the stuffed animal is watching me. Peeling my gaze from it, I shift my attention back to Mia.

"Was there anything else in the letter?"

"Yes, it said if I take care of her, she will take care of me."

When I look up and see Miss Campbell at the front doors of the school, I know I need to have a quick word with her.

"Sweetie, step out of the car for a minute. I need to speak to Miss Campbell."

"Please don't ask her to take Holly away. I need magic, Mommy. I need a friend."

"Don't worry. I just need to have a quick word with your teacher, and you and Holly should come with me."

Mia reluctantly gets out of the car and follows me.

Miss Campbell smiles as she sees me coming. She seems to be about to say something, but instead I speak first. "Miss Campbell, good afternoon."

"Good afternoon, Mrs. Watkins. It's lovely to see you."

"Oh, thank you," I reply. "Mia showed me the stuffed rabbit she found in her gym bag, and I just wanted to make sure it doesn't belong to anyone else."

The teacher smiles at Mia and looks back at me, shaking her head. "It actually came with a note that had Mia's name on it. Did she tell you about it?"

"But it looks like such a treasured toy. Are you sure there isn't a child who's missing it?"

Miss Campbell clasps her hands in front of her. "I don't think so because the note was specifically addressed to Mia." She leans in and whispers so that Mia can't hear. "It was an anonymous gift from Miss Simmons. She said it had once belonged to her daughter, who's too big for it now, and it had comforted her so much when she was little. She hoped it would do the same for Mia, and she asked me to put it in Mia's gym bag for her to find."

"That's really sweet of her. And she didn't want Mia to know it was from her?"

Miss Campbell shakes her head. "She wanted it to seem magical. I think it worked."

"You're right about that." I glance at Mia, who's now standing by a potted palm tree, rocking her rabbit back and forth. "I'm sure Mia will enjoy her new friend; she could certainly use one right now. I'll thank Miss Simmons when she returns from her leave." I smile at Miss Campbell, then pull out my purse. "I really need to pay you back for the groceries you paid for the other day. Please let me do this."

Before she can protest, I hand her some cash. She smiles, but looks a bit embarrassed as she accepts it. "If you insist."

"Thank you. Now, we should get going. Have a good day."

Back at the house, after spending some time at the playground, we find my mother in the kitchen, which is filled with the smell of spices and meat. Clearly, it's another one of her good days.

Mia runs over to her grandmother and my mom lifts her up into her arms. "Do you smell that, little girl?" Mom asks Mia.

Mia nods, her curly hair bouncing around her face.

"That's dinner. It's lamb stew. We can eat it with sweet potatoes or the fresh bread I baked this morning."

"Oh, that sounds wonderful, Mom," I say. My day has been mentally exhausting, so I'm happy to come home to a house filled with warmth and love.

My mother lowers Mia to the floor and turns to stir in the pot, and Mia grabs the rabbit from her school bag, a big gap-toothed smile on her face.

"Look, Grammy," she says, lifting the toy high in the air. "Someone gave me a magic rabbit. It was a surprise for me."

When my mother turns around, she's still holding the wooden spoon. Her eyes focus on the rabbit, and I watch the smile on her lips fade away. As if in slow motion, the spoon falls from her grasp and clatters to the floor. It splatters sauce all over the floor and Mia's pink shoes.

I watch in confusion as my mother's face turns as white as the flour she used to make the bread this morning. It doesn't take long for her hands to start shaking, her lips to tremble, and her eyes to become wild with what looks like fear.

"Mom?" I ask. "Mom, what's wrong?"

I stop in my tracks when she gives me a cold look.

"Leave me be," she says in a voice that's both shaky and authoritative. Her gaze returns to the rabbit, which Mia dropped onto the floor after my mother scared her. One of the rabbit's ears has landed on top of the dirty spoon.

"Grammy," Mia cries. "Are you sick again?" I can hear the worry in her voice. She's using words I used as a child when out of nowhere my mother withdrew from me.

My mother stumbles out of the kitchen, almost knocking over a chair on her way out. "I'm... I'm sorry," she mumbles.

I can tell Mia is on the verge of tears from the way she looks up at me. "Does that mean we won't have a fun day with Grammy?"

I lift her into my arms and hold her tight. "I don't know, baby. I don't know."

I ask if she wants to go for a walk, and she instantly agrees, but the moment we step out the door, we notice Celeste's car slowing in front of the house. I'm surprised because she had not called to let me know she was coming over, but seeing my friend is always a welcome sight.

"I wanted to surprise you with a visit, and maybe take you both out to dinner unless you've already eaten."

"Grammy spilled the sauce all over the floor," Mia fills her in. "Now dinner is all ruined."

"I see." Celeste gives me a frown, then smiles at Mia. "Looks like I showed up right on time, then. How about we go out for a burger?"

My daughter giggles and jumps up and down. "Yay! I want a cheeseburger."

"Yep, I think that's a good idea," I say. "I'll go get my purse."

I run back inside and grab what I need, then check on my mother in their bedroom, but I find her lying in a fetal position. Not wanting to disturb her, I tiptoe back to the door.

"Where are you going?" she asks suddenly, and I jump. "You're wearing perfume."

"We're going out for dinner with Celeste."

"Don't be late," she mutters without looking at me, and I nod, too numb to argue. Celeste is not a fan of my parents, and the feeling is mutual.

Outside, I find Celeste hugging Mia and whispering something into her ear as she smiles.

Later, when I tuck Mia in, she blinks her sleepy eyes at me and says, "Mommybee, if something bad happens to you and Daddy, can I live with Celeste? She said she'll take good care of me."

My heart freezes to ice, and I have to blink repeatedly to keep the tears at bay. "Nothing bad will happen, baby," I whisper. "Everything is going to be just fine. I promise." If I keep telling Mia that, maybe she will believe it for both of us.

She nods, and after a long moment, she smiles and closes her eyes. "Okay, Mommy."

As soon as I get back to my room, I call Celeste to ask about what Mia said.

"Why would you tell her something like that? She thinks something bad will happen to us."

"Oh no, I didn't mean to scare her. When you went to get your handbag, I was just telling her that before I came to your parents' house, I was taking a donation to the orphanage, and she asked what that was. When she heard it's a place for kids without parents, she asked if I would take care of her if—"

"I get it, Celeste. It's okay. She's been asking a lot for Keith, and I guess she's afraid to lose us."

"Yeah, I can see what you mean. I'm sorry. I shouldn't have mentioned the orphanage."

"Don't worry about it." I yawn. "Thanks for dinner, by the way. It was lovely of you to surprise us like that."

"Anything for both of you. Now, I better leave you to get some sleep."

After the call, I do fall asleep, but I dream of Keith lying in a coffin. His eyes are open and coated with tears as he repeats the words he said to me, just before he slipped into the coma.

CHAPTER 17

Four hours before my alarm goes off, Mia bursts into my room in tears. Yawning and blinking away sleep, I force myself awake. "Honeybee, it's really early. Why are you out of your bed? Why are you upset, sweetheart?" I ask.

She jumps into my lap and clings to me, her eyes red and swollen. "Mommy, Holly's gone. She's not in my bed anymore. She's all gone." She takes a deep breath and tears start to fall.

I push the blankets away, get out of bed, and pull her into my arms.

"You said she was a magic rabbit; maybe she's hiding under the bed. Don't worry; she's sure to be in your room somewhere."

I'm still confused by the way my mother reacted to seeing the stuffed rabbit yesterday. I didn't get a chance to speak with her about it, and my dad accused me of upsetting her so much that she had to take her anxiety pills to cope. I'm sure he was disappointed, like we all were, that she had retreated into her shell again before we could enjoy her company.

Mia curls her hand into mine as she used to do as a baby. "Mommy, can you come and look for her with me?"

I kiss her forehead and tuck her head under my chin. "Of course, baby. We'll ask Mr. Waddles to help us search."

Inside her room, she crawls under her bed and I peer into her closet.

"Mommy, she's not here." She curls up and sobs. "I need her."

"I know you do, sweetheart. She'll find her way back to you. She's a magic rabbit, remember?"

Mia's little face scrunches up in confusion as she looks at me. "But what if she doesn't, just like Daddy?" The tears come again.

I close my eyes and swallow the lump in my throat. "She will, and we have to believe that Daddy will too. Maybe I can take you to visit him again sometime."

She shakes her head vehemently. "No, Mommy. I don't want to see him at the hospital; he looks strange. I want to see him at home."

With my chest aching, I say nothing as I rock her back and forth and try to soothe her, but she's still inconsolable. After a while, I take her with me to my room and we cuddle up together. She doesn't say anything else, but her sobs continue. I wish I could take away her pain, but I can't, so I just lay completely still, listening to the sobs subside and, when she finally stops crying, I hear her breathing slow down, growing deeper and more even, even though I know she's still awake. I am exhausted, but I know that if I sleep now, I'll wake up late and miss dropping her off at school. So I stay awake, watching her until finally she falls asleep.

As soon as the alarm goes off, I kiss her warm forehead, then get up to dress and get ready for the day. It's only when I'm done that I rouse her awake, and the first thing she asks for is her rabbit. As we make our way to the kitchen, I pray that I will see my mother there, for the dark cloud to have passed. But only my dad is at the kitchen table, his hair and face rumpled, looking like he hasn't slept a wink.

He has a cup of coffee in front of him, and I smell a whiff of alcohol in the air. But he looks sober enough to talk to. Mia gives him a hug and he clutches on to her for a little longer than usual.

"My Holly rabbit is gone, Grampy," she murmurs, but this time she doesn't cry.

Dad looks at me and I shrug. Then he pats Mia on the head and promises to keep an eye out for Holly. After breakfast, I put Mia in the car and we drive off. She doesn't say a word the entire way until I pull up at the school, and then I turn to look at her in the backseat.

"Don't worry about your rabbit, honey. With so many people looking for Holly, I'm sure we'll find her very soon."

I see her mouth move, but she doesn't say anything or even unbuckle her seat belt as she normally does. My heart heavy, I get out of the car and go to the back door to open it.

"Come on, sweet girl. It's time for class."

Outside the school, the substitute teacher, Mr. Singer, welcomes her and they disappear into the building.

My next stop after school is the hospital. As I walk down the corridor to Keith's room, I see the regular nurses waving and wishing me a good day.

In light of what I found out yesterday, I almost don't recognize my husband as he lies there in a coma. I just don't know how to feel. Is the man I love and trust a cheater? A killer?

I pull the chair close to his bed and lean my lips against his ear. "Wake up, Keith. I need to know what's going on."

He doesn't move, doesn't give me any indication that I'm reaching him and, sighing, I rest my head on his chest. "Honey, I love you, but I'm confused. I trust you, but I need to know about the money you withdrew and the flowers you bought. Who were they for?"

I straighten up and look at my husband. He's so still, it's as if he is already gone, and I lean back in and stroke his cheek. I just want a sign that he's still in there somewhere. I press my lips to his and wait for him to return my kiss, but when he doesn't, I lift my head again then give it another try.

"Keith, you need to talk to me," I murmur against his lips. "You need to tell me what's going on."

My words are barely a whisper, but I'm too overcome with grief to speak louder.

"Please, baby, wake up and tell me you didn't kill anyone, and you weren't cheating on me. I need to hear it from you." I bite my lip and shake my head. "I need you to say you would never do something like that, and you would never do that to me, to us."

Tears burn my eyes, but I blink them away. I don't want to cry anymore, I don't want to give into that feeling of despair, but I've never been so scared in my life. As I rest my forehead on his chest, I continue to wait, to hope, to pray. Keith is still alive. But my stomach is in knots, and I'm beginning to lose hope even though I'm not ready to let him go. Not yet, not ever.

The scents of hospital soap and disinfectant fill my nostrils as I take a deep breath. Closing my eyes, I slowly exhale, forcing pleasant memories to flood my mind, erasing the image of my unconscious husband and the idea that he might have been unfaithful.

I think back to the day we met at the Willow Gate annual fair. I remember how nervous we both were the first time we spoke, and how I thought he was the most gorgeous man I had ever seen, and was amazed at the fact that he was interested in me. As I reminisce, I recall the day he proposed to me, our vineyard wedding six months later, and our romantic honeymoon in Maine. I remember baking him his favorite coconut and Greek yoghurt cupcakes on every one of his birthdays, and when I let him hold Mia for the first time, the look of awe on his face.

Keith is the perfect husband and hands-on dad. When Mia was a baby, he would wake up with me every night when I breastfed. Even when he had to work the next day and I begged him to go to bed, he always sat next to me and watched Mia suckle while stroking my back. Emotional support, he called it. He always made sure I didn't feel everything was on my shoulders, that we were a team when it came to raising our daughter or doing chores around the house.

I remember his words when he spoke to me, and the sound of his breathing when he whispered into my ear. There are so many precious moments I want to hold on to, so many happy times I want to cherish, and I cling to them like a lifeline. The last thing I want to do is give up on him, since that would mean giving up on us as well. So I force myself to remember, to never forget. I remain by his bedside for hours, afraid to leave him until Doctor Drew enters the room at two o'clock.

"Doctor, he hasn't opened his eyes in a month. When will he wake up?" I ask, desperate for anything that will give me some kind of reassurance.

Every day I visit him, talking to him, reading to him, and telling him whatever is on my mind. Keith doesn't receive many visitors aside from me and a few friends. Even though Silas writes every few days to check on his progress, he hasn't yet visited. I'm positive that Norman forbade him to do it. But it doesn't matter. They don't matter. I'm at Keith's bedside often enough to fill in their absence.

Every time I hope he will wake up and look at me, to answer my questions or crack one of his jokes.

After assessing Keith's chart, the doctor looks at me with sympathy. "Mrs. Watkins, I understand how hard it must be for you to see your husband in this state, but he will wake up when he's ready to."

Looking at my sleeping husband, I feel my stomach twist. "I've been waiting. How long—?"

"For some people, it takes a day, for others it takes a year. You just need to be prepared to wait."

I stare at him, horrified. "A year?"

Based on my extensive research online, I know he's telling the truth. I also know that for some patients, it can take longer than a year. There are even those who never wake up from a coma. Even so, hearing the doctor's words still hits me hard.

I also cannot help but think about the cost of keeping Keith in the hospital for up to a year. Although we have a lot of savings, thanks to Keith who insisted on putting money aside for a rainy day, I'm concerned that we won't have enough to last.

With a lump of fear in my throat, I fold my arms across my chest. "Aside from talking to him, what else can I do to help him wake up?"

Keith has to wake up. There is still so much we need to experience together. We have so many dreams, including one day purchasing a run-down building by the water that we would renovate into a luxury spa retreat. While I would take care of the spa, he would design and maintain a beautiful tranquil garden with waterfalls and fountains, creating a place for our guests to find peace and solitude.

Taking a moment to consider my question, Doctor Drew shakes his head at me. "Just keep doing what you're doing and be patient." He pauses to think. "There's no guarantee, but there is a chance that music might help. It's worth a shot. He may benefit more than you think."

I nod in agreement. "I'll give it a try."

As soon as Doctor Drew leaves the room, I sit back down in my chair and open the music app on my phone. When the sound of soothing jazz fills the room, I take Keith's hand and kiss it. "I know you're in there somewhere. I won't give up on you until you wake up. I'll never give up on us." I pause. "I have to leave shortly to go pick up Mia from school, but I'll see you soon."

I wait for a few moments, hoping he'll give me some indication that he hears me, but I get nothing back. I finally leave, and walking down the corridor, I'm aware that Keith may never wake up, but I need to keep praying for a miracle. I must hold on to any shred of hope like a lifeline.

In front of the school, Miss Campbell gives Mia a long hug and kiss on the top of her head before letting her go to come to the car.

We arrive home to find that my mother is no longer locked away in their bedroom but is sitting woodenly in front of the TV next to my snoring father.

"Hi, Mom. How was your day?" I keep my tone neutral, so I don't accidentally trigger her. I need to choose every word carefully.

Her eyes are lifeless as she half-smiles at me before turning back to the TV.

Giving up, I make Mia a snack and watch her eat, and when she's finished, I send her next door to Ruth, to get her out of the stifling environment. If guilt didn't have me in its grip, I'd pack up our bags and we'd go back to our house, but I have realized that even though initially I moved back home for the support, my parents need me more than I need them. When my mother emerges from her haze, I plan on talking her into going to therapy again.

Left alone with my silent parents, I occupy myself with tidying the house, washing the dishes and putting away the laundry, relishing the chores even though they are monotonous and tedious. If I don't fill my mind with something else, I'll just start thinking about Keith again, and I can't bear it.

I take out the garbage an hour later, planning to pick up Mia afterward from Ruth.

As I push the black garbage bag into the can, something gray and fluffy catches my attention, and it pokes out from between two other garbage bags.

Lifting one of the bags, I gasp in shock.

Who could have put Mia's rabbit in the garbage? And why?

CHAPTER 18

When I retrieve the stuffed rabbit from the garbage, I decide not to show it to Mia just yet, so I take it inside before I get her. Fortunately, the dirt on the rabbit is not too hard to remove, and I'm able to get most of it off using a damp washcloth.

After homework is done, dinner is eaten, and Mia is in bed, I ask to speak to my mother alone in the room she uses to quilt. Filled with sewing and knitting projects, colorful materials, and needles, it looks smaller than I remember it, and the scents of freshly cut pine, new yarn, and fabric glue waft through the air. Hanging quilts, colorful tapestries, and two crocheted dresses cover one wall. As my mother sits on her work chair, a padded recliner with a purple pillow, I close the door. I hold my breath as I pull out the stuffed rabbit from the plastic bag, and I wait patiently for my mother to look at me. Eventually she does. Her eyes mist over as she realizes why I want to speak to her.

Even without asking her, I know the answer to the question on my tongue; her tears and shaking hands already convey it clearly. I sit down on the only couch in the room and I put the rabbit on my lap, its face pointing in my mother's direction, so she can have a good look at it.

"Mom, why did you throw Mia's rabbit in the garbage? What do you have against it? It's just a stuffed toy."

"It's a reminder. I-It reminds me of... of..." Her lips are quivering and she can't quite form coherent words. Suddenly, she stops talking and presses her lips together in a thin line.

Either she's lost for words or she's trying to hide something from me.

As the silence between us grows uncomfortable, a heart-rending cry erupts from her as she covers her face with her hands. Confused, I stay on the couch, waiting for her meltdown to end, and when she eventually drops her hands back into her lap, I ask, "What does the rabbit remind you of, Mom?"

Sniffing, she wipes her eyes with her sleeve. "I don't know where to begin."

"Start anywhere. I just need the truth, Mom. What's going on?"

Her hands clench tightly in her lap, then she blinks once and speaks, her voice stronger than it was moments ago. "It reminds me of my daughter... your sister. But she's gone now."

"My sister?" I whisper.

My body and mind feel paralyzed.

As far as I know, I'm an only child. I stare at my mother. I wait for her to tell me that she was joking and that she didn't mean what she said. But she's no longer looking at me. Her posture is wilting by the second and she's crying again.

I'm afraid of going to her and taking her in my arms. I feel frozen, confused, lost. Sitting silently, I hear the TV in the distance, the murmur of a late-night talk show, and a long while passes before Mom's wet eyes meet mine. They are full of total and utter sadness, deeper and darker than I have ever seen.

"I'm sorry, Avery. Your sister is gone. I can't talk about her. No." She shakes her head slowly. "I can't tell you anymore."

"Why not, Mom?" Now that she's opened a door I didn't

know existed, I can't allow her to close it until she shows me what's hidden behind. "Please tell me what's going on." I'm trying so hard to stay patient with her.

"I don't want to." She closes her eyes and rocks back and forth, something Mia does when she's upset. Then she opens them and looks back at me. "It's too hard."

I push my own pain and fears aside and force myself to stand up to go to her, wrapping my arms around her shaking body. Making her feel safe might be the only way to get her to open up. "You can tell me anything, Mom. I'm your daughter."

While I hold her, her sobs subside and her breathing begins to calm. Although she's still shaking, at least she isn't crying anymore. I lead her to the couch and sit down with her, and for what seems like an eternity, we sit in silence, while I stroke her hair, comforting her without words.

Finally she pulls back and gazes into my eyes. She places her hand on top of mine and holds it tightly, her expression blank.

"You had a sister," she whispers. "Her name was Lynn." She takes her time saying every word, as if she's trying not to say the wrong thing.

"You said she's gone," I say cautiously. "Where? Where did she go to?"

"She's dead, Avery. She was just a little girl." Her words are soft, but they hit me like a sudden blow that jars me to the core.

Stunned, I stare at her and struggle to find any words to say. Could this be why my mother suffers so much mentally, and why my father drinks so much and is so protective over Mia?

"How?" I try to keep my voice steady, but it comes out as a strangled whisper. "How? How did she die?"

She squeezes my hand a little tighter, then pulls away. "I can't talk about it. I've told you enough, please, don't ask me any more questions."

I nod and hug her again, taking in her scent of sandalwood perfume, her warmth, her pain. "Okay, Mom," I say into her shoulder. "I understand."

Of course I can understand how painful it was to tell me that. I can't even find it in me to be angry with her and my father for not telling me about my own sister, because I can't even begin to imagine the agony of losing a child. As I hold my mother, feeling her shake and tremble with grief while I try to contain my own emotions, I have never felt such an overwhelming sense of empathy and compassion. It's probably the closest we've ever been.

"Mom," I say when she stops crying again, "I understand why you threw Mia's rabbit in the trash, but she's going through a lot. The toy comforts her."

My mother pulls back. "But it's a reminder of... Lynn had a rabbit just like that. It's too painful to see it."

"I know, but Mia needs a little comfort right now. And it was a gift. We can't just throw it away." I pause. "How about we allow her to keep it and it stays in her room?"

She nods hesitantly. "You keep it in her room, Avery," she says. "I don't want to see it ever again."

"You won't, I promise. I'll keep it out of your way."

"I'm tired. I need to go to bed." She gets up and walks toward the door, but stops and turns around before walking out of the room. "Goodnight, angel."

As I smile at her, I try to keep the tears at bay. "Goodnight, Mom."

The entire conversation upsets me so terribly that I sit on the couch for a long time, unsure of what to do. My parents kept a secret from me throughout my childhood, just as my husband has been keeping secrets from me. Do I really know anyone I love?

I wish I could scream, throw something, or cry—anything to

get rid of this frustration and anger—but I can't. The room is too stuffy, and, in need of fresh air, I get dressed and step out to go for a short walk, but I never make it to the front door. When I hear the sound of the TV, I change my mind about going out. I can speak to my father; he might be able to answer some of the questions my mother left open. I pray that he's awake and not drunk.

He's awake, but he's not watching television; he's just lying on the couch, staring up at the ceiling, his eyes open but too hazy and unfocused to see.

I step closer to him. "Dad?"

He turns his head toward me and his eyes clear up a little as he sits up.

"What is it, love?" he asks. Despite his slurred speech, he seems almost sober.

"Mom told me about Lynn."

He doesn't say anything for a long time, just stares at me. Then he nods and struggles to stand up. "Yeah?" His voice is sharper now, with a bitter undertone.

"Why haven't you spoken about her before?" My voice comes out louder than I intend, so I take a few deep breaths to calm myself down before continuing. "I had a right to know. She was my sister."

Averting his gaze, he picks up a cup of coffee from the coffee table and leaves the room, and when I follow him to the kitchen, I find him standing by the stove, holding on to the counter.

Finally, he turns to me and answers my question. "We didn't tell you because it's too painful." He reaches into a cupboard to retrieve a bottle of Jack Daniel's, which he pours into the cup of coffee. "We didn't want to hurt you."

"But knowing you kept a secret like that from me all these years hurts. I'm your daughter; you should have told me. How did she die? Can you at least tell me that?"

He shakes his head and takes a sip of his drink. "Let it go, Ave. Let bygones be bygones."

I don't get anymore information out of him because he proceeds to drink himself into a stupor and later, as I lay in bed, I hear him stumble around in the kitchen, looking for something more to ease his pain.

CHAPTER 19

My stomach still twisted up in knots, I park the car next to my father's white Camry. After dropping Mia off at school, I had planned to go straight to the hospital, but Miss Campbell made me aware that I'm still wearing the red and white checkered pajamas Ruth bought for me two Christmases ago. My mind was so scattered from last night's events that I hadn't even noticed. It was all I could do to drag myself out of bed this morning, take care of my daughter.

I shut off the engine, but I don't get out of the car. I'm not ready to face my mother, who is alone in the house because my father left early to go off somewhere. Lately he's been leaving the house without telling us where he's going, and I wonder if he found a bar that opens early in the day.

I stay in the car staring at my parents' house, and after sitting there for some time, deep in my thoughts, a knock at my window jolts me out of my reverie. Ruth is standing there with a smile on her face, so I roll down the window.

"Good morning, dear," she says. "Are you all right? It looks like you haven't slept for days."

She's right. All night I was thinking about my dead sister,

whether she was born before or after me, what she looked like, and how she left this world. My imagination even went so far as to envisage her little body surrounded by white daisies in a silk-lined coffin.

A sigh escapes me. "I... I was just going to get dressed and head to the hospital, but I'm exhausted. I don't know if I can..."

"Oh, love. I know it's hard. How about you come over for a cup of tea and ginger cookies?"

I look over at our house and then back at Ruth. Suddenly my heart feels lighter. Ruth might be the person I need to speak with; my parents have known her for years. She would surely know about their other child, and I'm desperate to be able to talk about her.

"A cup of tea would be really nice," I say with a grateful smile. "Thank you, Ruth."

Once inside, Ruth makes a pot of chamomile tea and puts it on the kitchen table. The house is neat and tidy and smells like freshly baked cookies on a Christmas morning.

"Avery, dear, you never have to thank me for being there for you." She lays out a set of elegant white china cups. "You've always been like a daughter to me."

She fills my cup with tea and I take a sip. "That means so much to me."

As a child, my mother used to give me chamomile tea when I had an upset stomach. Although I loved the smell, I hated the taste of the tea. After putting down the cup, I reach for one of the ginger cookies in the middle of the table, and take a bite. It has a chewy core and a crisp, sweet crust.

Ruth's chair squeaks as she sits down and picks up her cup, bringing it to her lips.

"These are delicious," I say as I chew.

"I baked them last night for you and Mia, and I was planning on bringing them by as soon as you brought her home from school. I assumed you were going to the hospital first."

"In my pajamas?" I manage a chuckle. "I came home to change."

"Oh dear." Her eyes take in my clothes. "You must be really tired if you forgot to change this morning. Did you hear anymore news about Keith?"

Leaning forward, I lift my eyes to hers. "I received some bad news last night, but it wasn't about Keith."

Ruth takes a sip. "Has Jodie taken a turn for the worse?"

I put the cookie down and breathe deeply. "It *is* about my parents. They kept something from me."

Ruth frowns. "What in God's name would that be to upset you that way?"

"Ruth, did you know I had a sister who died when she was a little girl?"

Ruth does not speak until she has finished her entire cup of tea.

Her silence tells me that she knows. Like my parents, she has known all this time and never said a word to me.

Even though I trust her completely, she betrayed me just as much as my parents did.

"Why didn't you say anything?" My voice catches in my throat and my eyes begin to sting.

She puts her cup on the table and places both her hands on it. "It wasn't my place to tell you. It was your parents' story to tell. I'm sorry, dear, but they had their reasons."

"But I deserved to know, Ruth."

Ruth reaches for my hand. "After losing your sister, your parents were devastated. They never recovered from the pain." She draws a deep breath. "Darling, I think it would be best not to bring this matter up again. We don't want your mother to spiral out of control; she barely makes it through the day."

Blinking away tears, I stare up at the ceiling. "Please, Ruth,

I at least need to know how my sister died. They won't even tell me that."

"I'm sorry, Avery, but I think it's best if we leave it alone. For everyone's sake."

I rise to my feet. "I have to go," I say, ignoring the tears welling up in my eyes, and I leave the house before she can stop me.

As I'm walking home, I feel the anger rising, choking me. Despite my best efforts to quell it, it boils over like a pot of hot water and spills from my eyes, scorching my cheeks.

By the time I get inside my room and lock the door, I'm in such a rage that I feel like I'm going to explode. I stand at the window, seething. The feeling that everyone has betrayed me is overwhelming, and my urge to scream is so intense that even when I press my hands over my mouth, the scream escapes. As my body rocks back and forth with sobs, I scream until my throat is raw. There's no way my mother doesn't hear me. And yet, she doesn't come because she knows why I'm upset, and doesn't want to continue our conversation from last night.

After my breakdown, I dress and leave the house without saying a word to her. I felt sympathy yesterday, but today I'm angry and too upset to consider her feelings.

I go to the hospital first, then meet Celeste during her lunch break at Burger Stop, a restaurant near the parlor. She knows something is wrong with me, but doesn't ask until we're sitting down with our food.

As I take a sip of my strawberry and chocolate shake, she finally asks, "Are you okay? Is Keith—?"

"No, he's not," I say quickly before she says the word. "Nothing has changed. He's still in a coma." I press a napkin to my lips.

Celeste squeezes my hand. "Then what's wrong? You're clearly upset."

People around us are laughing, joking, and enjoying their

food, and I envy them for how normal they are, while my life is falling apart.

I push away my half-eaten burger and wrap my fingers tightly around the napkin. "Last night, I discovered that I had a sister I never knew about."

Celeste's eyes widen and she leans in. "What? How? Where is she?"

Tears well up in my eyes. "She's dead. My sister died when she was just a child."

Celeste lets go of my hand and leans back in her chair. "How horrible. How did you find out?"

I take a deep breath and tell the story about the stuffed rabbit, and how if Miss Simmons hadn't given it to Mia, I would probably not have known the truth.

"Oh my God," Celeste says when I'm done. "I'm sorry, Avery, but at least you found out, right? Even if it's too late, you deserve to know. You have a right to know."

I take a long sip of the water that was brought together with my milkshake. "You're right, of course. I think I'm still in shock."

"Avery"—her voice drops—"I hate to ask, but how did she die?"

"They won't tell me. Not even Ruth will. It's like they want her memory to die with her."

"I can only imagine how painful it must be for your parents to relive that day."

"I know, but the idea of living the rest of my life wondering what happened to her is unbearable for me. Her name was Lynn."

"Lynn," Celeste says, almost to herself. "Have they shown you a photo of her, so you know how she looks?"

"No, and I didn't ask." I know my parents will not give me any photos, and I won't bother to ask them. I will have to find them on my own.

I finish my milkshake and rise to my feet. "Thanks, Celeste.

Talking to you really helped, but I need to go." I lean in to hug her. "I'm so happy that you and Donnell are dating. He's quite a hunk, and you two look so happy in that photo you sent me."

"Thank you, my love. I wish I could see you happy again too."

I lift my shoulders then drop them again. "I don't know if I'll ever be happy again. But I'm glad one of us is."

CHAPTER 20

It took four days for both my parents to be out of the house at the same time, but now I have the opportunity to dig through their stuff in search of Lynn's photos. So after Mia has gone to bed, I go to the storage room in the basement, where I start rummaging through boxes filled with things I've never given much thought to.

When I was a child, I was never permitted to go into the storage room, which was often locked. I never wanted to anyway since the room has always been so packed that I was terrified something would jump out at me. As both my parents tend to hoard things, the room is a mess and the smell of dust and mildew hovers in the air. In my search for any clue about my dead sister, I go through boxes full of clothing, dusty books, old newspapers, and outdated electronic devices. Things they no longer need are stuffed into boxes and pushed to the corners of the room. There are magazines from the eighties, more books, old VHS tapes, and even a radio with an antenna on top. Among the boxes are my baby toys that I no longer remember, as well as clothes I wore when I was a child. Sorting through the clothes, I reach the bottom. There is nothing there.

After going through four large boxes and not finding anything, I tell myself that I'm wasting my time. Maybe my parents destroyed any photos of their other daughter to bury the painful memories of her. I'm about to leave the room and return upstairs when I open one more box with a carved wooden box inside it, a memory box. Inside it, I find a photo album with a soft, white and cream fabric cover. With no idea what it contains between its pages, I sit down on the floor, put it on my lap and flip open the cover.

The first picture shows my mother smiling at the camera while holding a newborn baby in her arms. The baby in the photo, wearing nothing but a diaper, is not me. Although she has black hair like me, her eyes are blue like Mom's, while mine are brown like Dad's.

In between flipping through the pages, I close my eyes and search my mind for any memories I might have of my sister, but nothing comes to me. Were we even alive at the same time? Maybe my parents had me after their first child to try and fill the void her death left behind. I do remember having an imaginary friend, but I can't remember whether she was a girl or a boy, or even her name. Could it have been my sister?

I open my eyes and see the next picture annotated with the words "Her first birthday."

Several more photos are labeled in my mother's handwriting with black ink. It seems a little odd to me that none of them have her name on them, just short captions and sometimes the age she was when the photos were taken.

Her first day at nursery. Our baby girl with Santa.

Picture after picture of my sister doing ordinary things, like playing with a doll, riding a tricycle and eating ice cream.

Lynn is sitting on a table next to a chocolate cake on her second birthday, her hands and face covered in cake. On either side of her, my parents are beaming, my mother wearing a necklace with a silver locket. Her hair is pulled up in a ponytail and she's wearing a simple blue dress with a thin, white belt, while my father is in jeans and a black T-shirt. He has his arms around my mother and Lynn.

As I watch them, a pang of jealousy cuts through me. It would be great to go back in time, to live my life all over again from the beginning, without having to deal with all the pain that came later. I'd love a chance to see my father's eyes clear, untainted by alcohol, to know my mother the way she was back then, happy and full of love and life.

In my entire life, I have never felt loved enough by my mother. When I was a little girl, I did everything in my power to please her, including being the best in class, being a good girl at home and in public, and helping out around the house when she wasn't able to, cleaning, cooking, and even wiping up my father's vomit.

Occasionally it worked and I got what I wanted. Whenever she wasn't ill, she told me she loved me, embraced me, kissed me, and read to me at night, but it was never enough. I always craved more than she was capable of giving me. I understand now that part of her heart died with Lynn, and not even a new child could bring it back to life.

The last picture shows my sister when she was five years old. Standing in front of a Christmas tree, she's smiling widely enough to reveal the missing tooth in her mouth. She must have died at that age because there are no more photos after that, just blank pages without memories to fill them. My eyes are filled with tears and I cannot contain them, so I grieve for the sister I never knew, the girl who was taken away before I had the chance to know her. It would have been nice to have had a sister to play with or to talk to when I felt lonely or sad. The two of us could have been confidants, sharing secrets and communicating in a secret language.

While I'm glad I found the photo album, knowing it exists doesn't make me feel any better. I still have questions. As I'm about to snap the lid shut, I catch a glimpse of a folded piece of paper at the bottom of the box, where another photo of Lynn, sitting on a swing this time, is also lying face down. It must have fallen from the album when I opened it.

I carefully unfold the paper and read the words on it. Four words that knock the wind from my lungs.

You took a life.

CHAPTER 21

Inside my head, I repeat the words Keith said to me in the hospital.

"I took a life."

I feel a chill run through my body and I can't breathe. Holding my head in my hands, I wait for it to pass. Then I read the note again. Trembling, I put away everything except for the piece of paper, which I slide into my pocket, and I leave the basement.

As I lie down in my bedroom, I pull out the piece of paper and read the message again.

"You took a life," I read out loud.

I try to make sense of the words, and they burn into my mind. The more I try to work it out, the more confused I become and the more I'm afraid of what it might all mean. Did one of my parents write Keith the note? But then how did it end up in the box? And what exactly is it that they know?

I long to be able to pick up the phone and talk to Keith. I feel sure that if only he could talk to me, he could explain everything. But he's unreachable, and I have no choice but to confront my parents when they get home.

.   .   .

Just before midnight, I hear the sound of a car pulling into the driveway and my heart starts pounding frantically, my breathing erratic. Once I regain my composure, I stand up from the bed, pacing the room as I rehearse the words I'm going to say, the questions I have to ask. I walk to the window and look out into the night. Though I can't see the driveway from my window, the sound of the car door slamming once, then twice, makes me jump nervously. A moment later, the front door opens and closes, then I hear their voices.

I shiver and sit on the bed again, staring at the note in my hand and trying to gather up the courage to go and talk to them.

You took a life.

I fold up the paper and curl my fingers tightly around it. As I sit there, sweat trickles down the middle of my back, and my stomach hurts. It takes me a good ten minutes before I'm brave enough to walk out of the room, and as soon as I enter the hall-way, I see my mother disappear into their bedroom without seeing me. Instead of following her and demanding a conversation, I walk down the stairs. I'll speak with my father first.

As I walk down, I only hope he isn't too drunk to have a coherent conversation. I pass through the empty living room, and then walk into the empty kitchen. Stepping out the back door, I enter the backyard. I take a moment to adjust my eyes to the darkness. The moon is almost full, but covered by clouds, and the stars are nowhere to be seen. I rub my arms with my hands, my skin feeling a chill even though the night air is comfortably warm.

My eyes scan the yard for my father, and at the back of the yard, I spot him sitting on a table with a beer in front of him. His mutterings sound like a conversation he's having with himself, like he's trying to convince himself of something. He's so caught up in his thoughts that he doesn't notice me standing not too far from him. He sets his beer down on the table, then rubs his hands over his face before picking it up again.

Finally, I can't take it anymore. There's no way I'm putting this off.

"Dad," I call and his head whips around.

"What are you doing out here at this hour?" he asks and looks away again. His back hunches as he stares into the darkness like he's expecting to see something or someone.

I can see he's still angry with me for bringing up the past, pouring acid on wounds that have not healed. Taking a few steps toward him, I stop when I reach the edge of the table. "Are you okay?"

When he doesn't respond, and drinks instead from his can of beer, I take a seat at the table with him. This conversation has to happen.

"Why aren't you in bed?" he asks again, avoiding my question.

"I have something to discuss with you."

"As long as it has nothing to do with the past, that's okay with me. You know how your mother and I feel about that." His tone is like a slap to the face and it takes everything in me to control the frustration that's starting to push itself to the surface. I can't argue with him, not when I need him to open up to me while he's sober enough for a conversation.

I open my palm to reveal the piece of paper, and it feels like a bomb about to go off. "Dad, I found this in the storage room. It's a note."

He shoots me a look, but it's hard to read his expression in the dark. "What were you doing in there? You know you're—"

"Yes, Dad, it's true that I wasn't allowed to go down there as a child. But I'm an adult now. Do the same rules still apply?"

"They do," he says, gritting his teeth.

Drawing in another breath, I forge ahead. "The reason I was down there is because I needed to look for photos of my sister. You can't hold that against me."

I hear a soft crack as my father squeezes the can of beer with his hand, but he says nothing. But I can almost feel the anger flowing off of him in waves, and I know I touched a nerve. He doesn't want to discuss this, but I won't let him off the hook.

"Dad, I did find photos of her in a memory box, but I also found this." I put the note on the table between us. Now that the moon has emerged from behind the clouds, he will be able to read the words, which are big enough to fill the page. As he leans over to pick up the paper, his eyes narrow and he stares at it for some time without speaking.

"Did you write that?" I ask, my pulse pounding, my mouth turning dry.

"I don't know what this is," he says in a deadpan voice, but he won't look at me, and he's still holding the paper in his hand, which is shaking slightly.

"Are you sure?" I ask. "I feel as if you are not telling the truth."

"I don't know what you mean," he says, but I feel his tension radiating from him. It electrifies the air between us.

Before I can continue, he gets up from the table so fast that, in his haste, he knocks over his beer and the liquid spills as it hisses into the air.

Shuddering, I glance around me. Everything around me is dark and empty, except for the misshapen shadows. Putting the note in my pocket, I stand up. I won't give up until I get to the truth.

Running after my father, I stumble a few times as if I've also had too much alcohol. And by the time I catch up with him, my muscles are screaming with fatigue, and my lungs are burning. All I want to do is fall into bed and sleep, but I'll never be able to rest with all the questions drowning me.

"Dad, please." I put my hand on his arm, but he brushes me off.

"I said I don't know anything about... about it."

"But—"

"I have nothing to say, Avery. Go to bed." He walks more quickly toward the back door.

"Dad!" I call, but he doesn't slow down. A moment later, he's in the house and the door slams closed behind him.

Anger and guilt roil inside me as I stand outside for a while. Guilt over what, exactly? I didn't do anything wrong. His behavior just now confirms that he's hiding something, and I march into the house determined to find out what that is. Another bottle of beer is in his hand as he sits on the couch, watching a movie with the sound off. I doubt he's focused on it. My arms are crossed over my chest as I stand in the middle of the living room. He doesn't say anything or even look at me.

"Dad, I know you don't want to talk about this, but it's important." Despite my heart pounding against my chest, my voice is steady. I toss the piece of paper next to him on the couch. "I know you're hiding something from me."

Instead of picking it up, he looks at me with his face contorted.

In an ice-cold voice, he asks, "What do you want to know?"

I sink onto the couch, on the other side of the note, and it sits between us like a wall, a barrier that neither of us can cross. While I stare straight ahead at the TV, my hands are clasped in my lap.

"Before Keith went into a coma, he told me something strange." I inhale sharply as my stomach begins to rumble. "He said 'I took a life.'" My eyes begin to water as I pick up the note again and stare at it through my tears. My hands tremble as I hold it up for him to see. "This note says almost exactly the same thing. Who wrote it, what does it mean, and why was it hidden in your memory box?"

He shifts in his seat without looking at the paper, and when he looks at me, something flashes in his eyes, but I can't tell what it is.

I bury my head into my hands, trying to stop the tears. "Talk to me, please. I can't stop worrying that my husband is a killer, and this has to be connected to what he said. I need to know the truth. I know you are hiding something from me."

After what feels like an hour, he leans toward me and places his hand on the middle of my back. I sit up straight and look into his eyes. "I'm so sorry," he croaks. The pain in the space between his words is so stark and raw that it steals the breath from me. Something about his voice seems foreign, like it belongs to someone I just met.

I watch his eyes as he takes a few breaths. "I don't know what to tell you," he says, trying to hold it together.

"I don't need the whole story now. I just need the truth." My voice is small and weak. "What does the note mean? And what connection does it have to Keith? Just answer me at least one of those questions. Did Keith kill someone?"

Waiting for his response, I feel as if I'm standing on the edge of a cliff and, in just a moment, I'll slip and tumble into the void.

I watch my father's back heave up and down with each ragged breath, then he releases a huge gust of air. "No, he didn't." He lowers his head, his chin hitting his chest. "Keith is a good man. I'm... I'm not."

"Dad, what are you talking about?"

His shoulders slump forward as he presses his face into his hands, and when he speaks, his voice is muffled and broken by sobs. "I killed someone. I did."

"What?" I grip my knees as if they could save me, my fingernails digging through my skin. "Who did you... kill?" It makes me cringe to say the words; they sound absurd.

A few more deep breaths, then he wipes his eyes with his sleeve.

"Your sister," he says. "I killed your sister."

CHAPTER 22

JODIE: 31 YEARS AGO

The morning Jodie Gregor's life changed forever, she woke up at 6:30 a.m. with a bad feeling in the pit of her stomach that warned her that something was off or about to go wrong. She didn't know what or when it would happen, but she could feel it in her bones.

As she did every morning, she opened the window to let fresh air into the room, and sat back down on the bed where she spent a few minutes in prayer. Afterward, she sat in silence so that she could listen to the birds outside the window and the rustle of leaves in the wind, while trying to understand what it was she was really feeling. She didn't like it one bit.

Her mother, Monica, had always told her that the greatest tool she had at her disposal was her instincts and she had to trust them. She repeated the same words to Jodie when she was on her deathbed, a few breaths away from checking out for good.

"Your instinct is never wrong, my child. I wish I had listened when my gut warned me against getting involved with your father."

Jodie's father had been a married man her mother had met

at a party, but he'd had no ring on his finger. Against the alarm bells in her head, her mother had fallen head over heels in love with him and become pregnant. Only then had he confessed he was married and did not want his family to find out about the child that had been conceived out of wedlock. That had been the last time they'd seen each other. He'd left, and Monica had raised her daughter alone.

Since the day her mother had died from kidney failure, Jodie had promised herself to listen to her intuition, no matter how crazy it seemed. Before making a major decision, she would always pause and listen to her inner voice. Her gut was the tool she turned to when her heart needed advice. It was her gut she listened to when she chose to follow in her mother's footsteps and become a nurse. Her gut she turned to when she contemplated moving to Kenya for one year to work for the Doctors Without Borders volunteer program.

If she had not gone, chances were she would not have met Harry Gregor, a farmer's boy turned accountant, whom she had bumped into at the airport in Nairobi, when her mission was complete and she was about to take a flight back home. He had been in Kenya attending a friend's wedding. They'd started dating soon after, and he'd proposed a year later. After they'd married, she'd moved from her hometown of Montclair, New Jersey, to start a life with him in Willow Gate.

And now, her gut was telling her something was wrong.

She stretched her arms above her head and tried to shake off her unsettling feeling. Still carrying the knot in her stomach, she got out of bed and went to check on her five-year-old daughter, Lynn, the love of her life. Her little girl was still asleep, her arm flung over her face, and Jodie bent down and kissed her lightly on the forehead. When she walked into the living room, she saw her husband on the couch, sipping coffee. His face was pale and his eyes were bloodshot and tired. A pile of blank papers, coffee mugs, and accounting ledgers lay in front of him. She knew he had been up all night working.

He worked as an accountant at a small firm that paid him well, but they had a lot of clients. Harry's days were long, and on nights when he did not stay late at the office, he would often bring work home with him.

Jodie tied the belt of her bathrobe tighter around her waist. "Honey, you really have to take a break. You can't continue to work like this. You're making yourself sick."

"I know," he said, rubbing the stubble on his cheek. "But I have a client who's in deep trouble. I have to figure out a way to help him."

"By getting yourself sick? You need to get some sleep, Harry. You can't help anyone if you're not well."

"I'm fine, sweetheart. Trust me."

"You have to stop saying that because you're not. You should think about going on leave even for a few days." Jodie kissed him on the forehead. "I'm going to go shower. I'll make you breakfast when I get out, but don't forget that I'm leaving for work soon. You need to be present for Lynn."

He nodded and went back to his work. It saddened her that he didn't make much time for their daughter anymore, and Jodie often worried that their daughter would grow up resenting him for not putting her first. But today, even though it was Saturday and Ruth, their neighbor, was home, Jodie wouldn't ask her to babysit Lynn as she normally did. Harry had promised he would be a hands-on dad today, and after lunch he planned on taking her to the playground.

As Jodie was getting ready to leave for work, Harry and Lynn were in the bathroom and he was singing the hippopotamus song that always made Lynn laugh out loud.

Jodie smiled, but deep down, something still nagged at her.

She carried the feeling with her all the way to the hospital, and at one point on the drive it was so strong that she almost turned the car around, to go back home to see if her family was all right. But she told herself she was being silly and that she would call home during her break. As soon as she entered the hospital, she squashed the feeling of unease. Being a nurse required her full attention; she had to be at the top of her game to ensure that her patients always received the best treatment possible.

The moment she walked into the Emergency Room, she was met with chaos. It was like a war zone inside. Patients in wheelchairs and on gurneys were being wheeled in, while family members stepped in and out of waiting rooms. In the hallway, a woman with a broken wrist and a teenage boy with a bleeding nose waited for their names to be called by the triage nurse. The knot in her stomach tightened as she greeted her colleagues, but she managed to keep it under control, to switch off her emotions and get to work, keeping her anxiety hidden.

At her lunch break, she couldn't bear it any longer. Her gut told her that something was very wrong and she needed to get home immediately. Without telling anyone, she grabbed her bag and rushed out of the hospital. She needed to know that everything was fine, that her worries were unfounded.

But that was not the case.

When she opened the front door, she heard Harry crying in the kitchen, and she ran inside to find her daughter lying lifeless on the floor, a pool of vomit next to her body.

CHAPTER 23

AVERY

My father's confession echoes in my head and pierces my heart. "It's not true," I whisper. "You can't mean that." The words are heavy and sour on my tongue, making me sick to my stomach. I want to shake him, to yell for him to tell me the truth, but it's right there in front of me, in his hunched posture, the empty eyes, and the expression of anguish on his face.

"It's true." His face crumples, but he meets my gaze head on. "I did it. I killed my own daughter. I'm a monster."

"Stop, Dad." I reach out to grab his arm, still reeling from the shock of what I'm hearing, and refusing to believe it. "You're not a monster. Please don't say that. You didn't kill anyone." He must have had more to drink than I realize. There is no way that he can be thinking clearly.

He shakes his head, tears swimming in his eyes. "I'm guilty. I killed my own daughter. But Keith... he's innocent."

I press my fists against my eyes and release a slow breath, feeling as exhausted as if I've been running a marathon. "I don't understand, Dad. What is going on? Why would you say you killed someone... my sister? Exactly what happened?"

He looks at me with horror and guilt painted across his face.

As the sharp blade of pain cuts deep into his features, the lines around his mouth and on his forehead seem to deepen into his tanned skin with every passing second. Although his gaze is on me, his brown eyes have a faraway look, as if he's seeing something terrible that I cannot see. It's almost as if he's reliving the incident he's telling me about over again.

"Your husband is innocent. That's all you need to know."

Standing up, he goes to the kitchen and returns with a bottle of booze in hand, but instead of coming back to the couch, he walks out through the front door into the night. I know he will drink himself into a state that will make it impossible for him to answer any further questions. I'm too exhausted and shaken to go after him, and it would be best for me to wait for him to be sober before bringing up the topic again. I go to talk to my mother, but I find her fast asleep and when I try to wake her, she just mumbles incoherently.

I go to my room and, sitting on my bed, I groan and lean forward, resting my forehead on my hands. My strength has run out tonight, my headache has reached explosive levels and I feel like all I can bear to do is lie down and sleep. Surely tomorrow my father will tell me he didn't mean what he said about killing Lynn. I believe in his innocence just as I believe in Keith's. The man who raised me would never kill anyone, let alone a child, and certainly not one of his own. The idea is impossible. I can't understand what has gotten into them both, but I have to believe there's an answer, an answer I can bear.

My brain niggles at a chilling thought.

Three days before Keith was hit by the car, he had come to see my father, who'd wanted him to fix his old computer, and he planned to return again the day of the accident. What if something happened between the two of them?

What if...?

There's no way. My own father couldn't possibly hurt my

husband, a man who had been nothing but kind to him despite openly condemning his excessive drinking.

Desperate to speak to someone, I pick up my phone to call Celeste and I finally tell her everything that happened tonight as well as Keith's and my father's confessions.

"Oh my God," she says when I'm done. "I have no idea what to say."

"And I don't know what to think." I pinch the bridge of my nose. "I'm so confused right now."

"Avery," Celeste says in a quiet voice, "what if Keith found something on your father's computer that proved he really did kill your sister. Maybe he returned to confront him on the day of the accident." She inhales sharply. "What if—?"

"He ran him over to shut him up?"

"I'm not saying... I just mean." She sighs. "Maybe that's what Keith was trying to tell you in hospital. I don't know. I'm sorry. I really don't want to paint your father in a negative light."

"He already did that himself," I say, my voice breaking. "He confessed. Now I'm not sure what to do with what he told me."

"I don't want to tell you this, but, as your friend, I need to." Celeste pauses as she takes a deep breath. "I think you need to contact the police."

"That's not an option. I can't do that to him; he's my father." I'm pacing again, my stomach churning with every step.

"But, Ave, what if he really did run Keith over? And what about what he says he did to your sister? You can't just ignore this. At the very least, talk to Liam."

I bite into my lip. "I'll have to think about it, but I need more evidence before I can make a decision."

"You don't need to decide right now," Celeste says. "But anyone who put your husband in a coma needs to be held accountable." She clears her throat. "Either way, you can't let your father get away with what he did to your sister. And you need to protect yourself and Mia."

"He'd never hurt her," I whisper... But if he really did kill his own daughter, how can I be so sure?

"I hope you're right. But I feel like as long as you don't know how she died, you need to assume the worst and protect your child."

After Celeste and I end our call, I immediately go to my closet and start pulling out clothes. I know she's right: as long as I don't really know what my father did, Mia and I cannot stay here. We have to leave, and it has to be tonight.

I chaotically stuff my clothes into my suitcase, without folding anything properly. Mia's clothes are in my room, so I don't have to wake her up until the time comes to leave. I throw them into a bag, my hands shaking and tears spilling over onto my cheeks. As soon as I'm done, I hurry down the dark corridor to her room, which is right next to mine. Tiptoeing over to her bed, I feel my heart pound in my chest. I cannot believe I'm afraid of my own father. But why shouldn't I be? He said he killed his first child and he refuses to tell me how and why.

Mia looks so peaceful as she sleeps, her mouth parted as she snores. I kiss her forehead and bend down to pick her up, and although she murmurs something in her sleep, she doesn't wake up. I tuck her little body closer to me as I head back to my room, and then I lower her gently into my bed.

"Mia," I whisper softly. "Wake up, baby. We need to go."

My mother will be upset when she wakes up in the morning to find us gone, but I can't find it in me to care at this point. I no longer feel safe in the house and nothing and no one will make me stay. Mia stirs a bit, but does not open her eyes. She only wakes up when I pull a pullover over her head and put socks on her feet. After we're done, we walk out the door, my arm wrapped around her tiny body as I promise to never let anyone hurt her.

"Mommy, where are we going?" she asks, her voice hazy with sleep.

"To see Ruth," I reply, the decision coming to me in an instant. My first instinct was to go back to our own home, but as much as I want to be far away from my parents, I also want to be close enough to discover the truth.

Mia's eyes light up when she hears Ruth's name. "Will I sleep there?" she asks and I put a finger to my lips.

"Grammy and Grampy are sleeping, so we need to be quiet, okay? We'll be staying with Ruth for a little while."

"Okay, let's go. Let's hurry." She pulls at my hand with excitement.

When we're standing in front of Ruth's door, I look back at the house I grew up in, thinking of all the secrets it hides. Could my father have killed their little girl and kept it a secret all these years? Could he have tried to kill my husband and kept the truth from me? Did my mother know everything, all along? What kind of people would that make them?

Monsters, a little voice in my head says.

Mia rings the bell before I do, and the lights come on in Ruth's house. After the door opens, Ruth appears before us in her rollers, looking confused. I haven't spoken to her since the day she refused to tell me about my sister's death, but I don't hold anything against her anymore. She was just being a good friend to my parents, and when all is said and done, her house feels more like home to me than anywhere else right now. When she sees the suitcase in my hand, she frowns and starts to speak, but I shake my head slightly. I can't explain to her what happened, not in front of Mia.

She gets the message and smiles, reaching out to embrace Mia. "How nice of you two to surprise me with a visit."

Mia rushes into her arms and Ruth holds her close.

As soon as I have put Mia to bed, Ruth makes me a cup of coffee and asks me what happened. But despite my desire to tell her, I find myself unable to do so. I don't want someone else putting pressure on me to tell the police when I'm not ready to do so, and I think it's best not to involve her until I have answers to all the questions floating around inside my head.

"I just... My parents and I had a bad fight. I hope we can stay here for a few days. If you don't mind."

She nods and pats my hand, but I don't miss the worry clouding her eyes. "Of course, honey. You and Mia are welcome to stay as long as you need."

Later, as I'm closing the blinds of the guest room that I will be sleeping in, I catch sight of my mother through our living-room window. She's holding a bottle to her lips with her head tilted back. I can't tell what it is from a distance, but by the way she's holding it, like my father does, I'm sure it's not water. For the first time in my life, I'm pretty sure I'm witnessing my mother not only drink alcohol, but straight from the bottle, and that terrifies me even more. This can't end well.

CHAPTER 24

I spent the past two hours sitting at Keith's bedside, silently begging him to awaken so I can ask him if he knows what my father did, if he can shed some light on all the secrets swirling around me. But his eyes remain closed as the minutes tick by. Doctors and nurses come in from time to time to urge me to get some fresh air, but the only breaks I allow myself are to walk around the room. My eyes are drawn to a faint mark on the door, trying to figure out who has left it. Was it a disgruntled patient, a member of staff, or a visitor?

Around 1 p.m., I do leave the room, but only to get some coffee. I haven't slept since my conversation with my father last night, and I'm in desperate need of caffeine.

At the coffee machine, I fill a white styrofoam cup with black coffee. There's something strangely comforting about the thin stream as it hits the bottom of the cup and, as I wait, my eyes are drawn to my reflection in the machine's shiny silver metal.

I'm a catastrophe with my hair in a tangled ponytail that I hurriedly crammed into one of Mia's pink rubber bands this morning. I have panda-like dark circles around my bloodshot eyes, and I look like I haven't slept in weeks. I'm far from presentable, but if you can look like a mess anywhere, it's a hospital. From the dispenser, I grab a packet of artificial sweetener, tear it open, and pour it into my cup. My coffee tastes like a poor imitation of itself, but it will do for now, and I sip it on my way back to Keith's room.

Near the entrance to the ICU, I pass a rounded corner and almost collide with a man standing close to the wall. It takes me a moment to realize that it's Liam. Today, he's wearing civilian clothes and he's also sporting a day's worth of stubble. I want to tell him about my father's confession. I want Liam to call him in for questioning—the police will be able to uncover the truth—but I won't do that. I can't. Despite what he said, I'm still not completely convinced he was telling the truth. He is still my father and if I do not have concrete evidence that he committed the crimes he confessed to, I cannot turn him in.

"Avery, are you okay?" Liam's eyes are full of concern.

I put on a smile as fake as the coffee in my hand. "I'm trying to be."

"Nothing's changed, huh?" The words seem to be pressing down on him because I watch his shoulders tense as he speaks. "I thought I'd pass by to see how he's doing. How are you holding up, really?"

My gaze lingers on him for a moment before I respond. "I'm doing fine, Liam. Just scared and tired." My voice sounds hollow to my ears.

He hugs me then and, after we let go, we go to Keith's room together. As Liam watches his friend, his expression changes from worry to pain, then he clears his throat and looks at me. "I know he's going to make it, Avery. He's a fighter. One of these days he'll wake up and crack one of his unfunny jokes."

We both laugh, but there isn't much humor in it.

"Have you eaten today?" he asks me.

"Not yet," I say. Food has been the last thing on my mind.

He wags his finger at me. "That's not good. Let's get you something to eat."

Liam leads me out of the ICU to the cafeteria, where I get a grilled-chicken sandwich and an order of fries, and we sit down at an empty table. I force down the fries even though they taste like rubber. My body needs energy. For a while, we eat in silence, then Liam puts down his fork and wipes his mouth with a napkin. "You mentioned a while ago that you're back home with your parents. I hope you and Mia are getting the support you need."

"It's... yeah. It helps." I take a bite of my sandwich to distract him from my lie. I'm not entirely lying, though. Ruth is part of the family and she is helping me. "I'm just trying to keep my head above water."

"You're a strong woman, Avery. You'll get through this." He picks up a fry and bites into it. "Have you thought more about what we talked about a while back?" I raise an eyebrow and he elaborates. "If you think anyone might have wanted to harm Keith?"

I swallow slowly and take a sip of water as I think of my father, and I see everything like a movie in my mind. While Keith cycles away from their house, I see my father get behind the wheel of his car and drive after him. I shut my imagination down and bring my attention back to Liam. "No. No one jumped out at me. Have you found any leads?"

Shaking his head, he puts down the half-eaten sandwich and wipes his mouth again. "The person we're looking for is smart. They're very careful, but at some point they're going to make a mistake, or guilt is going to get the better of them."

I pick up my chicken sandwich, but I'm no longer hungry. "Thank you for coming to see him, Liam. I really appreciate it."

"He's my best friend. I'll always be here for him, no matter what. You know that. And for you and Mia too."

Both of us return to the ICU, and I tell him I have to pick up Mia from school.

"You do that," he says, looking at Keith. "I'll stay a little longer. Maybe I can annoy this guy into waking up."

A smile crosses my face. "Let's hope you succeed." I tilt my head to the side. "Last time you told me about a domestic dispute case you were working on. How's that going?"

"I'm glad to say that justice is being served and the kids have found a safe home. Hopefully the emotional and physical damage caused by their parents can be undone. Some parents hurt their children every day without even knowing it."

"You're right about that. I'm glad to hear they're safe. I'll talk to you later."

He nods and I leave him there, walking out of the hospital in a hurry before calling Celeste when I get into my car.

"I did it," I tell her. "After you and I spoke last night, we moved in with Ruth."

"That's good," she says, "but why didn't you just go back to your house?"

"I want to be close enough to find out what's really going on."

"So you're still not willing to go to the police?"

I stare at the steering wheel as I try to figure out what to say. "I can't just go to the police with my worries."

"But isn't a confession sufficient evidence?"

"I just don't know what to think. Dad was drinking when he told me." I sigh. "I still get the feeling there's a lot more to it than what he said, and I don't want to send my dad to jail without knowing the truth."

"Well, you know my feelings about this," Celeste says. "I trust your judgment, though."

"I know you do. I'll let you get back to work. Talk later."

"Okay. Take care of yourself. Love you."

"Love you too," I reply, then I end the call, start the car, and head to the school.

When I get there, Mia runs up to me and gives me a big hug. She gets heavier every day, but I pick her up and squeeze her. "How's my princess doing?"

"Great," she says and kisses my cheek.

When we get into the car, I glance back at the school in time to see Miss Campbell waving, and I wave back. Mia won't stop talking about her, as always.

"You know what, Mommy? She helped me do a drawing for Grammy and Grampy."

"Oh, right," I say as I slow down at a red light. "That's nice."

People are all around us outside the window. There must be some kind of event going on because so many of them are holding brightly colored flags and balloons. As they pass by, I can't help but notice how happy they appear, laughing and joking, and in a flash, I feel a powerful urge to join them, to throw away my troubles and be like them. But as soon as the light turns green, I turn my attention back to the road.

When I arrive in front of Ruth's house, I realize I was so caught up in my thoughts that I had not even noticed the trip.

As soon as I stop the car, Mia leaps out and runs up to Ruth's front door. "Come on, Mommy. I'll show you the picture, then we can take it to Grammy and Grampy. It'll be a surprise."

Ruth is out playing bridge with friends and, after I let Mia in, I remain outside for a while, staring at the house I grew up in. As if on cue, my mother emerges in her bathrobe, her hair tangled and wild. I can see she's been crying. She texted me earlier to say good morning, but she did not ask me to come home. Perhaps my father told her what had happened last night and they're both relieved to have me out of the house so I won't continue to dig for the skeletons they're trying so hard to bury. Still, I feel the urge to go to her, to hug her, to apologize for leaving her last night. But I can't do it. I simply wave and walk into Ruth's house, the taste of iron on my tongue from my bitten lip.

I stand in the kitchen doorway for a moment and listen to Mia who, with childlike glee, shows me her picture. It shows a river flowing under a bridge. The banks of the river are full of colorful flowers, and an oversized blue bird sits on the railing of the bridge.

"This is so pretty," I say to Mia and she beams.

"Let's show it to Grammy and Grampy," she says. "It will make them happy again."

CHAPTER 25

Before I take Mia's drawing to my parents, I wait until Ruth returns home. I was tempted not to go, but Mia was so excited to show them the picture and, as it turns out, I have a few more things to pick up from the house anyway.

"I want to come with you," Mia says when I walk to the door.

"I know, baby, but Grammy and Grampy are having a nap right now. I'll just sneak in there and put the picture on the fridge. When they wake up, they'll be so surprised."

"That sounds like a great idea," Ruth says, backing me up.

I still haven't told her what the argument with my parents was about and she didn't ask any more questions.

Mia squints her eyes a little, saying, "Okay, but make sure they don't hear you."

"I'll be very quiet," I promise her.

"I'll stay here and play with Holly." Mia presses the rabbit to her chest.

Ruth lays a hand on Mia's head. "Why don't you, me, and Holly have a tea party? Is that something you would enjoy?"

In excitement, Mia shifts from one foot to the other. "Yes. That sounds fun."

They disappear into the kitchen and I leave the house, feeling oddly nervous. Never in a million years did I think that one day I would be afraid of seeing my own parents. I'm not sure if I'm afraid of them, or of the secrets they have buried. I still have my key, so I quietly let myself into the house and hurry up to my room.

Behind my closed door, I stop to listen. Earlier, when I was in Ruth's kitchen making Mia a snack, I saw my mother's face at the living-room window, and the car is parked in the driveway. It seems we all just want to stay out of each other's way.

I toss the picture onto the bed face down and throw open the closet to get what I need. Last night, in my hurry to leave, I didn't have time to put back the hangers on the rest of our clothes, so some of them are lying on the floor in a rumpled mess. My mother would have a fit if she saw them. She is obsessed with wrinkle-free clothing and putting things away properly. The woman irons everything, including underwear and handkerchiefs. She would iron a shirt or pants until it looked as if it had never been worn before. Maybe it's her way of feeling in control.

I grab what I need and throw it all into a large duffel bag, and just as I'm reaching into the closet for more of Mia's clothes, the door creaks open. I freeze, but don't look back. I sense it's my mother since my father stumbles around, especially after a drink or two, while my mother is always light and quiet, moving like a cat. Often, when I was a child, she would come up behind me and playfully tug my ponytail before I'd even realized she was there.

The sound of her uneven breathing makes its way to me, and although I want to turn around and face her, I'm afraid of what she may say to me, or what I may say to her. Do I really want to know the truth? Will I be able to handle it when I already feel like my world is crumbling down around me?

"Avery," she says in a voice I don't fully recognize. She sounds weaker than I have ever heard.

I still don't turn around, and my throat aches as I try to swallow the lump lodged inside it.

"We're sorry," she continues, her words drenched in tears. "Please don't... Come back home."

Turning around, I face her. She squints back at me with red and irritated eyes, quivering lips and hanging shoulders. Her hair is dishevelled and her clothes are dirty. My mother looks a mess when she's depressed, but it's never usually this bad. I stare at her for a long time, unsure what to say. I'm not ready to forgive her for keeping such life-changing secrets from me—I don't know if I ever can—but I don't think I need to say that. She already knows; it's in her eyes.

"No, I can't do that," I say softly, my voice choked. "Not until I know the truth about what happened to my sister." I bite into my lip again in a feeble attempt to stop the tears from falling. "Dad told me he was responsible for what happened to her, and until I know exactly what happened, I can't come back to this house."

She shakes her head and looks down. She won't do it; she won't tell me more than she already did. I hold my breath as she moves closer and reaches out her hand to touch mine, but I jerk it away before she can. My jaw clenches and I take a step backwards, the duffel bag still in my hand.

"Avery," she says again, sounding more like herself, "you don't understand."

"I don't, and since you aren't ready to explain, I can't stay here. Nor can I keep Mia around you until I know what happened. Until I know if my own father had something to do with what happened to my husband, too."

All of a sudden, I don't feel anything. No pain, no anger. I just feel... nothing.

"I have to pack," I say as I return to the closet and grab Mia's T-shirts, pants, and leggings, and place them in the duffel bag. As soon as the bag is full, I grab Mia's drawing from the bed and walk out of the room without looking back.

"Avery, please," she says in a desperate tone. "Please don't do this. Your father... He didn't mean what he said."

I stop in my tracks and turn to face her again. "That's not true, Mom," I say, my shoulders trembling but my voice steady. "Don't lie to me, please."

Her gaze moves from me to the window and remains there. "I'm not," she replies. "I just want you to understand how difficult it was for us."

"Difficult for you?" I shout, unable to control the volume of my voice anymore. "Have you even stopped to consider how all this affects me? I'm sorry, but as long as you're not ready to tell me the truth, I can't be here. I won't put my daughter in danger like that."

She inhales sharply then rubs her face roughly with both hands. "You don't understand. Come back to the house and we'll explain."

"You can explain right now. Get Dad if you can't do it alone. I'm ready to hear you out."

Wringing her fingers, she looks away. "He's... ummm—"

"Drunk? Hungover?" I throw my hands in the air. "Yeah, because he was so busy drowning his guilt, wasn't he? I used to wonder why he drinks so much, what he was trying to escape. Now I know. I need to go, Mom. I'll be back when you're ready to tell me the truth. If you're not fast enough, I'll go straight to the police."

I push past her and go downstairs to the kitchen, and she follows close behind, still pleading with me. The kitchen is a mess with dishes piled up in the sink and the smell of last night's dinner lingering in the air. On my way to the fridge, I step over a crumpled tissue and an empty bottle. I lift two hamburger magnets off the fridge door and use them to hold the drawing up.

"Mia drew this for you," I say when I turn around. "I need to go."

I'm about to walk through the door when I hear my mother gasp, and as I turn around, I see her staring at the drawing on the fridge. Then she jumps away as if she has been burned, shaking her head, and runs through the back door into the yard, letting out a choked sob. Through the window, I watch her drop to her knees in front of the willow tree.

I do not understand how an image of a bridge over a river could upset her. But then again, I know more than anyone how strange and sudden her behavior can be. Normally I would go after her, but that's not going to happen anymore. I need to get back to my daughter.

CHAPTER 26

JODIE: 31 YEARS AGO

"She choked," Harry said to Jodie when he looked up to see her standing in the kitchen doorway. "I wasn't paying attention and she... she choked on a chicken bone."

Jodie ran to her daughter's side and tried to revive her, but her efforts were in vain and when she checked her daughter's pulse, there was none to be found. After lying next to her daughter for half an hour, Jodie could no longer bear to look at her body. She did not want her last image of her daughter to be one of her lying there with vomit all over her. She didn't want to believe that she was dead. She couldn't be. She just saw her this morning. She read a bedtime story to her last night.

"She's dead." Harry rocked back and forth. "You should have been here to save her, Jodie." His voice grew louder and more agitated. "You should have been here."

"Don't you dare say that," Jodie screamed, her voice raw with grief and anger. She wanted to slap him for blaming her. Instead, she turned away from him and curled up next to her daughter's body. After what felt like forever, Jodie detached herself from Lynn's body and looked at her husband with disgust. "It's your fault. Your goddamn work has always been more important than our daughter. That's all you care about."

In a sudden fit of rage, she hurled an object at him, her face twisted into a mask of grief, but he ducked and it struck the wall behind him.

Harry wiped sweat, snot, and tears from his face with a kitchen towel and stared at his wife. It was the first time he had seen her so angry. She was always the quiet, gentle one. "No, that's not how it happened," He protested, his face red with guilt and anger.

"Why don't you explain to me how it happened then? Don't you dare blame me for this. Your daughter is dead. She was in your care." Jodie was so enraged she felt like attacking him again.

"I'm sorry," he said, more tears streaming down his face. "I know it doesn't change anything, but I'm so sorry."

She laughed, a hollow, cold sound. "Sorry doesn't make up for what you did. Sorry... it doesn't make this better. You should have been there. You were so focused on your job that you forgot your daughter needed you."

Harry dropped to his knees and broke down in tears, and with fury still boiling inside her, Jodie glared at him. To see him in such despair only fueled her fury. She wanted him to feel more pain than she was experiencing.

"Jodie, I'm sorry," he whimpered. "Please, forgive me."

Her eyes filled with tears as she shook her head. "I don't know if I can." She walked out of the kitchen to avoid seeing her little girl helpless and motionless on the floor.

He followed her, and when she threw herself on the couch and began to weep, he came to hold her, but not wanting to be comforted by the man who was responsible for her daughter's death, she fought him. He held on to her until she stopped struggling and buried her face into his chest, and wrapped in each other's arms, they grieved for their lost child.

"You shouldn't have left her alone with me," Harry said, even though his voice was thick with guilt. "You knew I didn't sleep much last night. I was—"

"Shut up." Jodie pushed him away from her. "How dare you try that again? Making it my fault."

"I'm just saying—" Before Harry could finish talking, she slapped him hard across the face and he jerked away from her, his hand pressed to his cheek.

He looked at her for a moment, then closed his eyes and wept bitterly.

Jodie cried as well and screamed until she was exhausted, lying on the couch, staring into space. It was a long time before she looked at her husband, her eyes empty. In a soft voice, she said, "Lynn's not dead. She'll come back to us, you'll see."

As if a button had been pressed, the pain on her face melted away and she smiled. Harry watched in shock as she got up, put the cushions back where they belonged, and walked toward the stairs. "I'm going to tidy her room and change her bedding. I'll put on the one she likes, the one with the butterflies."

Harry did not speak as she walked away.

Inside Lynn's room, Jodie took a moment to admire the glow-in-the-dark stars, then opened the curtains wider to let more sunlight in. If the room is bright during the day, they will glow more at night. Then she picked up Lynn's toys and placed them in the see-through toy box next to the bed. She made the bed up, plumped up the pillows and gave the curtains a tug to get rid of the wrinkles. She folded Lynn's T-shirts and shorts, putting them neatly in the drawer and her children's Bible on her bedside table before gathering the dirty clothes to put in the laundry basket.

"Perfect," she said, wiping at tears that flowed even though she wasn't crying.

Why should she? Their little girl would return to them.

When she turned to go to the door, she saw Harry standing

in the doorway. She gave him a kiss on the lips and walked past. "I'm going to take a shower, then I'll go for a quick drive."

Harry nodded, his body trembling with sobs.

Jodie hummed a tune as she stood in the shower, letting the water wash over her, washing away all the tears. She was still humming when she walked into the bedroom and found Harry sitting on the bed, crying. For a moment, she stopped as something inside her chest seized up with pain. Then she shook her head and smiled at him.

She sat on the bed beside him and held his hand. "You don't need to cry. Everything is fine. Why don't you go get some work done?"

He took a shuddering breath, then cupped her face with his hands. "Baby, Lynn is dead. We need to call—"

"No." Jodie pulled away and stood. "That's ridiculous. A bad dream, that's all it is. Our Lynn is fine."

Harry got to his feet and grabbed her by the shoulders. "Jodie, honey, wake up, please," he said, shaking her. "I'm telling you, she's died."

She bit hard into her lip until it throbbed. "Don't you say that word again to me. Not ever."

As she dressed, she ignored him. As it was a warm day, she chose a white blouse and a blue plaid skirt. She brushed her hair into a ponytail and picked up a pair of sunglasses from the bedside table and put them on. She could still hear Harry calling for her when she went downstairs, begging her to listen to him, but once she stepped through the front door his words were cut off.

When she started the car, she saw Ruth through the window, and rolled down her window to greet her. Ruth and her husband Elijah—who died five years after they were married—had no children. So Jodie let her borrow Lynn as much as possible, and her daughter certainly didn't mind having two women doting on her.

"When will you send Lynn over? I made her favorite cookies," Ruth said.

"Tomorrow," Jodie replied as she put the car in gear. "Yes, I'll bring her over tomorrow.'

CHAPTER 27

AVERY

It's a beautiful Wednesday afternoon, so after picking Mia up from school, she and I are spending the day at Rodeo Park, which is just a ten-minute walk around the corner from our street. The air is pleasantly warm and is sweetened by the scent of cut grass, and the sky is a clear blue. Lush and green tree leaves rustle softly in the breeze as bees and insects hum.

The park is mostly grass, with a small playground and a forest nearby, which has a large pond that Mia loves to throw pebbles into so she can watch the ripples she makes. Last time we came, I was distracted and not present for my daughter, after finding out about the money Keith withdrew from our account and the flowers he bought. My goal for today is to do better. On this beautiful day, I will spend time with my little girl, and will do my very best not to be distracted.

As we walk through the grass and trees, we look down at our feet to see if we can find ladybugs. Birds are chirping, people are talking and laughing, but, despite my best efforts, it all gets drowned out by my thoughts. Mia is skipping alongside me now, holding Holly the rabbit in one hand and one of her favorite dolls in the other. Her hair is up in a ponytail, and she's wearing blue-jean shorts and fresh flowers in her hair.

She had been sobbing when I took her to the hospital with me to visit Keith an hour ago. She sometimes handles it well, and other times she breaks down crying or throws a tantrum to vent her frustration. She still doesn't understand why her father won't wake up when she talks to him, and it's heartbreaking to watch.

Mia waves at a dad carrying a baby girl on his chest in a carrier. More people are enjoying the weather today, including dog walkers, joggers, and parents with their children. I bend down to pick up an empty water bottle someone has dropped on the ground, and toss it in a nearby trash can. Whenever I walk past garbage, I feel compelled to pick it up. It has been a habit of mine for as long as I can recall.

In the shade beneath a large tree, I spread out the picnic blanket and we settle in. In front of us is a large grassy area, and both Mia and I have a clear view of the playground on the other side of the pond. A family of ducks swims around in the water, while a couple of young lovers lie on a blanket in the grass several feet away. Mia is sitting cross-legged with Holly and her doll on her lap as she sings quietly to herself while watching the ripples on the water.

Keith's accident was a tsunami that carried everything in its wake, and now it threatens to pull me under. I try my best to let my churning thoughts go and to focus on my daughter. My sweet girl. My baby. Tears pool in my eyes as I watch her play, but my mind keeps wandering back to Keith. It's so frustrating that I can't let it go for even a minute. I hate that I miss him so much.

But today is about Mia, not about me. She needs me to be here for her, to be strong for both of us. Especially as I'm keeping her away from her grandparents. Over breakfast this morning, she told me that she misses them, and I didn't know what to do.

I reach for her now and give her a big hug.

"Let's go play at the playground, sweetheart. You can bring Holly and Doll with you."

"Yay, let's go." She holds up Holly and the doll and asks me to carry them for her.

"I can carry Holly, but you have to carry Doll yourself."

In the end, she chooses Holly and leaves Doll on the blanket. "We'll be right back," she says.

Hand in hand, we walk around the pond to the playground. Mia stops at the small gate and points to the slide. "I want to go down the slide, Mommy."

"You go ahead, sweetheart." I sit down on a bench nearby. Her squeal of delight pierces the air as she slides down the metal slide and runs back up the small hill to do it all over again. Her face is elated, as if this is the best thing she's ever done. My body is stiff and uncomfortable as I shift around in my seat. My bare legs and arms are in the sun, but I feel cold. Mia smiles at me, her hazel eyes wide and her cheeks rosy with happiness. Her joy gives me another pang of guilt for not having been there enough for her.

Then the vibration of the phone in my pocket causes me to jump upright. When I see it's a call from the hospital, I instinctively feel like my heart is about to burst. There is only one bar left, so hopefully the call won't drop. The hospital only calls when it's urgent.

Mia is still busy enjoying herself, unaware that I've stopped watching.

I press the phone to my ear. "Hello?"

"Mrs. Watkins, this is Doctor Drew. I'm calling to let you know that your husband's condition has taken a turn for the worse."

In an effort to breathe, I bend over and encircle my throat with my hand. "What does that mean? Is he awake?"

"No, I'm afraid not. His condition has deteriorated, so I suggest you come to the hospital right away. We're doing all we can for him, but I have to be honest with you, Mrs. Watkins. He—"

"He's going to die, isn't he?"

After a brief silence he says, "The outlook doesn't look promising."

"Okay, Doctor. I'll be there in about forty minutes or so. Thank you."

I hang up the phone and put my head in my hands, the doctor's words still bouncing off the walls of my mind. This can't be happening. I need to tell Mia that we have to leave, but I cannot move. I'm frozen on the bench, my body and mind no longer functioning.

"I should tell Mia," I whisper to myself, struggling to get my legs to work.

I don't want to take her to the hospital, but if her father is going to die, she has to come with me, to say goodbye.

Looking up, I murmur, "Mia."

There's no sign of her at the slide or anywhere else I look.

"Mia?" My voice is louder, more panicked. "Mia, where are you?"

Jumping to my feet, I run around the playground, my breathing frantic and my heart pounding hard in my chest as I shout her name: "MIA!"

I turn in a circle, looking for her, looking for anyone who can help me find her. I run to the pond and back to the playground, but she's nowhere to be found. I am unable to focus on anything as the world around me spins, and I close my eyes, desperately trying to get control of my breathing and stop the dizziness. As I stand there, trying to pull myself together, several people surround me, parents asking if I need help.

"I'm looking for my daughter. She was at the slide a few minutes ago. I got a call and she's disappeared. Please help." I pause to catch my breath. "I've looked everywhere. She's not here. She's gone."

"Sit down, miss," someone suggests. "You're in shock."

I shake my head. "She was just here. She was at the slide," I say, my voice rising. "MIA!"

I start pushing my way through the crowd in desperation. I must find her.

"Ma'am, can you describe your daughter for us?" A woman with short, black hair with blue tips and dark eyes steps in front of me.

"She's seven years old. Her hair..." I pause, trying to remember what Mia was wearing. "She's wearing jean shorts, a pink, long-armed T-shirt, and pink shoes. She was carrying a gray stuffed rabbit."

While other people go on the search, the woman nods. "You should call the police. We'll do everything we can to find her." She pauses. "Are you sure she was at the slide? Perhaps she wandered off somewhere else."

"No. She was...I was..." I swallow hard. "She was at the slide."

Someone suggests driving to the police station and putting out an Amber Alert. But I can't leave the park, not without my daughter. My phone rings again and I reach for it, my hands trembling. I don't even look at the screen to see who's calling. Maybe they know where Mia is. "Hello?"

"Avery, it's me... Mom."

My heart leaps into my throat. "Do you have her?" I ask, shaking with panic. "Do you have my daughter?"

I know my mind is jumping to conclusions, but I can no longer trust my parents at all. What if one of them followed us and took her away? Or maybe Mia somehow walked back home and went to see her Grammy and Grampy without asking me?

"Mia? What are you talking about?" Her voice is still as broken as it was yesterday. "I just wanted to let you know I am ready to tell you everything."

"Mia's missing, Mom. We're at the park and she disappeared. Do you have her?"

"What? No, I don't know what you mean." Her voice is shrill and panicked.

As I pace around, I press my hand to my forehead. "Mom, I have to go. I need to call the police."

"No," my mother replies quickly. "Don't call the police. I think I know where she is. Come home."

CHAPTER 28

I drive back to our street in five minutes instead of ten. In case my mother is wrong, I gave the woman who was helping with the search my number, asking her to call me if they found Mia, and when I pull into the driveway of my parents' home, I'm surprised to see my mother on Ruth's doorstep. I get out of the car and run to her. She looks like she's just woken up and her hair is still as tangled as yesterday, her eyes red and swollen.

"Mom, you said you know where Mia is. Is she in the house?"

My mom bangs on the door instead of answering me. "Ruth, come out here."

I take hold of her arm and turn her to face me. "Mom, wait. What's going on here?"

Her eyes are full of rage as she shakes me off and continues to bang on the door. "She took her. Ruth... she has Mia."

"What are you talking about?"

She forms a fist again and slams it against the door. "Ruth, if you don't let me in right now, I'll call the cops."

As I search my bag for my key, I try to nudge my mother aside to open the door, but she is hysterical and won't budge. I only get access to the door when my mom runs to Ruth's backyard, but before I can insert the key into the lock, the door is swung open.

Ruth's eyes are wild with panic as she peers over my shoulder and says, "Thank God you're here, Avery. Where's Jodie? I couldn't open the door. She was banging on it something crazy."

"She said you have Mia. We were at the park and she vanished."

"I don't understand, dear." She presses a hand to her chest. "Whatever do you mean?"

My mother appears and pushes past me, pointing a finger with a broken nail at Ruth. "I know you took her. Where is she?" she demands.

While they argue on the doorstep, I storm into the house and call for Mia. No answer. Inside the kitchen, I hear their raised voices.

"You've got some nerve, Jodie, to accuse me of something so awful." Ruth's voice is raised. "Why would I do such a thing? Just what is wrong with you? Mia lives here. Why on earth would I—?"

"Don't play dumb with me, Ruth. I know you're hiding her somewhere. You're just doing everything you can to hurt me, aren't you? First the rabbit, then the drawing, now you're hiding my granddaughter."

I make it to them in time to defend Ruth. "Mom, Mia drew that picture at school with the help of her new teacher, Miss Campbell, the teaching assistant. And the rabbit was a surprise for her left in her gym bag by her teacher. She told you that on the day she showed it to you." I pause. "Now please stop fighting and help me find my daughter."

They both turn toward me. My mother's face is red with shock and Ruth's is blank, but she seems to be holding back tears. When neither of them say a word, I hurry past them to go to the car to get my phone. "I'm calling the police."

My mom runs after me and grabs my arm tight as she pulls me back. "Don't call the police. I know where Mia is."

"You said that before, Mom. I can't waste any more time. I need to find my daughter."

"I know. I know." My mom sounds desperate and I can see the distress in her eyes. "But I don't want you to go to the police; they will only slow you down."

"Why should I believe you? You told me before that you knew where she was, but you didn't. Instead, you're accusing an innocent person of taking her."

My mother looks back at Ruth, who's still standing in the doorway, her mouth parted. I'm sure she wants to say something, but she doesn't.

My mother drops her hand from my arm. "I know I got it wrong before, but now I'm very sure I know where Mia is. Please, just give me a few minutes to talk to Ruth, then I'll tell you."

I bury my hands in my hair. "My God, why would you need to talk to Ruth first? What the hell is happening here? If you want to apologize to her, can't it wait until we find Mia?"

"Please," she begs with her hands pressed together. "I know I'm a mess and I've let you down, but I need you to trust me. I know where Mia is, and I don't think she's in danger."

"Fine," I say, releasing a shaky breath. "Do what you have to do, but please hurry. I'll be waiting in the car and if you don't tell me in five minutes, I'm driving to the station."

I get into the car and call the hospital to check on Keith's condition while my mother and Ruth go into the house. I can't believe I'm about to lose him on the same day I lost our daughter. I long for him right now, I know he would tear the earth apart to find his little girl. He would know exactly what to do.

"How's my husband?" I ask when Doctor Drew is put on

the line. "I wanted to come right away, but something happened to my daughter and I—"

"Mrs. Watkins, don't worry. Your husband is stable again. I'll explain everything to you when you come in."

"I don't understand. Wh... What happened before? You said he was about to die."

"He woke up briefly, but he suffered a stroke. It was a minor one, but the pressure of the situation could have killed him."

"Is he still in a coma?"

"I'm sorry, but yes."

I nod. Even though Keith is still in a coma, a wave of relief comes rushing through me, causing me to slump back into the seat. "Thank you, Doctor, for everything you're doing for my husband. I'll come as soon as I can."

I hang up and stare at Ruth's front door, and watch as my mother walks out and rushes into her own home. Shaking my head, I dial Liam's number. I should have done this a long time ago.

Voicemail.

My mother runs up to the car, holding up a piece of paper, and I roll down the window impatiently. "What is going on?"

She hands me a map with a red circle around a spot just outside Willow Gate. "This is where Mia is, I'm sure of it. There's a river with a bridge over it. It's not far, just a little ways down the road on the west side of the town. About a mile from here."

"What on earth? How can you be so sure that she's there? And who has her?" I ask, staring at the map in my sweaty hands. "If you're wrong, we may lose more time than we have. Mia's life could be in danger right now."

My mother drops her gaze to the ground, shifting from one foot to the other. "I just know she's there. Please go, and don't call the police."

I glance at Ruth's house, my senses on high alert. I want to ask her if she knows anything about this, but there's no time to waste.

"Okay," I say, putting the car into gear.

"Call me and let me know if you find her," my mother says, stepping away from the car. "I love you and I'm so sorry—"

I don't hear the rest of her words as I'm already driving away. On the way to my daughter, I call Celeste and explain what happened and she immediately tells me to call the police, or at least Liam. Even though my mother asked me not to, I agree with her, but then my cell phone battery dies. I'd like to think Celeste will alert Liam or the cops, but she thinks I'm about to do that.

My hands firm on the steering wheel, my fear and anxiety grip me so tightly that I can barely think straight. The only thing on my mind is finding Mia, and I drive faster than I should. I barely notice the landscape as I drive on autopilot, the map on my lap.

I feel stupid for listening to my mother. What if I don't find Mia in time? When I drive past a gas station, I make a stop there and ask the bored-looking woman at the counter if she knows where the river is and how far it will take me to get there.

She puts her finger on the map. "You go north of here, take a left on the next road, and you'll see the bridge on the right after about three miles."

The directions are clear in my head and I thank her and run to my car. I don't want to lose more time. Only when I reach the main road do I realize that I should have asked to use the woman's phone to call the police, in case Celeste didn't do it already. But I can't turn back now. Mia is waiting for me, and the clock is ticking too fast.

Time is running out.

I follow the directions given to me until I eventually see a thin silver ribbon winding its way through the landscape. As I turn toward it, my anxiety increases and I wish I had someone with me. Why didn't my mother offer to come? There's a dirt road along the river, but it ends a few feet away from the bridge and the water. I turn off the engine. As I open the door, a gust of wind blows in, sending my hair tumbling into disarray. The sound of rushing water fills the air, drowning out all other sounds.

Mia could be anywhere. She might be sitting on the river bank, or she might be in the middle of the river. She could be alone, or with her kidnapper. That's if she's even here.

I'm not sure what to expect and every possibility scares me to death. I exit the car and walk across the bridge that connects the two sides of the river, and my steps echo off the wood as I cross to the middle.

When I stop and look down, something inside of me shifts.

I know this place. Everything in me is telling me that I've been here before, but I can't quite put my finger on it. Then I hear the sound of a child's laughter carried on the wind and my heart almost explodes with joy. My mother was right.

I glance over the edge of the bridge and see Mia. She's sitting on the ground with her legs outstretched toward the water, running her hand over the fur on Holly's head. I can hear her laughing as she throws the rabbit's head back and forth, watching the ears flapping in the wind. Someone is with her, a woman. She doesn't need to turn for me to know who she is.

She's wearing the same clothes she wore when I dropped Mia off at school yesterday morning. A flowing gypsy skirt and a striped black and white top.

Miss Campbell.

My heart thumping, I sprint off the bridge, not stopping until I feel the ground beneath my feet. Then I break into a run, down the grassy area next to the river and then through the tall grass. Mia's laughter keeps me going, the sound of it so pure, it brings tears to my eyes. Once I'm a few feet away from them, I call for her again.

"Mia, Mia! It's Mommy," I say as I near the water, but my voice is low, choked by tears. My entire body is shaking with relief and fury.

"Mia," I try again. My voice quivers with emotion and my heart is in my throat. "I'm here. Mommy's here."

This time, she turns her head in my direction, her eyes wide with surprise. Then she jumps to her feet, her rabbit falling onto the grass. She starts running toward me and I smile, opening my arms to her.

"Mommy," she cries, throwing herself into my embrace.

I hug her tight and I can hear my heart pounding so hard it vibrates through my whole body.

"You found me," Mia says, looking up at my face, her eyes sparkling with joy. "How?"

"I just guessed," I say, my eyes shooting daggers at the teaching assistant, who surprisingly doesn't look at all scared to be caught kidnapping a child. "Are you okay, baby? Did she hurt you?"

With one arm, I draw Mia to me and with the other, I reach into my pocket for my phone, my eyes still on Miss Campbell.

"You took my child. You're in a lot of trouble," I say between clenched teeth. "I'm calling the police." It's only after I threaten her that I remember my phone is dead.

"No, please don't," she says, pushing herself to her feet. Her voice is calm and steady, but I can see fear and sadness in her eyes now. "Don't call the police, Avery. I'm your sister."

And just like that, my memories of this place rush back to me and the phone drops from my hand and into the grass.

CHAPTER 29

CASSIDY: 31 YEARS AGO

Mommy walked into the living room and switched off the TV. I looked up at her, confused.

"No, Mommy, I'm watching cartoons," I said, pouting and folding my arms across my chest.

"Not anymore, sweetie." She sat down next to me, and started brushing my hair, separating the curly strands into three parts. I didn't like it when she did that; it made my scalp itch, like ants were crawling on me.

"Are we going out?" I asked, scratching the back of my head.

"Yes, honey, we have places to go. Now please sit still."

As she started braiding, I crossed my arms again. Curiosity got the best of me, and I asked, "Are we going to visit people?"

"Not today." She waited until she finished the braid and put her hands on my shoulders. "We're going to the store to get some groceries."

"I don't want to go to the store. I want to watch TV."

"I'm sorry, honeybee, but I can't leave you at home all by yourself." She stood up and took my hand. "They have sales today at the grocery store. We need to get there before they run out of the good stuff."

I looked up at her and sighed, knowing I was not going to win the argument. "Fine," I said, standing up.

"Don't you want to wear a dress?" she asked when I was putting on my clothes, eyeing me warily. "It's really hot outside."

"I don't want to. Dresses are stupid and dumb." I hated them because they tickled my legs when I walked, and they got in the way when I wanted to run around. Trousers were better because I could put rocks and sticks inside the pockets.

"We'll talk about your language later, young lady. Now, let's get out of here."

After I had on my shoes and went to get my rabbit, we climbed into our yellow Volvo. I didn't like grocery shopping alone with Mommy. It would have been more fun if Georgia was with me. But she went to a sleepover party at her friend Sandy's house. If she were around, we would play hide and seek to keep ourselves busy because we were not allowed to look at the yummy candy or the toys. Georgia said it was because we were poor. She said that when Daddy went away, he took all our money and now we were on food stamps.

The car ride was long and boring so I pressed my face against the window. There weren't many cars on the road, and a few people were walking down the sidewalk.

"Let's sing the song from school," I said to Mommy, licking the window without her seeing me.

"Okay," she said. "Do you know the words?"

"Yes, Mommy!" I replied, and we sang about a grandma who swallowed a fly, then about a girl who had a hat that was too big. Finally, we sang about a dog who swallowed a large, large bone.

Mommy laughed and sang along, in a low voice. I liked it when Mommy laughed. She was very sad when Daddy went away, but now she was happy again. During the drive, we saw a bridge and a river and I begged Mommy to stop. I wanted to splash my feet in the water, but she said we didn't have time.

"If you behave at the store, maybe we'll drop by on the way back home."

"Okay." I pressed my rabbit's ear to my mouth and whispered, "We have to be very good so we can go to the river." I kissed the top of its head and looked at Mommy in the mirror. "Can we stay for a really long time?" I used my baby voice, the one I knew Mommy liked.

"We'll see, honey. Now, can we continue singing?"

We sang another song all the way to the store, and when we arrived at the store parking lot, Mommy turned off the car and carried me out.

"Remember that I need you to be really good, okay? And stay near me. If you can see me, it means I can see you too."

"I promise," I said, putting my arms around her neck.

"That's my big girl." She put me down again so she could get a shopping cart.

While I waited for her, a man with a cane was standing nearby and kept smiling at me. I smiled back, hoping Mommy didn't see. She didn't like it when I spoke to strangers, and to me, smiling was like talking.

When we entered the store, I touched everything I could reach: the toys, the magazines, the candy, the egg that was lying on the shelf... everything. Mommy took the egg from my hand and scolded me.

"If you want to go to the river later," she said, as she grabbed a bottle of milk and put it in a cart, "remember what you have to do."

I sighed and put my hands behind my back. "I'll behave, Mommy. Can we go to the river? Pleeease?"

She tucked a strand of my hair behind my ear. "If you help me, maybe."

"Okay, Mommy." I held on to my rabbit and waited

patiently as she shopped. Sometimes she stopped to ask me to pick out some things and asked me to put them in the cart. I did what she wanted, but I pulled the stickers off first, and pressed them to my forehead and arms.

"Stop doing that, Cassidy," she said, wagging her finger at me.

I dropped my head to my chest, bored again. "Why?"

"We need them so the cashier will know what we're buying and how much it costs." She put the stickers back on the cans, packets, and bottles. Then she held up two cartons of juice. "Orange juice or apple juice."

"Grape juice," I said and she shook her head and made the choice for me.

I was almost tired when Mommy finally finished shopping and it was time to go out to the car, but when I remembered that we were going to the river, I walked even faster. I wanted to sing again while Mommy drove, but now she wanted silence.

While driving, she kept looking at the envelope she had put on the passenger's seat when we left the house earlier. She said there was an important letter inside, but she had not opened it for two days, even though she carried it everywhere with her. Georgia said Mommy was scared to read it because it was from Daddy, and he was maybe writing to tell her that he had a new family now, and he would never come back to us.

Mommy stopped the car by the river and I opened my seatbelt before she turned off the engine. She took my hand and we walked to the water.

The sun was warm and it felt good on my face, and when we reached the edge of the river, Mommy turned to me and held up the envelope. "Honeybee, I need to read this important letter, but I want you and rabbit to stay here. Watch the ripples and listen to the water. Don't go in, do you hear me? I'll be watching you."

I nodded. "Yes, Mommy."

She smiled, kissed my forehead, then she walked a little bit away from us in the direction of the bridge while opening the envelope.

"Let's walk around a little," I said to Holly, my rabbit. I held her hand and started walking around in a circle.

When Mommy was looking in the other direction, I stopped for a moment, holding the rabbit up until it was looking in my face. "Do you want to go in the water?"

I brought her mouth to my ear and listened. She didn't speak loudly, so I had to listen very carefully. She only talked to me and no one else. Daddy had bought my rabbit for me before he went away. He said it was a magic rabbit and it would make me happy when I was sad.

Holly told me that she wanted us to go in the water.

"But Mommy will be angry," I said, wagging a finger.

But Holly told me it was okay. Mommy was looking the other way, and was now busy reading the letter.

Before Mommy could turn around, I quickly took off my shoes and socks and dipped my feet in the river. It was cold, but I liked it. It was fun to wiggle my toes in the water. I felt something slimy and it tickled, but I didn't care. I had to be quick, though, so I wouldn't get caught. While I played with Holly, I heard Mommy yell a bad word. I looked, but she was talking to herself, and she couldn't see us.

When I took another step forward and stopped, Holly told me to go all the way in to see if we could cross to the other side. There were some pretty flowers by the river bank. Maybe we could pick some for Mommy, then she wouldn't be too mad at us.

"Okay," I whispered, taking another step. "But if Mommy sees us she'll shout and we'll get into trouble."

I was about to keep walking, when someone grabbed my shoulders from behind and pulled me out. I didn't scream because I thought it was my Mommy, but when I looked up and saw the woman's eyes, they were not brown like Mommy's.

"Shhh!" the woman said when I opened my mouth to call Mommy. "Don't be scared, baby. I'm here now. I bought you some lollies today, the purple ones that make your tongue look funny. They're in the car. Should we go and get them?"

I nodded. I was a little scared, but her smile made me feel better and I liked lollies and the lady was nice. She was wearing perfume and it smelled sweet, like candy floss.

She lifted me up and we ran to the car, but then I remembered that Holly fell in the water when the woman pulled me out. It was okay though because I'd be back soon to get her. I would ask the woman to give me another lolly for Holly.

When we got to the woman's car, she put me inside and gave me my lolly. But then she locked the door and drove away.

"Let's go home," she said. "Daddy is waiting for us."

CHAPTER 30

AVERY

Memories are clouding my mind, confusing the hell out of me, but I push them aside for now as Miss Campbell nears me.

Holding up her hand, she says, "I'm sorry for taking Mia, but you know I would never hurt her."

"Who are you and why did you take my daughter?" I ask, grabbing Mia's hand and taking a step back.

I've known for a while that she cares for my child, but I never thought it would turn into an unhealthy obsession that would lead to something like this. And why is she calling herself my sister?

"She's Miss Campbell, Mommy," Mia answers.

Miss Campbell stops walking and brings her hands together. "I was worried, and I was upset. I didn't understand why you didn't recognize me. I just wanted to talk to you, to get you to remember."

I lift Mia into my arms and take another step back. "I'm sorry, but... I don't know what you're talking about. Why would you take my child?" My eyes start to burn as I shake my head in confusion. "And why did you call me your sister?"

Miss Campbell glances away, clearing her eyes of tears. Her

voice is barely above a whisper when she speaks again. "It's me, I'm her. And I didn't understand why you sent your husband instead of coming to see me yourself."

"My husband?" It takes me a moment to swallow and find my voice. "Wait, what about him?" I ask, stunned.

Miss Campbell sniffs. "I wanted to get to know you, but you sent him to meet me instead. I didn't understand why you didn't come, and I was angry." Her crying has intensified, and it's not just a few tears, but full-on sobbing. "She was dying and you didn't come. You didn't care. And at the school, I waited and waited for weeks, but you didn't even recognize me."

I place my hand on the back of Mia's head and draw her close. I don't want to hold this conversation with her around, but I can't let her out of my sight.

"I'm sorry, but what are you going on about?" I pause and feel the color drain from my face. "Did you have something to do with what happened to my—?"

"No, I had nothing to do with that. Why would you even say that?"

I feel like I'm going to be sick. Could she be the woman Keith sent flowers to? She's incoherent, and I feel like I'm missing something here that would make sense of everything.

I shake my head. "I'm sorry," I say. "I don't know who you are, and I don't know what you're saying." My lips are dry and cracked, and I try to wet them with my tongue, but it doesn't help. This is all too much for me. My head is spinning from everything that's happened today. "You must have me confused with someone else."

Miss Campbell must see the bewilderment in my eyes, because she gasps and sinks heavily onto a patch of grass. "Oh my God," she says. "You don't know."

"Know about what?" My voice is trembling with both frustration and fear as I hold my daughter closer. I've had enough of people not telling me exactly what's going on.

Through her tears, she looks up at me and smiles. "Cassidy, I'm Georgia, your sister. You don't remember me at all?"

Frowning, I take hesitant steps toward her and she doesn't break our gaze. Her eyes are glassy and her mascara has run down her cheeks.

"Georgia" repeats in my head, over and over again. "I'm not Cassidy, I'm—"

"I'm sorry. I thought you knew about me."

She gets to her feet again and comes to me, but before she can say anything else, I shake my head. We can't continue this conversation around Mia.

"I'll take her to the car," I mutter. "Then we can... Then we can talk."

On my way to the car, my head is awash with emotions that jumble and collide, blending into an incoherent mess. After opening the car door, I change my mind about putting Mia inside since it's so hot outside and I have no idea how long my conversation with Miss Campbell will last.

When she's playing with Holly at a safe distance, but out of earshot, I take a deep breath, fold my arms across my chest and meet the other woman's gaze. "You said your name is Georgia?"

She nods and reaches out for my hand. "That's right. I'm Georgia."

I pull my hand away and take a few steps back, trying to process what I have just learned, the memory that came flooding back to me by the bridge. Did I really imagine having a sister named Georgia? The questions come pouring out, one after another. "Why do you keep saying you're my sister? And why do you think I sent my husband to meet you? I never met you before you started at Mia's school."

Georgia takes a step back and presses a hand over her heart. "I thought he told you."

"Who? My husband?"

She purses her lips, then nods. "When he found out about

me and Mom, I thought you did too. He sent money and flowers. It was anonymous, but I knew it was him."

"What?" I bury my hands into my hair and slump against the car. "My husband knows I don't have a sister. Well, I didn't know until my mother—"

"Our mother," she says.

I shake my head. "Please, explain everything to me. I'm really confused right now."

We stand side by side at the front of the car, facing forward, and Georgia tells me her story. It helps that we don't have to make eye contact. If I'm going to process this properly, I can't be distracted by Georgia's emotions when I'm dealing with my own.

"Your name is not Avery," she says. "It's Cassidy. When you were four, Mom took you to the river and you vanished. We thought you drowned and were carried away by the river."

Pressing my body against the car for support before I lose my strength, I blink to get rid of the black dots in my vision. The memories are coming again, forcing me to see deeper and darker truths. The river, the bridge, the grocery store. "The rabbit," I whisper.

"Holly," Georgia says next to me.

"You mean..." My voice drifts off.

"Yes. It was from me, not Miss Simmons." I can hear the smile in her voice. "Holly was your magic rabbit; I thought she would jog your memory."

I don't say anything as I stare at Georgia in disbelief, and she continues to tell me that the only thing the police were able to find were my shoes and the rabbit.

"Since Holly was found in the middle of the river, everyone thought you had drowned and"—Georgia sniffs and pulls a tissue out of her handbag—"all those years, we thought you were dead until your husband showed up. He told me you were alive."

I take a deep breath and look up at the sky. If I have a sister who's still alive and didn't grow up with me, what does it all mean? How do my parents fit into this story? My mind zooms in on the scene of the woman who pulled the little girl inside my head from the river and lured her to her car with the promise of lollipops. Her face was that of my mother, the woman who raised me.

I blow out a breath. "This can't be happening." I don't know what to think, I'm not sure I want to know. But my mind is starting to put together the pieces of a puzzle I didn't know existed.

My sister. Georgia. Holly. The words and names keep echoing through my head, and they don't make sense, and I don't want them to.

Georgia finally speaks again. "After your husband came to the house, I followed him."

"To our house?"

I feel instead of see her nodding. "Then I saw you and little Mia."

I turn to look at her now, her profile broken by the tears in my eyes. "How could you be so sure it was me?"

"Your husband had given me a photo of you." She curls her hands in her lap. "And Mia... she was the spitting image of you as a child. And since you were alive, I realized someone must have taken you. I thought you had found out about us but you were not ready to meet us yet." She pauses and takes a deep breath. "I continued to watch you and when I saw a teaching assistant job advertised at Mia's school, I took it. I wanted to be close to my niece."

I don't speak, I can't speak. Could my childhood really all have been a lie? Or is Georgia the one who's lying?

A tear escapes from the corner of my eye and slides down my cheek. "This is all too much to take in," I finally murmur. "I'm sorry. I don't know what to think."

Georgia scoots closer and lays a cool hand on top of mine. "What do you mean?"

"I mean, I don't know if I can trust you. This is all so crazy." I let out a bitter laugh. "I don't know if I can accept that you're my sister. I have no proof."

She squeezes my hand. "That would be simple to prove. We can do a DNA test."

That's it. If she's willing to do that, then she can't be lying, and the people I know to be my parents are not who I thought they were.

"Why did you take Mia?" I ask, looking up at her and remembering the fear I had felt at finding my daughter missing.

If she's really my sister, why would she want to hurt me like that?

"I thought if I could get you to this place, it might make you remember. And I hated the thought of Mia staying with the people who kidnapped my little sister."

CHAPTER 31

THE WATCHER

I don't want to do this, but I have no choice. The situation is out of control and the time has come for me to take action. Waiting any longer is not an option.

I snatch the leather suitcase from under the bed and flip open the cover, listening to the dull thud as it hits the wooden floor. Next, I scan the contents of the case: a few dresses for Mia, two pairs of shoes, a pair of sunglasses to disguise her with until we're well out of town. I will dye her hair a different color at some point so that nobody will recognize her.

My fingers sweep over three new children's books to keep her company and two of her old toys.

Content, I unzip the side pocket and pull out the money, a few hundred dollars in tens and twenties. When I have counted each note to make sure it's all there, I tuck the wad of cash back into the pocket. I need to have enough cash on me in case, while on the run, we don't get a chance to go to a bank.

I check the contents of the case one more time, making sure I've chosen everything I need. I can't risk not being prepared.

Satisfied with my choices, I zip up the case again and run

over the carefully thought-out plan in my mind, one I have been putting together for months.

My goal is not to hurt anyone, it never has been. My job is to protect children, to make sure Mia is safe. But if I have to hurt someone, even if it's Avery, to get Mia away, then that's just what I'll do. I'll do what I have to do to protect the little girl, no matter what it takes.

I gave Avery many chances to prove to me that she can take care of the child, but she was distracted yet again, and Mia was taken. She now has to face the consequences.

I lift the suitcase off the floor and head for the door. Less than a minute later, the suitcase is in the car and the trunk is closed.

As soon as I get Mia back, we'll be on the road for a long time before anyone can find us.

There are many places we can go, safe houses in small towns, in the woods, even as far away as Canada. The farther we go, the less likely anyone will catch up with us.

CHAPTER 32

JODIE: 31 YEARS AGO

Twenty minutes after Jodie left the house, she found herself at the Kirkook River. She and Lynn came there a lot to play "pooh-sticks" like she did with her mother as a child. Jodie got out of the car and noticed a yellow Volvo parked at the other side of the bridge. Walking along the river's edge, she watched the current rush downstream. It would be so easy to jump in and get swept away by the water, but she could not do that when she had a daughter to raise.

Jodie stopped walking when she saw a little girl in the river, paddling in the shallows. She was holding something in one hand that looked like a stuffed animal. She heard someone shouting as she walked closer, and saw a woman walking away from the river, staring at a piece of paper that fluttered in the wind.

Jodie ignored her and focused on the little girl.

"My baby," she whispered over the roar of the water. "I'm here, my sweet girl."

She knew it. She knew she would return.

She picked up her pace and ran to her because the river was too dangerous. As the girl was so engrossed in whatever game she was playing with her toy, she didn't notice her at first. Jodie had to get her out of the water before she went too deep. The last thing she wanted was for her little girl to get hurt. She gently grabbed her shoulders from behind and for a moment the little girl struggled. But she stopped when she saw her face and relaxed.

They had to get back to Harry. He would be so happy to see their daughter again.

A few minutes later, Jodie glanced in the rearview mirror at the girl seated safely in the car seat, and a smile crept up on her face. She had her daughter back. Harry would be so pleased.

"Do you like your lolly?" she asked the child. The girl nodded, but something in her expression had changed. She had lost the sparkle in her eyes and now her face was solemn.

Jodie turned back to the road. "Are you okay, darling? What's wrong, sweet girl?"

"I want my Mommy," the girl said in a small and timid voice.

Jodie's breath caught in her throat. "I'm your mommy, sweetheart."

"I want my real mommy," she said in a louder, more determined voice, and continued to ask for her mother.

Jodie didn't say anything further, just kept driving. Soon they were home and Jodie helped her out of the car and took her inside. Ruth was not outside to see her bring the girl home, and as soon as they were behind closed doors, she pulled the child, who was now crying softly, into her arms and held her.

"Shh, baby girl, don't cry. Everything will be all right. You're back home now."

The girl pulled away from her and looked up at her with tears running down her cheeks. "You're not my mommy."

Jodie shuddered as a chill ran down her spine, but she put on a smile and brushed back the flyaway strands of the girl's hair. "I tidied your room and put on the nice butterfly bedding that you like on your bed. Do you want to see it?"

The girl nodded and allowed her to lead her up the stairs and into Lynn's bedroom. Then she stood there, looking around as if trying to remember something. Jodie moved to the bed and picked up a stuffed whale, sitting down with it on the edge of the bed. "Do you like it?"

"The walls are pink," the girl muttered, her voice monotone, her eyes still roaming the room.

"I know. You like pink, don't you? It's your favorite color."

The girl folded her arms across her chest and pouted. "I don't want to stay here. I want to go home."

"Home?" Jodie felt the ice that had settled in the pit of her stomach earlier climbing back up her throat, freezing everything in its way.

The girl looked down and shuffled her feet. "Yes, our house, with my mommy and Georgia," she said. "My mommy is waiting for me at the river."

"You're being silly. This is your home, with Daddy and me." Jodie tried to keep her voice steady, but she was shaking inside. "The woman at the river was not your mommy. I am. Now don't you say that again. It makes me sad."

The girl ignored her and started toward the door. "I'm going to my mommy and my rabbit, Holly. She fell in the river."

Jodie felt a wave of determination wash over her. She wouldn't let her daughter go, not this time. So she got to her feet and grabbed the girl's arm, pulling her back. "Come, Lynn, this is your home, where you belong."

"My name is not Lynn." The girl's voice had a sharp edge to it now. "It's Cassidy."

Jodie knelt down in front of her and made her look into her eyes. "Cassidy is a lovely name, but it's not yours. Your name is Lynn, but if you don't like it, your second name is Avery. You know what, we'll call you that. So, come on, Avery, let's go and look for Daddy."

As she stood up, she grabbed the girl's hand, but the child yanked it away before bursting into tears.

Jodie opened a drawer and found a box of tissues, and it took thirty minutes for her to clean her up and calm her down. Then she dressed her in Lynn's clothes, a purple T-shirt and red shorts, and tucked her in bed for a short nap. Tired from all the crying, she slept almost immediately.

Only then did Jodie go downstairs to find out where her husband was. She looked for him in the living room, the den, and the study. Then she walked into the kitchen and came to a sudden halt. Lynn was still on the floor where she had left her, her body lifeless, her eyes closed. Jodie felt bile rising in her throat and tears flooding her eyes. She fell to her knees and reached out to touch the girl's face, but her hand froze in mid-air. She could not touch the face of the dead little girl.

Staring at the body, she thought of the girl sleeping upstairs and shook her head. Her daughter was alive. The girl on the floor was just an empty shell. Standing up, she turned her back on the body and walked out the back door before throwing up in the bushes. As she straightened up to wipe her mouth with the back of her hand, she noticed Harry sitting on the garden bench, a bottle of alcohol next to him. Jodie was startled because her husband did not drink, not even when they had visitors. She hurried to him and noticed that he was crying, his head in his hands.

"Harry?" Jodie said, walking toward him.

"She's gone, Jodie." His words came out in a hiss. "Lynn's dead."

"No, Harry." Jodie sat down next to him. "She came back to us. She's upstairs sleeping."

Harry lifted his head, and it lolled a little to the side. "What...? No, Jodie, our girl is—"

"Sleeping upstairs," Jodie said more firmly. Her hands were shaking so she pushed them between her knees to stop them. "Come with me. I'll show you. She came back to us, Harry. She's as right as rain."

"What are you talking about?" Harry's voice was slurred as his eyes widened.

Jodie watched Harry get unsteadily to his feet and she scurried after him into the house and up the stairs. In their daughter's bedroom, he stopped in front of the bed and stared at the girl sleeping in the middle of a pink bedspread.

Jodie picked up a light blanket from the end of the bed and covered her body. "See?" she whispered. "She's asleep. She was so tired after we played at the river."

Harry looked at his wife as if he'd never seen her before, then closed his eyes and took a deep breath to steady himself. "That's not Lynn," he insisted, his face drawn with tension. "She's gone."

Jodie's lips trembled as she began to sob. "No, she's not. She's right there." She pointed to the girl.

Harry brushed a hand over his face, pulled his wife into the hallway, and grabbed her by the shoulders. He was suddenly sober again. "That girl in there is not our daughter, Jodie. It's someone else's child. Where did you get her from?"

Jodie ignored his question and continued to make him understand. "I know she doesn't look like Lynn, but our daughter is inside that girl. I knew it as soon as I saw her. Since she looks a little different, I think we should call her by her second name, Avery, to signify a new beginning for all of us." She shook her head as fresh tears began to stream down her face. "She came back to us. Please, Harry, don't take her away from me."

Before he said anything, she closed her ears to shut him out and ran to their bedroom. When he came in after her eventually, she dropped her hands and looked him straight in the eye. "We need to bury the body."

They did exactly that. That night, Jodie cut off a lock of Lynn's long hair for safekeeping before they buried her in the garden under the weeping willow tree, and they kept the new child: Lynn, returned to them in a new body.

Jodie warned Harry that if he called the police and took her child away, she would kill herself, and to bury his own grief and guilt, he started drinking. He just could not accept the fact that his daughter was dead and no amount of alcohol could make her come back. In a way, Jodie was relieved that her husband was becoming a drunk. It meant that he would stay out of the way while she raised Avery.

The night after Jodie brought the girl home, she watched the news and learned that the girl was assumed to have drowned in the river. The news reporter, a woman with short, curly hair, who stood on the opposite bank of the river from where the incident occurred, looked into the camera.

"A search is underway for Cassidy Campbell, a four-year-old girl who is believed to have drowned in the Kirkook River between the towns of Little Lake and Willow Gate. She was last seen wearing blue jeans and a brown T-shirt. Her shoes were found along the river's edge, and what appears to be a stuffed rabbit was found in the water."

The camera panned to a picture of a gray rabbit with black eyes, then switched back to the reporter.

"Our hearts go out to the girl's family, and we pray that they will find the strength to cope with the loss of their beloved daughter and sister."

While her husband was knocked out by alcohol next to her, Jodie stared at the screen and knew that everything was going to be just fine. No one would come looking for the girl as she was believed to be dead, and she would grow up and make Jodie's life complete.

But for now, until things cooled off and the police stopped searching, they would have to be careful.

The next day, they packed their bags and left town, and they spent seven months on a disused farm Harry had inherited from his grandparents. They had planned to stay for at least a year, but then Jodie started dreaming of the willow tree in their backyard and what was buried underneath its shade, and she felt it was a sign for them to return home. Harry wanted them to stay away for good, but she knew the willow tree would keep whispering for her to come back.

Even though she told herself that no one would come looking for the girl, Jodie was still plagued by the fear that her secret would be discovered. She never imagined that the choices she made would one day have such terrible, deadly consequences.

CHAPTER 33

KEITH: THREE DAYS BEFORE THE ACCIDENT

Keith shrugged on his leather jacket over blue jeans and picked up his black helmet from the hall table.

"Are you going biking?" Avery asked as she walked into the house after dropping off Mia. "I thought you were working from home."

"I changed my mind, I'm taking the day off. Sometimes it's good to go with the flow."

Keith owned one of Willow Gate's largest landscaping companies, but, unlike Avery, he was not a workaholic. He was determined to enjoy his freedom. That was, after all, the reason he became an entrepreneur in the first place.

"You're such a show-off," Avery said with a grin. "While some of us are working, you are out gallivanting."

Keith walked over to her and gave her a kiss on the lips. "I'll have fun for the both of us." Then he stood back and cocked his head. "In the spirit of having fun, are you looking forward to celebrating with Celeste this Friday?"

"You bet I am. Can you believe Opal Touch is a year old?"

"I'm so proud of you, baby." Keith pulled her into his arms.

"You've worked so hard and you deserve to celebrate. Where are you guys going again?"

"The Lobster Roll, baby."

"But that's our place." Keith feigned disappointment. "Can't you eat with your friends somewhere else?"

Avery laughed. "No, honey. Celeste wants to try out the place and there's nothing that says celebrating to me like their grilled lobster salad."

"True, and maybe a celebratory cocktail to go along with it?"

"I don't think so," she replied. "No alcohol for me. I'll stick to lemon water or soda." She glanced at her watch. "I need to go get dressed for work."

Keith followed Avery upstairs to their bedroom and pulled her toward him. He sat her on his lap and turned her to face him. "Your not drinking doesn't stop your father from drinking. It's not like you drink to get drunk."

She sighed and rotated her neck. "I know. I just... I don't know."

"I wonder if he'll ever stop," Keith said, even though he knew the truth.

Avery kissed his cheek and stood up. "I don't think so. He's too far gone, in my opinion. Ruth said that, as a child, I called his alcohol 'daddy juice.'"

"Daddy juice? I've never heard that before."

"I don't think I've told you before. It seems silly, yet sad too, don't you think?"

"You should stop torturing yourself about it," Keith said, running his hand up and down her arm. "You can't prevent your father from drinking. He's an adult, and he's responsible for his actions."

When Keith first started dating Avery, he tried to stop her father from drinking because it really destroyed her, giving her one more thing for her to deal with on top of her mother's depression. Keith was so determined to rescue Harry that he even accompanied him to AA meetings, but Harry never showed up for the third meeting and, later that day, Keith found him in a bar, drunk. He tried a few more times over the years to help him, but kept hitting a brick wall. Until he had no option but to accept that this was a battle he couldn't win.

"I'm sorry, son," Harry had said to Keith once. "I really am. But I'm an alcoholic and this is just the way I am. If you're going to be a part of this family, you have to accept me like this."

Harry embarrassed them by showing up drunk at their wedding ceremony and interrupting the pastor. When the pastor asked if anyone objected, Harry shouted, "I do! Avery is too good for him."

Keith asked his best man, Liam, to drive Harry home so that the wedding could continue uninterrupted, and the next morning, sober and crying, he apologized to both of them. However, the damage had been done and there was no turning back.

"I know he's responsible for his own choices," Avery said. "Now I really need to get going. It's a busy day."

Keith watched as his wife pulled out a black skirt and white blouse from the closet and laid them on top of each other on the bed.

"So, where are you going?" she asked as she held up the blouse to see if it needed ironing.

"I'm going over to your parents' house, actually."

"Really?" Avery asked in surprise. "Why?"

"I promised your dad I'll help fix his computer."

Avery laughed and shook her head. "He should really let that thing go. It breaks down at least once a month; it can't even run the software we use these days. I offered to buy him a new one, but he's too darn stubborn."

"Avery, he's been using it for fifteen years. As long as it

keeps coming back to life, why not let him keep it? I better go and try to revive it."

"You're biking there in this heat? Why not take the car?"

"Why not bike? It's a great day out. I'll burn off calories."

Avery laughed. "I guess we'll always have this discussion. I don't even know why we have a car for you."

"Good point. I did suggest we sell it and get me a motorbike, but as I recall, you refused."

"No way, you lunatic. You'll kill yourself doing stunts with that thing."

Keith kissed her again and walked out. He rode his bike down the streets of Willow Gate, remembering the day he first saw Avery. It was one of those random days when you met someone and immediately knew they would change your life. They met at the Willow Gate annual fair, the highlight of the year for the small town for both residents and visitors. It also served as a means of introducing newcomers to the community.

The two-day event drew thousands of visitors from all over the country, and the town lived off the money it brought in for months.

Keith was one of the newcomers. Well, almost. After being away to study landscape architecture at UC Berkeley, he had come back home to accept a position at his father's landscaping company.

Keith was forced to partake in the festivities by his school friend, Liam, who, despite being a rule breaker in school, had become a police officer.

During a game of tug of war, he saw Avery and immediately zeroed in on her, forgetting about the competition. Although he initially tried to ignore her, he kept getting distracted as he stood by the rope waiting for his turn. Until she also noticed him. She wore a high ponytail, a pair of scuffed blue jeans, and a white T-shirt with a large Granny Smith apple on the front. She completed the look with flip-flops. When their eyes met, he just knew she would be his wife.

Keith's father died of a heart attack two months after they were married, and he took over the business. While he became the town's most sought-after landscaper, he never gave up his freedom. He had no regrets. He had a beautiful daughter, a lovely wife, and a flourishing business. What else can a man ask for?

While whizzing through town, he closed his eyes for a moment to enjoy the sun and wind on his face. It was a feeling of freedom he had never experienced in a car, and he also enjoyed watching the scenery of his hometown. Several magazines rated Willow Gate in the top ten best places to live in the United States for two consecutive years, and Keith was proud of it.

White houses surrounded green lawns and flowerbeds were filled with flowers of all colors and sizes. Ponds and lakes dotted the small town, and the wetlands provided a habitat for a variety of animals. As he drove by the church where they got married, a structure that looked like an Italian villa, he was getting closer to his in-laws. They lived a little farther away from the town center in a neighborhood made up of single family homes.

He parked his bike by the front door and was just going to knock on the door when he saw that it was slightly ajar. As he walked inside, he expected Jodie or Harry to meet him. He called them, but they didn't answer. Jodie was probably still sleeping off the numerous pills she took every night.

In the living room, Keith found his father-in-law holding a photograph. Next to him was an empty bottle of cheap whiskey.

"Harry," Keith said, disappointment in his tone. He had hoped to find him sober.

Harry looked up at Keith with wild red eyes, then took a deep breath and said, "I took a life. I killed her."

As soon as he heard the words, Keith's mind immediately flashed to Avery and Mia, even though he knew Harry couldn't be referring to either of them; Mia was safely at school and he had just seen Avery. But it was hard to ignore the overwhelming feeling in his gut that they were in danger somehow.

CHAPTER 34

Keith stumbled backward. Was it the alcohol talking or had his father-in-law just confessed to a murder? Why would anyone say something like that, drunk or not? Afraid to ask Harry to explain or even to approach him, he gazed beyond him through the glass doors leading out into the garden.

Gray clouds hung heavy with moisture, casting a gloomy mood over the scene. The sky promised rain. The lawn was brown and dry, the hedges were overgrown, and the red maple looked as though it was dying. The only tree that was flourishing was the weeping willow tree next to the garden table where Harry loved to drink. Keith needed to convince Harry to let him see to the garden and get it all in shape, but he doubted he would say yes. He constantly offered free landscaping services to them, but they never used them.

"I did it," Harry repeated, as if he was having trouble remembering and needed to keep on hearing the words. "I killed her."

"Who, Jodie? Did you hurt Jodie?" Keith turned back to him and watched him shake his head before he sipped from his bottle, then continued to talk to himself.

"I—I did it. It was my fault."

Even though Keith was relieved Jodie was not hurt, he was getting more and more frightened, and he had no idea what to say to Harry.

"Dammit, Harry, you're scaring me right now. Who did you...?" He blew out a breath. "Who did you kill?"

Keith couldn't even believe those words were coming out of his mouth. He wanted to believe that his father-in-law was experiencing some sort of psychotic breakdown, but something told him there was a grain of truth in what he said. The man was so insistent.

But how could it be?

Harry looked at him with eyes that were like two pools of still, dark water. His face was ashen, his lips pale, and his trembling hands clutched the couch's arm.

"My daughter is dead." His voice broke. "It was an accident, but I'm responsible."

"What are you talking about?" Keith's voice rose with his rising panic. "Avery is fine. Nothing has happened to her."

Harry shook his head, then dropped the photo onto the frosted glass coffee table. "She was in my care and I killed her."

Keith couldn't believe his ears. Harry was definitely not thinking straight. As he looked down, he felt his hand tremble as it picked up the photograph, wet from Harry's tears. A girl on a swing looked up at him, carefree and happy. She wore her black hair in two thin braids behind her back, and her eyes were a denim color. Keith looked up again, and his throat tightened, but he managed to speak. "Who is this girl?"

Harry took a long drink from a bottle he pulled from somewhere behind him and wiped his mouth on his sleeve. "She's dead in the kitchen, Keith. My little girl is dead."

Keith dropped the photo and ran to the kitchen, fearing what he might discover there, even though he didn't believe a word Harry said. Jodie was in a heap on the floor, sobbing like her husband. She didn't even look up at Keith.

What the crap was going on here?

Keith knelt down beside her and gently touched her shoulder. "Jodie, what's going on? What are you doing on the floor?"

Jodie flinched and looked up. Her eyes were red and swollen and her nose was running, the tears and snot mixing on her dry, cracked lips. She had clearly been crying for a long time. As her eyes squinted at him, her face crumpled. He had seen her fall apart many times before, but this was something else.

"Harry killed her," she murmured.

Keith blinked several times, completely puzzled. He felt as if he had just landed in a strange film, and in frustration he raked his hands through his hair. "Can someone tell me what's going on?" he demanded.

Jodie was inconsolable, Harry was drunk, and Keith was trying not to lose it. Jodie swayed back and forth when he helped her to her feet, and, taking her to the kitchen table, he sat her down in one of the chairs. He then went to get her a glass of water, which she didn't touch.

He pulled up a chair next to her. "Jodie, what did Harry mean when he said Avery is dead?"

Jodie clutched at her chest, and her face crumpled. "Our Avery is dead."

"Your Avery? You daughter Avery, my wife Avery? Is that who you're talking about?"

Jodie shook her head and wouldn't stop, like a patient refusing to take their medication.

Grabbing her hands, he gave them a gentle squeeze. "Stop it, Jodie. Just stop it right now. You need to tell me what happened here."

She stopped again and met his gaze. "No, not her. My daughter." Jodie's voice was hoarse, broken.

Keith let go of her hands and closed his eyes. When he opened them again, he was on the verge of bursting and yelling in frustration. "You only have one daughter, Avery. And she's alive. I can call her right now. Do you want to speak to her?"

Jodie didn't say anything. She just sat there, her face like a mask, her body like a statue, and her hands gripping the edge of the table. When Keith pulled his phone from his pocket and turned it on, Jodie's hand shot out and slammed into his. It slipped from his fingers and clattered to the floor. He stared at Jodie in horror. There was something fierce and maybe even dangerous in her eyes that he had never seen before.

"Don't call her," she said.

"Why not, Jodie? I just wanted to prove to you that Avery is fine. I saw her before I came here." He stood up and picked up his phone. "Something strange is going on here and if you won't tell me what that is, I need to get you help or call the police."

Jodie's eyes grew wide and wild. "No, Keith," she said, and her voice was shaking. "No police, please."

Keith clenched his jaw in anger. "Then. Talk. To. Me."

"Avery, your wife, is not our daughter... our real daughter."

Keith spun around and faced the door where the voice was coming from.

Harry stood in the doorway. His eyes were still red and wet, and his face was pale and drawn. He leaned against the door frame. Despite still being drunk, he also seemed to have clarity.

"Harry, don't do it," Jodie whispered, but her husband shook his head.

"Jodie, it's time. Keeping this secret is killing you and killing me. I can't keep it inside anymore." He drew in a deep breath and turned to me. "Our daughter's name was Lynn. She died in this kitchen thirty-one years ago." His words were clearer than Keith had ever heard them before. "Right there." He pointed to Jodie's seat. "We were so crazy with grief that we... we found another child to raise."

"Avery?" Keith whispered. "My wife is not your daughter?"

Harry nodded. "Her real name was Cassidy."

"Cassidy..." Keith's eyes darted around, his body cold and his face sweltering. "Where did you get her?"

"We took her." Harry turned and went back to the living room, leaving Keith with Jodie and the weight of the terrible secret he had just revealed.

Keith wanted to scream. He wanted to run. He let out a long sigh as he ran his hands through his hair. "You kidnapped Avery?"

Jodie grabbed his hands. "Please, don't tell the police. We loved and still love her like our own child. You know that."

Keith yanked his hand away. "You don't love her. You lied to her all those years. You made her believe she was someone she wasn't. How could you do something so cruel to that girl, Jodie? To any child?"

She averted her gaze, her shoulders slumping forward. "It was my fault. I did it all. I took her from her real mother."

Keith was unable to hear any more. He had to get out for fresh air, so he stepped out into the garden through the back door. Despite Jodie's sobs behind him, begging him to understand, he kept walking. Outside there was a warm breeze, scented by the flowers in Ruth's garden. The leaves on the trees rustled softly, but there were no birds singing or insects buzzing. Keith couldn't focus on anything outside his troubled mind. Harry had confessed to killing his own daughter, and he saw no reason not to believe him.

CHAPTER 35

After a while outside, Keith heard Ruth calling him, wanting him to stop for a chat, but he didn't have the energy to speak to her. Ignoring her, he walked back to the house where Jodie waited outside the back door, her face red and streaked with tears. "Keith, please don't do this."

"What do you want from me, Jodie? I've just discovered that you and Harry have been keeping a terrible secret."

In truth, he had no idea what to do with the information. Should he pick up the phone and call the police?

Jodie wiped her nose with the back of her hand. "Don't go to the police, please. You know we love Avery."

Her words cut Keith's heart like a knife, but he didn't feel any pain, only anger. "Stop saying that. You lied to her for over thirty years. You kidnapped her."

He walked past her and sat at the table, his head in his hands. Avery needed to know, but where would he even begin?

Jodie pulled up a chair next to him.

Seeing her start to speak, he looked up and held his hand up to stop her.

"How did she die?" He paused to swallow. "I need to know how your daughter died."

Jodie dropped her gaze to her hands on the table and told Keith the entire story. It was pointless to hold back now.

"Did you call the police or take her to the hospital?" Keith asked when she was finished and her voice trailed off into tears.

Jodie bit her bottom lip and shook her head. "It was too late. We just... We buried her."

"And took another child." Keith rubbed his forehead.

Jodie nodded. She had stopped crying; in a sense, it was almost as if she was relieved the truth had come out. As though keeping it inside her had been more painful than she could bear.

"I was so devastated. I wasn't thinking straight." Jodie reached out to touch Keith's hand, but he pulled away.

"I don't want to hear any more," he said. "It no longer matters. I need to do something about this."

"If you tell Avery now, it would ruin her life and Mia's," she continued.

Keith held up a trembling finger. "Don't say their names. Just don't." He closed his eyes, pressed his fist to his forehead, cursing under his breath. "Can you leave me alone for a while? I need to think."

Jodie got up and walked out of the back door, closing it behind her, and Keith didn't say another word. He didn't call the police. He just sat there in stunned silence.

The people he believed to be his father- and mother-in-law were not.

How could he not tell Avery? After having the truth being withheld from her for so long, she deserved to know. He decided that he would talk to her first and she would have to make the decision about what to do next.

Just as he was standing up, both Jodie and Harry entered the kitchen, and he stared at them for a moment.

Finally, he said, "The police need to know what you did. And Avery deserves to know the truth."

They nodded, resigned to their fate.

"Please, let us tell them ourselves," Jodie pleaded with him, "but we need a little time to prepare and to spend time with Avery and Mia before—please."

"How much time?" Keith asked, his tone stone cold.

"Just a few days... three?"

Three days. Three days in which he would look into his wife's eyes and not be able to tell her that her life was about to be turned upside down. Three days when she would smile and not know that, in a moment, everything she thought she knew about herself would turn out to be a lie.

Taking a deep breath, Keith felt as if he was suffocating. "Fine. But not one second more. If you don't come clean and confess within three days, I'll go to the police myself. I'll tell them, and Avery, everything I know."

He walked out of the kitchen and slammed the door behind him. He could no longer bear to be in the same room as them. As he stepped outside, it began to rain but he rode his bike and let it take him wherever, not caring that he was getting soaked. He rode to the park they often took Mia to when they visited, where he leaned his bike against the trunk of a tree by the duck pond and took a seat on the bench. His clothes soaked through from the rain as he stood there for a long time. He looked up and saw more dark clouds gathering.

The pain in his heart was so intense that he thought it would break him. Although he wanted to cry, he could not. He couldn't tell Avery yet what he knew, but there was one thing he could do while he waited.

He hated having to speak to Jodie and Harry again today, but he picked up his phone anyway because he needed something from them. The full name of the child they'd kidnapped.

CHAPTER 36

THE WATCHER

Having closed the garage door and turned on the light, I remove the leather bag from behind boxes of tools, old cabinets, and buckets of paint. A spider scurries across my bare arm and I swat at it, more annoyed than scared of the creature.

I remove the gun from the bag, a silver pistol that feels solid in my hand. It feels heavier than I recall from the last time I held it, at the shooting range two days ago. I know that the weight is just as much in my head as it is in my hand.

As I wrap my fingers around it, I study the thin metal of the barrel and the glossy black handle. It's a small gun, but it's enough to do the job.

At the shooting range, I have shot hundreds of rounds with it. In the silence of the garage, I still hear the sharp crack of my shots, the sound of the bullets as they left the barrel and punched through the targets. I can still feel the sense of satisfaction when I hit the bullseye.

Touching the cool metal with my thumb, I breathe in the scent of gun oil and steel.

I'm not nervous or afraid. I'm confident that what I'm doing is the right thing for Mia.

I have no qualms about shooting someone to save the life of an innocent child. I hope I will not need to use the gun, but it helps to be prepared.

To make sure I'm not caught in a situation where I'm unable to act quickly, I pull back the slide to check if the gun is loaded. It is.

A distant car horn interrupts my thoughts, but I ignore it.

I set the gun on a paint bucket carefully, then reach inside the bag again to make sure everything else is still there. An extra box of bullets, more cash, a new burner phone, a flashlight, extra batteries, and a camping knife. Everything is neatly tucked away in the bag's many pockets.

I pick up the gun again and put it back in its place, careful to make sure it's secure and hidden from view unless I need it.

Now it's time for me to get Mia.

CHAPTER 37

KEITH: ONE DAY BEFORE THE ACCIDENT

Two days after hearing Jodie and Harry's confessions and reading all of the old articles about Cassidy Campbell's disappearance, Keith tracked down the address of her family's home. They lived on Lauren Drive, in Little Lake, a small town only forty-five minutes away from Willow Gate. Between the two towns ran the river where Cassidy was believed to have drowned. Little Lake was a simple one-road community, a quiet farming town except for a small store on the main road.

The Campbells lived in a small house at the end of two dirt roads, surrounded by fields and open land. It looked like a renovated and modernized farmhouse, and there were quite a few similar homes in the area, as well as some actual run-down farmhouses. Keith parked his car on the side of the road and walked up the dirt road to the house. He rang the doorbell and waited with his hands in his pockets, wondering if he was doing the right thing.

The door was opened by a woman wearing a light-green sweater and blue jeans. Although her hair was blonde, he detected dark roots showing. For a moment, Keith was speechless, transfixed by her eyes. Avery's were brown, while this woman's were amber, but they had a similar shape. There was no way to miss the resemblance. He just knew that she was Avery's sister. Her pretty face was masked by the sorrow in her eyes.

As he stared, the woman frowned, scrutinizing him. "Can I help you?"

"Hi, sorry." He cleared his throat. "I'm Keith Watkins and I'm looking for someone who used to live here. A Kathy Campbell."

"My mother," she said, narrowing her eyes, and crossing her arms across her chest. "She's not in. What is this about?"

Keith hesitated before speaking. "I... Ummm... it's about Cassidy Campbell, her daughter who went missing thirty years ago. I have information about her."

She looked away, biting her lower lip in distress. Her sister's disappearance was clearly a painful topic for her.

She opened her mouth to say something, but then seemed to change her mind. She frowned, then stepped aside. "Come on in."

The two of them sat in the living room after she led him inside the house. It was very modest, with only a few pieces of furniture and a large window that overlooked the fields.

"I'm sorry to bother you," he said. "I know this is a very painful subject."

"It is. It's been a nightmare; my mother never recovered from it. I'm Georgia Campbell. Who are you and what do you know about my sister?"

A woman with no time for beating around the bush. Just as straightforward as Avery.

"Your sister's my wife," Keith blurted out. Maybe he should have eased her into it, but he didn't want to drag this out more than he needed to.

He heard a sharp intake of breath and Georgia's face

drained of all blood. Her eyes widened, but she didn't say anything as she stared at him, her face twisted in confusion.

"She's alive," Keith continued.

She put her hand over her mouth and shook her head. "Y-your wife? It's impossible. Cassidy drowned."

"No, she didn't," Keith said. "Georgia, I know this is a lot to take in, but it's true."

He would not talk about the kidnapping just yet. He will let Harry and Jodie confess their own crime. If he told Georgia that her sister was kidnapped, she most certainly would go straight to the cops.

"How do I know if you're telling the truth? Why should I believe anything you're telling me? You're a stranger. I shouldn't have—"

"I'm telling you the truth. I can prove it." Keith reached into his back pocket and pulled out his wallet. Inside was a passport photograph of Avery. He took a deep breath and handed the photo to her.

She took it and studied it, biting her lower lip. A tear slid down her cheek. "Her eyes..." her voice drifted off. "They're the same."

"It's her," he said, nodding. "Your sister really is alive, but she goes by the name of Avery now."

"Why? What happened to her?" She was still staring at the photo, unable to look away from the proof of the miracle unfolding in front of her. "Where was she all this time?"

Keith squeezed his eyes shut and opened them again with a sigh. "I'm sorry, but that's not my story to tell."

"I don't understand." She finally looked up at him, a deep frown between her brows. "Why won't you just tell me?"

Keith rubbed the back of his neck roughly as he pondered what to say to her. "I just think... I think yours sister should tell you herself."

"Well, where is she? When can I see her?"

"You'll see her again in a few days. I promise. I just wanted you to know she's alive. You can keep the photo."

Nodding, she stood up and walked over to the window. Her eyes were still glued to Avery's photo. "I can't believe this. All these years we've been living in the shadow of my sister's disappearance." She turned to face him again, with tears making her eyes shine. "My mother was numb with grief. She stopped caring, stopped living."

"Where's your mother now?" Keith asked.

"She's in a hospice in Willow Gate. She's suffering from ovarian cancer."

Keith's chest contracted. "I'm sorry to hear that."

Georgia shrugged. "She's in the end stages; I'm not sure how long she has left. A couple of days, months, maybe a year. The doctors keep changing their opinions."

"I would like to see her, to talk to her."

"I'm taking her out of the hospice early next week. That's why I'm here this week, preparing the house for her return."

Keith frowned. "Why are you taking her out?"

Georgia sat down again and sighed, looking down at the floor. "Meadows Hill is expensive; so is every other place I looked up. I can't afford to keep her there. I'm pretty much tapped out financially."

"I need to go," said Keith, getting to his feet after a few moments. "There's something I have to do."

"But wait, what about my sister?" Georgia followed him out the door. "When can I meet her?"

"Soon. I'll keep in touch, I promise."

When Keith left, he drove straight to the bank and withdrew ten thousand dollars to send anonymously to Georgia Campbell. Then he drove to Seeds & Buds and asked for a bouquet of flowers to be sent to his real mother-in-law at Meadows Hill.

Knowing that Avery's mother was sick and could die any

moment changed everything for Keith. The next day, he would go back to Harry and Jodie to tell them that he had changed his mind and would tell Avery the truth.

That night, he woke up because Mia had a nightmare and he went to comfort her. As soon as she fell asleep again, he left the room.

While walking to their bedroom, where Avery was sleeping soundly, he passed the hallway window and saw something outside, a car he thought he recognized, although it was difficult to tell for sure since it was dark. A figure sat inside the car staring up at the house, someone he knew.

The car was gone by the time he ran outside. Convincing himself that he had imagined it, and too distracted by the drama surrounding Avery and her parents, he put it out of his mind.

But the next day, when the same car sped toward him seconds before it slammed into him, knocking him off his bike, he knew he had not imagined it. Not the car, and not the person behind the wheel.

At the hospital, moments before he slipped into a coma, after saying the first words that were on his mind, he wanted to say more. He desperately wanted to warn Avery that she and Mia were in danger, but even though every fiber of his being screamed with panic, darkness descended upon him. It was like he was yelling silently, trapped behind his skull, begging for someone to hear him. No one did.

CHAPTER 38

AVERY

Trying to process what I just heard from Georgia, I slide off the trunk of my car and take a few steps away from it. My parents are not really my family. I was kidnapped as a child. It's too much for me to comprehend and I can't handle the weight of the truth. Covering my mouth with my hand, I fall to my knees.

When Georgia, the sister I never knew I had, touches my shoulder, I jump, wiping my eyes and turning around to face her.

"I'm sorry. I didn't mean to upset you." She offers me her hand to help me back up, and I take it and let her pull me to my feet.

"I'll be fine. Just give me a minute." I brush my hair from my face and attempt a smile. "This is just a lot of information to take in in one go."

"Of course, it was for me too when I found out." Georgia takes a step back.

I let out a breath and turn away, staring at the glimmering river, following its path from the clifftop down to the bridge. The place where I had been stolen and made to live a life that wasn't mine. Everything makes sense now; the pieces have finally fallen into place. Keith found out I was kidnapped and was run over before he got a chance to tell me. My mother doesn't drive, so the only person who could have done it is the man who pretended to be my father.

"I took a life."

When I heard the words from Keith's lips, I thought he was speaking about himself. But my father confessed to taking a life, and he must have said the same thing to Keith who was just repeating it to me that day, trying to tell me what he knew.

I turn around again to face Georgia. "I need to call the police. My phone is dead. Can I use yours?"

My parents kidnapped me, and my father attempted to kill my husband. I cannot forgive them; no one should be allowed to get away with such crimes. My eyes prickle with tears as I try to convince myself that turning them in is the right thing to do, but when Georgia places the phone in my hand, my childhood flashes before my eyes. There were slivers of happiness amidst a life with parents who were battling their demons.

I remember my mother's smile on her happy days.

I remember the warm hugs my father gave me when he was sober.

I feel sick at the thought of them behind bars.

Georgia realizes that I'm struggling and takes the phone away from me. "I know this is hard to do, but they took you away from us. I can't let them get away with that. I can't."

Nodding, I turn away again as she talks to the police, giving a brief overview of everything and the address of the house I grew up in.

"Georgia," she says finally when they ask for her name, "Georgia Campbell. Cassidy was... *is*... my sister."

. . .

Before heading back to the house, I also call Liam, who, even though he's out of town for the day, makes calls to set things into motion so fast that when we arrive at the house, two police cars are already there, parked outside the home I used to call my own, about to arrest the people I called my parents while Mia sleeps innocently in the car.

The neighbors have come out to watch, pointing and whispering, gossiping about the people they thought they knew. The McPhersons, the Daniels, Ruth, and countless others open their front doors with faces full of worry, which soon turns into confusion, then shock. My instinct is to turn around and leave, to forget that this is even happening, but Georgia's hand on my shoulder keeps me rooted to the spot.

A police officer steps out of the house and takes a few steps down the path, stopping when he sees Georgia and me. A moment later, two more police officers walk out with my parents, hands behind their backs. After years of lies, it will take me some time to stop thinking of them in that way.

They appear older, tired, and worn out, and I almost feel sorry for them. But I know that I will never forgive them for what they did to their own daughter, to me, to Keith. They look at me, my mother's face streaked with tears, then turn away.

Georgia pulls me closer. "It's okay." she whispers. "They can't hurt us now. You're safe. You're with me."

My parents are driven away, and the officer who had walked out of the house first approaches Georgia and me. He's tall and thin with silvery hair and round glasses on his face.

First, he looks at me, then at Georgia. "Is one of you Cassidy Campbell?"

I nod. "Me. That was me. I'm Avery now."

"Hello, I'm Officer Trent." He takes a deep breath. "I know this is difficult, but would you mind coming inside with me for a minute? I need to ask you some questions."

My arms tighten around my body as I shake my head. "I don't mind. But can we talk next door?" I point to Ruth's house.

I feel as betrayed by the house I lived in, which harbored so many dark secrets, as I do by my parents. I carry sleepy Mia from the car and the officer follows Georgia and me to Ruth, who welcomes us home. Hers was probably the only real home I ever had.

Georgia and Ruth occupy Mia while I sit in the living room with Officer Trent, who tells me that he was one of the officers called to the scene all those years ago, when I vanished at the river. I tell him as much as I can remember about what happened in the past few days, and he stops me several times to ask more questions I cannot answer. I'm exhausted by the time he leaves, and I wish I could just go to bed and never wake up again. But I have a husband in a coma and a little girl who needs her mother. I can't even imagine what it would feel like if anyone took Mia from me and I never got to see her again.

Georgia and I still have so many things to discuss and, after the policeman leaves, she takes me in her arms and holds me silently, rubbing my back. "I'm so sorry you have to go through this."

When we pull apart, I say, "Please, tell me about our mother." She's already told me that our father hasn't been in the picture for years.

Fresh anger stirs in my stomach and I clench my jaw when she tells me about our mother's grief and the cancer. The time I could have spent with my own mother was stolen from me. "Can you take me to see her?" I ask.

"I'll do that, but I think you need to rest first. I'm leaving now, but I'll be back later. We can visit her then."

She's right, and I'm too exhausted to even argue.

I follow her to the door, and she turns and hugs me. "I'll see you later."

I close the door and, when I turn around, Ruth is standing

there with tears in her eyes and her arms open wide. I breathe in her strength and let her hold me for a long moment.

"My darling, Avery. I'm so sorry about your parents."

"They were not my parents."

"I know; your sister told me everything. I feel terrible for not seeing what was going on. Who would have thought that they were capable of such terrible things?"

"But Ruth, you must have known, surely. You have been their neighbor for all these years, and you told me you knew Lynn."

"I did know." After staring at me for a moment, she blinks. "Not that you were kidnapped, but I knew you were not Lynn from the start. When I confronted Jodie, she told me you were Harry's daughter from an extramarital affair. She said she had forgiven her husband, and they would raise you together. Following the loss of her daughter, I figured Jodie needed another child to focus on. And you were such a sweet child. It was a pleasure having you around."

"Ruth, why didn't you tell me? You and I were so close." My voice is unsteady and I swallow hard, trying not to cry.

"They made me promise not to tell you that Jodie wasn't your biological mother."

"But where did they say my mother was, the woman who supposedly had an affair with..." I can't call him my father and Harry doesn't sound right either, not yet.

"They said she died years ago, so you were placed in foster care." She shrugs. "Perhaps I should have told you, but it's not in my nature to break promises. And it was none of my business. You understand that, don't you?"

I nod, but my heart is heavy. "I'm sorry they dragged you into this."

"And I'm sorry for what they did to you." Tears roll down her cheeks as she tucks a strand of hair behind my ear.

"It's okay," I say with a heavy sigh. "I feel so terribly betrayed. But justice will now be served."

"And that's fair." Ruth replies. "But you, dear, should stay here for a while, a week or two. After everything you've been through, I'd like to take care of you and Mia."

A few hours later, Liam visits and takes me aside.

My father has confessed to hitting Keith with his car.

CHAPTER 39

THE WATCHER

I pay Keith a visit at least once a week. Today is one of those days. I come to check on him, to make sure he's still asleep.

He's a distraction for Avery, preventing her from being a good mother to Mia, and the longer he's in a coma and alive, the harder it will be for Mia to move on. And he was never the best of dads anyway. I once saw him riding his bike way too fast when Mia was on it with him.

He might be prepared to risk his own life riding around on his own, but he should never be so reckless with his own daughter's safety. Some people don't deserve to have children. Children should be protected at all costs.

As I stand by Keith's bed, I whisper, "Don't wake up."

I know that the chances of him waking up after being in a coma for over a month are slim, but I'm tired of waiting for him to die.

With my lips clenched, I pull out a syringe from my pocket, uncap it, and fill it with air. According to an article I read on the internet, a nurse killed patients by injecting air into their arteries. Who knew that something that carried life-saving oxygen could be so deadly?

I'm about to find out if that's true.

I'm just bending over Keith when I hear someone outside singing, and footsteps approaching his room.

Looking for a place to hide, my eyes dart around the room. At the far end is a closet, so I quickly run to it and sneak inside. Through the crack in the door, I watch a nurse enter and stand by Keith's bedside. The woman sings to him while she checks first the IV bag, then the drainage bag, and she says a few words to him before walking out of the room again, singing softly once more.

I wait a few minutes before coming out of hiding. My palms are wet with sweat, and my heart is pounding in my ears.

I can't do it. Today is not the day, my nerves are too frayed now. I need a few hours to regain my composure before I can try again. Tomorrow, I will be more cautious and vigilant. I will not fail.

CHAPTER 40

AVERY

I tighten my fingers around the stem of the Seeds & Buds bouquet. Our mother's favorite flower is the rose, Georgia told me, so I bought a bouquet of buttercream roses, blue hydrangeas, and eucalyptus leaves. Meadows Hill Hospice has a beautiful and tranquil botanical garden, a long circular driveway, and a paved walkway. I was here for the first time three days ago.

On the gate is a large sign that reads, MEADOWS HILL HOSPICE—LIFE SUPPORT AND COMPASSION. The lobby has a fake fireplace, dark wood floors, and bright walls, and across from the doors is a long counter behind which a woman sits at a computer.

"I'm here for Kathy Campbell," I tell the nurse at the desk. "My name is Avery Watkins."

Upon discovering who I truly am, I considered changing my name, but everyone already knows me as Avery. Besides, a different name would only confuse Mia. Avery is just a name, and doesn't have to be connected to anything.

The nurse reaches for a clipboard on the desk and smiles. Her eyes are naturally squinty and she has deep laugh wrinkles.

"You're her long-lost daughter, aren't you? We haven't met, but I feel like I know you. Kathy hasn't stopped talking about you since your last visit. She is still in room two-two-four; I'm sure she'll be thrilled to see you again. Come with me."

Even though I know where the room is, she gets up and guides me down the stairwell and through a hallway. To keep up with her long, quick strides, I have to jog.

"I'm so glad you were able to find her while she's still with us," she says, turning to me. "Most of our residents are near the end of their lives. In three years of working here, I've seen very few people recover once they've been admitted with an illness."

My stomach twists. I hope she doesn't tell that to all people who visit. Finally, she stops at the door and knocks, then steps away. "Go on in," she says and walks away.

I take a deep breath, turn the knob, and walk inside. The plain room has pale-yellow walls, burnt-orange floors, and white curtains at the window. Wearing a hospital gown and soft, white socks, the woman who gave birth to me lies in the bed pushed against one wall. The bones in my mother's pale face are sharp and her head is shaven. She looks tiny, wasting away from the cancer. A portable oxygen tank is parked next to her bed along with an IV pole and a small table cluttered with miniature containers of medicine.

When she sees me, she smiles and lifts her hand to wave me over. "Cass— Avery?" her voice is scratchy and weak. "You're back?"

"Of course," I say. "I promised I would come back." I step over to the bed and place the flowers on the nightstand. Despite looking so frail, there's a sparkle in her eyes that reminds me of mine when I'm happy.

"Those are beautiful blooms." She beams at me. "Thank you."

I nod and breathe in deeply, feeling as though I'm inhaling all the oxygen in the room. Last time I visited her with Georgia, she barely said a word to me because she was crying so much. Now she extends her hand to me, and I take her thin fingers into mine. She squeezes them softly as a tear rolls down her cheek, and I wipe it away with a tissue from a box on the windowsill.

My mother laughs as she lifts the tissue to her face. "I'm sorry. I do nothing but cry most of the time, which is why my face looks like a dried-up apple. But you can't blame me, can you? The daughter I thought had died was actually stolen." She takes a ragged, deep breath and lets it go. "Now my little girl is here and I'm about to die."

I pull out another tissue from the box, this time for my own tears. I still don't know what to say to her, but it feels right to be here.

"I'm sorry, honeybee," she says. "The day you vanished, I wasn't paying attention because I was reading a letter from your father. He wrote to tell me he wanted a divorce. But that's no excuse. I failed you so badly." She dabs her eyes with the scrunched-up tissue. "Was your life at least enjoyable with those people?" she asks.

Honeybee. So that's where I got it from?

I choke back a sob. My desire is to tell her the truth, that the people who raised me were too focused on their guilt to provide me with everything I needed, but she does not need to hear that. She needs, and wants, to hear something that would ease her own guilt.

"Yeah," I say, thinking about only the happy times, most of them with Ruth. "I was happy."

"Good." She rests her head against the pillow and stares at the ceiling. "But I'm still happy they're going to rot in jail."

The thought of Jodie and Harry behind bars makes my heart ache. I did go and see them, but there really wasn't much to say between us. Maybe I just wanted closure, but I don't feel like I got it.

My phone vibrates, so I take it out of my bag and look at the caller ID. It's the hospital, so I excuse myself and step outside to take the call. I had just been there before I came to Meadows Hill.

"Mrs. Watkins," an unfamiliar voice says. "Your husband has regained consciousness, and he's asking for you. Please come to the ICU."

"But he was still in a coma when I left," I say, breathless, as I press my back against the wall and clutch my chest. "What happened?" I ask, afraid to go there and find they made a mistake.

"I saw him with my own eyes," the person says. "He's talking, breathing on his own, and his vital signs are stable, so we're hopeful. When you get here, the doctor will tell you all about it."

"Okay," I whisper. "I'll be there as soon as I can."

After hanging up, I stare at the phone for a few seconds, trying to digest what the woman just told me. My emotions are mixed, and I'm both excited and terrified.

I am breathless and shaking when I return to my mother's room. Lifting her head a few inches from the pillow, she licks her dry lips. "What's the matter, Avery? Are you all right? Did something terrible happen?"

"I'm so sorry, but I already have to leave you. The hospital called. My husband woke up, and he's asking for me."

"Oh, honeybee," she says. "That's wonderful news. I'm so happy for you."

"I'll come back tomorrow, and I'll bring Mia this time."

"I'll be right here waiting for you," she says. "Go and be with my son-in-law."

In the car, I call Ruth to tell her the good news, and she's just as surprised as I was when I got the news. "Oh Avery, that is just wonderful. You deserve some good fortune after all that you've been through. Call me again when you see him for yourself. I should go back to Mia now."

"Okay." I grip the wheel tighter and smile. "I'll talk to you soon."

"Goodbye, dear," she says.

By the time I reach the hospital, I'm out of breath and even though the August temperatures have cooled down a little, I feel hot. Doctor Drew is waiting for me in the ICU.

"Please tell me he's still awake," I say. I won't be able to handle more disappointment.

Doctor Drew gives me a wide smile. "He's still a bit weak, but he's awake and talking."

The doctor leads me through the ICU, down a hallway, and into a different room, which is a little smaller and not as bright as the others, and it has a private bathroom. My husband is sitting up in bed and looking out the window. I've never seen him look so small and fragile; he's not the big, strong man I know him to be.

Apart from an IV line in his left arm, the tubes that were attached to his body when I left are now disconnected, and the machines that had been beeping have fallen silent. I freeze and blink a few times to make sure I am not hallucinating. He's still bandaged up in places and his face is pale, but his eyes are wide open and he's staring at me.

I approach him slowly and stop at his bedside. "Baby?" I say cautiously.

"Yeah," he says with a weak smile. "Hi there."

My chest swells with joy, and I put my arms around him, my eyes filled with happy tears. I lift my head again and look into his face. "Baby, I'm so glad you're awake. My God, I'm so happy to see your eyes again."

"I'm sorry." His voice still sounds weak and hoarse, but it's clear. "I'm here now."

As I press my cheek against his chest, I wrap my arms around him again. "Just focus on getting better, so you can come back home with me. I missed you so much."

After holding on to each other for a while, I let go and take out my phone. "I promised to call Ruth after I saw you with my own eyes. She'll be so happy you're awake."

"No." He closes his eyes and swallows hard as if saying the word is causing him too much pain. "Ruth... she's the reason I'm here."

CHAPTER 41

"She ran me over," Keith insists. "I saw her."

His words seem to merge into one and press into my chest, into my heart. That's exactly how I feel right now, like my heart is no longer functioning.

"What are you saying, baby? You can't be right."

Over the sound of blood rushing through my ears, I can barely hear my own words. It can't be true.

"She wanted to stop me fro—" He looks at me with blazing eyes. "I'll explain later. Where's Mia?"

"With Ruth," I say, my mouth suddenly very dry. "She's safe with Ruth, I promise. She's not the one who hit you. It was my... my father. He confessed."

Keith starts to shake his head then winces. "He lied. Get Mia away from her. Call the police. Go now."

"Okay, okay." I want to ask him to explain, but I'm not sure that I want to know. I'm sick to my stomach at the idea that Ruth tried to kill Keith. I trust her implicitly.

Leaving the room, I call her, still refusing to believe she did what Keith said she did. I don't understand why she would want to harm him. It makes no sense.

"Hello, Avery," she says when she picks up the phone. She rarely calls me Avery without the name being accompanied by a "dear."

"Hey, Ruth. Are you and Mia okay?" I ask. Hopefully, she can't detect the fear in my voice, which sounds high and strange to my ears.

"We're fine." Her words should reassure me, but something in them is vaguely discordant. "Why do you ask?"

"Just checking." I grab the wrist of the hand holding the phone and squeeze it tight.

"Did Keith wake up?" she asks and when I say nothing, afraid to tell her, she goes silent as well, but I can hear her shallow breathing, faster than usual.

"Ruth... Are you there?"

"Yes." Her voice quavers. "Well, I'm quite busy at the moment. Please tell Keith I'll come to see him later. Give him my love, will you?" Even without me confirming it, she must sense Keith is awake.

"I will. Can you put Mia on the phone, please? I want to hear her voice."

"She's busy right now." The tremor in her voice is replaced by an unfamiliar cold edge that stings me like a hard slap. "We're having a movie day. You can speak to her later. Goodbye."

I squeeze my eyes shut. "Are you sure everything is okay, Ruth? You don't sound yourself. I need to speak to Mia. Keith told me to give her a message."

Panic spurring me on, I start running toward the hospital exit. I nearly collide with a woman who is wheeling herself in front of me, but I catch myself.

The hollow feeling in my gut has expanded, making it difficult to breathe.

"As I said before, dear," Ruth continues, "Mia is busy. So am I. I'll speak to you later."

"Ruth, wait..." I say, but the line is already dead.

The uneasy feeling in my stomach turns into a rock and a cold, prickly sensation crawls up my spine. I try calling Ruth again, but she has switched off her phone. Keith was right. In my gut, I know my daughter is in danger, with the woman I trusted all my life, the woman who was like a mother to me.

When I get into my car, I call Liam and tell him about my conversation with Keith and that Ruth sounded odd when I called her. Liam is overjoyed that Keith is awake, but springs into action when I tell him about Ruth.

"I'm worried about Mia," I say. "Ruth is up to something."

"Okay," Liam says. "I'll get a car and we'll go to the house now. You stay with Keith."

"No, Liam, I need to be with my daughter."

I only just got Keith back, but I know he would want me to go to Mia.

During the drive, I call Georgia since I know she doesn't live too far from the house.

"Avery, I'm not late, am I?" she asks. "I'm on my way. I'll be there in a few minutes."

Ruth and I had invited her to lunch, and I totally forgot.

"Please hurry. Mia is in danger. She's at the house with Ruth."

"What do you mean?"

I quickly tell her what I know.

"Oh my God, you can't be serious." Her voice sounds shrill in my ear. "Okay, I'll probably get there before the police do. I'm only about three minutes away."

The drive to Ruth's house seems to take forever, and I can barely see through the tears that are smearing my vision. I try calling Ruth once again, but her phone is still switched off.

Once I arrive, I find Georgia's silver Honda parked outside the house. Next to the Honda is a police cruiser, with a blue flashing light mounted on top, but nobody is inside. Ruth's car is nowhere to be seen.

When I kill the car engine and get out of the car, my skin turns to gooseflesh and cold fingers run up my spine. Before I can use my own key to enter Ruth's house, Liam opens the door.

"Where's my daughter?" I ask, out of breath. "Is she okay?"

"She's fine, just a bit shaken up."

I don't stay long enough to find out what happened. Instead I run into the living room and burst into tears of relief when I see my little girl sitting in Georgia's lap, hugging Holly to her chest. She's safe and unharmed.

As soon as she sees me, her face lights up and she runs to me. "Mommybee," she yells.

"Oh, my baby," I say, hugging her tight and kissing her face. "Are you hurt?"

"No, Mommy. But Ruth was very mean; she wanted to take me away."

I peer over her head at Georgia, who mouths that she will explain later.

I quickly put cartoons on the TV for Mia, and Liam and Georgia follow me to the kitchen, where we sit at the table and talk in hushed tones.

"Georgia got here before us," Liam says. "Thank goodness for that. Looks like Ruth planned to run away with Mia, and she wouldn't let anyone stop her. But Georgia wasn't about to let her take her, not even when Ruth pulled out a gun."

"I was so sure she was going to shoot me," Georgia adds. "Luckily, when she heard the sirens, she got scared and I succeeded in wrestling Mia from her."

"Where is she now?" I ask, fear gripping my spine.

Liam runs a hand through his hair. "She's driven off, but she can't be far away. A team has been sent to help search for her."

"Georgia, I'm so sorry I put you in danger." I squeeze my

sister's hand with tears in my eyes. "I feel terrible, and I'm so grateful to you."

Georgia shakes her head and blinks away her own tears. "Don't feel bad. I'm just so happy Mia is fine."

"I can't believe Ruth has a gun, and that she was going to kidnap my daughter." I look at Liam and then Georgia, my heart racing. "Why? Why would she do that? And why would she want to kill Keith?"

Georgia clears her throat. "Maybe Ruth was involved in your kidnapping. If that's the case, it makes sense for her to try to shut Keith up, and then to run; otherwise she might end up behind bars like Jodie and Harry. And I think she loved Mia to the point of obsession and just couldn't bear the thought of being separated from her. The other day, when I visited with you, Mia called her grandma, and Ruth looked like she was the happiest person on the planet."

Liam gets to his feet and walks to the door. "I'm going to call the station now to tell them what we know and suspect. I'll also contact the officers on the road to see if they have any information about Ruth's location. She'll be in handcuffs soon enough and we'll get a confession out of her."

As soon as he's gone, I turn to Georgia and hug her. "Thank you so much for coming. I don't know what I would have done if she had taken Mia from me. You saved my daughter."

"I'm so glad I got here in time." She rubs my back. "That woman is deranged. I've never seen anyone act that way before. She was like an animal when she was trying to grab Mia from me."

Georgia looks down at her hand and I notice two parallel scratches on her wrist.

"Did she hurt you?"

"No, it's nothing." She waves her hand. "Scratches go away. There are wounds that take a lifetime to heal, if ever."

She's right about that. If I had lost Mia, I don't think I would ever have recovered from the loss.

In the evening, as I pack our things to leave Ruth's house, I find Keith's journal hidden under a stack of books in one of the cupboards. The most recent entry in the journal was from 25 June, the day before the accident. In the past, Keith's attempts at writing non-rhyming poems made me laugh, and he often wrote them in his journals. But this is an ordinary diary entry and laughing is the last thing I want to do when I read it.

> *She needs to know, but am I ready to break her? But if I don't tell her, that would make me just as bad as they are.*

Back in my own home, I still don't feel safe, and before bed, I stare out the window for ages, my heart hammering as I scan the street for any sign of Ruth.

In half an hour I'll have to leave the house to be with Keith at the hospital while Georgia looks after Mia. I've locked all the doors and windows and checked them twice.

As long as Ruth is out there, I'll live with the fear that she will return to get my daughter. Something tells me that she won't give up that easily.

CHAPTER 42

JODIE: 31 YEARS AGO

In the daytime, Jodie was able to escape the truth of what had happened to her daughter, but at night, it haunted her so badly that she feared falling asleep. Soon, the effects of her dreams followed her into the waking hours, infecting her with the same sorrow she had experienced the day she'd walked into the kitchen and had seen her daughter lying dead on the floor.

She finally accepted the truth, but she couldn't let the girl she brought into their home go. She was brought into her path for a reason. The girl was sent to her and Harry to ease their pain, and they would raise her as their own child.

Ruth, their neighbor, knocked on their door the same day they returned from Wisconsin. She was confused as to why they would leave town for months without saying a word to her, even though they were friends.

"Jodie, I was surprised that you did not even ask me to water your plants as you normally would."

"It was a last-minute decision. We had to go away on an urgent family matter."

Ruth raised an eyebrow. "That took you seven months to resolve?"

When Jodie said nothing, she peered past her shoulders. "Where is the little one? I sure missed seeing her sweet face. I think I saw her out in the garden."

Before Jodie could stop her, Ruth walked through the doors leading into the garden, calling Lynn. Jodie followed and tried to explain to Ruth that, lately, the child preferred to be called by her second name. Ruth stopped and looked back at Jodie.

"Why would she want that? Lynn is such a pretty name."

"So is Avery," Jodie said, her throat tightening. "She has grown and changed so much in the last few months."

Ruth said nothing more as she continued her search for the girl. "Lynn?" she said anyway when she found her.

Avery looked up. She had been playing with the dog, who was licking at the head that had come off her doll's body.

Ruth took a step back, her hand pressed to her chest. "And who are you?" she asked and Jodie's stomach clenched with nerves.

Avery said nothing, but got up and ran into the house.

Ruth turned to Jodie. "Who is that, Jodie?"

Trying to stay calm, Jodie twisted her wedding band around her finger. "That's Lynn... Avery. I apologize for her behavior, but we've been away for so long that she has suddenly become shy around people. It must be a phase. She's also afraid of loud noises, and people getting too close to her. I guess you scared her."

Even though Jodie worked hard every day to make the child feel loved, there were times when she was afraid even of her. She was saddened by it, but she knew it would change with time.

"Well, that's strange." Ruth's expression was a mixture of sadness and confusion. "The girl looks nothing like your daughter. She looks like an entirely different child, if you ask me." She squinted a little. "Are you all right, my dear? You look a little peaked."

"I'm fine. I've just been a little under the weather with a cold, that's all."

Ruth nodded, then tilted her head to the side. "What's the matter, Jodie? You are not yourself. I know we have not seen each other for months, but I still consider you my friend. You can tell me anything."

"Everything is fine." Jodie suddenly felt exhausted. "I'm sorry. I have to go lie down. The journey was exhausting."

She turned and hurried into the house, closing the door behind her. Ruth knew her way out.

Through the window upstairs, Jodie watched her neighbor walk back to her house. A few months ago, she would have been happy at her unexpected visit, but now she was terrified. She couldn't let her come inside again.

Letting out a breath, she went to Avery's room and pulled her onto her lap. "That lady scared you, huh? I know you don't like strangers, and that's good. They can be dangerous, and I want you to stay away from her. You understand?"

Avery looked up at her sullenly, but she nodded and leaned against her.

Jodie smiled and held the child close, rubbing her back. "I love you, Avery. I love you so much."

It was a relief to her that the child no longer threw a tantrum when they called her Avery. After a lot of repetition, she had finally come to accept it as her name. The only problem was, she sometimes still asked for her mother. But it had trickled down to maybe every two days now, and Jodie and Harry continued to tell her that they were her parents. As long as no one interfered, Jodie felt that they would be fine. The girl would learn to love them as much as they loved her.

But sometimes, things don't go as planned.

An hour after Ruth dropped by, she returned, and this time,

she asked to sit down with Jodie, claiming it was important. Jodie wouldn't let her into the house again, so they stayed outside on the porch while Avery was inside the house drawing.

"Are you sure you want to have this talk out here where everyone can hear?" Ruth asked.

After a moment's thought, Jodie led Ruth to the back of the house and they sat down at the table.

"What is it you want to talk about, Ruth?" Jodie asked, getting straight to the point.

"Well... I was hoping you could tell me what's really going on."

Jodie clasped her hands in her lap. "What do you mean?"

"Don't play stupid with me. You know full well what I mean." Ruth leaned forward. "First you disappear with no explanation, then you return without your daughter. And who is that little girl in your house?"

Jodie's heart skipped a beat, but she kept her composure. "As I already said, she's our daughter, of course. Who else would she be?"

"Are you sure about that?" Ruth leaned back again and cleared her throat. "I know you have been gone for a while and that children change as they grow, but there is no way on God's green earth that that girl is Lynn Avery." She pushed her shoulders back. "The other neighbors may be easy to fool since you never really interacted with them, but I've spent a lot of time with your little girl. And I can tell the difference between her and someone else."

"I..." Jodie pressed her lips together and willed herself to stay calm, but inside she felt as if her chest was being crushed. "I don't know what you're talking about, Ruth."

"You're hiding something, Jodie, and I think I know what it is. I think that you and your husband stole that little girl from wherever you disappeared off to. And now, you're trying to pass her off as your own. The thing I can't quite figure out is, where did you leave Lynn? Where is your daughter?"

"She's... She is my child." Jodie could no longer hide the fear in her voice. She began to shake and her eyes filled with tears. "I swear, Ruth, it's her."

"Don't lie to me. That girl has the same dark hair as Lynn, but it's not her. Tell me the truth, for heaven's sake." Her tone had turned menacing. "If you don't, I may be forced to go to the police. If I do, you know what they'll do, don't you? I have half a mind to go over there right now and see what they have to say about it."

Jodie took a deep, shaky breath. "Please, Ruth, don't."

"You have a choice," she said. "You can tell me who that little girl is, and where the real Lynn Avery is, and I won't say anything. Or—"

"Okay. I will tell you, but please give me a moment." She left Ruth standing in the living room and went to tell Avery to go upstairs and draw in her room.

"I'll come up to you in a bit, okay? You can open the new coloring book Daddy bought you."

After the child was safely in her room and the door was closed, Jodie led Ruth into the living room and they sat side by side.

Jodie closed her eyes and bowed her head. "Several years ago, Harry had an affair that resulted in a child. It took me a long time to forgive him, but I eventually did. The child's mother has died, so Harry and I have decided to raise her together, otherwise she will end up back in foster care. I want her to grow up believing that I am her mother."

"I see," Ruth said softly. "But the child has the same second name as your daughter. How can that be?" She grasped Jodie's hand tightly. "That's a rather fascinating story, my dear, but it's not true, is it? You're lying, Jodie. Your hands are sweating, and you're trembling." She let go of Jodie's hand again. "You can either tell me, your friend, the real truth, or you can tell it to the police."

Jodie clasped her hands in her lap and inhaled deeply. "Okay, I will tell you the truth, but I'm begging you not to go to the police. And you can't tell anyone. No one."

Ruth nodded. "Okay. I promise."

Jodie took a deep breath and started talking. "You're right. The girl isn't Harry's daughter." She paused to wipe away a tear. "I found her at the river."

"What do you mean you found her?"

Jodie shrank back in her seat and clutched her hands to her chest. "She was going to drown. If I hadn't pulled her out of the water, she would have." Sobs tore through her so she couldn't continue.

"Dear God." Ruth put a hand on Jodie's shoulder and dropped it again. "That's just terrible. So you brought her home? Where are her parents?" Her eyes suddenly widened, as though a thought just slammed into her. "Please don't tell me it's that child who was believed to have drowned in the Kirkook River." A gasp escaped her. "Dear God, it is, isn't it? No wonder she looked familiar. I've seen her before, on the television. She didn't die. *You* stole her."

"They don't care about her," Jodie said quickly as panic rioted within her. "They let her go alone in the river."

Ruth was quiet for a long time, then she asked in a deeper voice, "Where's your daughter, Jodie?"

Jodie leaned forward, her arms around her cramping stomach now. "Lynn... she's dead. She choked and died."

"Jodie." Ruth covered her mouth with her hand and her eyes began to swim with tears. "What are you talking about? How can she be dead?"

Jodie closed her eyes and told Ruth exactly what had happened, and when she was done, she covered her face with her hands and sobbed even harder. "Please don't let them take her away from me."

Ruth was too shocked to do anything but sit there. It was a while before she spoke again. "So you kidnapped a child."

Jodie lifted her head up and wiped her nose roughly. "I love her like my own. She's doing well here with us. Please, Ruth, I'll do anything if you don't go to the police."

"You're sick," Ruth said absentmindedly. "If anyone finds out about this, you're going to prison."

"No, I can't go to prison. I can't." Jodie got up from the couch, her chest heaving. "You promised me that you won't tell anyone. You said we were friends."

Ruth told Jodie she needed to think about it, and left.

She came back that same evening, her eyes red from grieving for the little girl she'd loved.

"I won't report you to the police, but I need you to do something for me," she said.

"Anything," Jodie said. "Anything you want."

"I want to be a part of that child's life, to be as close as a relative. She will come to visit at least twice a week, and sleep over at least once a week."

Jodie sank onto the couch, too numb to even speak. "But that's—"

"That's all I need in return, Jodie. If you don't agree to it, I will call the police, and tell them everything."

Jodie bowed her head and nodded. When she spoke, her voice was low and broken. "Okay."

And so it started. In the years that followed, Ruth was just as much a part of Avery's life as her fake parents. Avery grew up and forgot the past as she adjusted to her new life, but Jodie's mental health deteriorated as she aged, and Harry turned more and more to drink in order to cope with the death of his daughter and the weight of the secret they kept. But when they were incapable of looking after Avery, Ruth was always there to step in. She even had a room in her home for the little girl, and she copied the Gregors' house keys and came and went as she pleased, frequently taking Avery out without permission.

As Avery grew older, Ruth found subtle ways to drive a wedge between her and her parents so she could be closer to her instead. And she was, so much so that when Avery gave birth to her own child and Ruth asked to be the godmother, Avery was all too happy to oblige. Although Ruth's involvement felt intrusive, there was nothing Jodie or her husband could do about it. Not a single thing.

Jodie and Harry watched as Mia played next door with Ruth. After shooting daggers at their neighbor, Harry growled, "I'm done with that woman. Mia visits her way too often. She should have been brought to us today, not her."

Avery had dropped Mia off at Ruth's after school as she and Keith were going on a date and she planned to pick her up again later. It infuriated Harry and Jodie, but they had no choice but to tolerate it.

Jodie accepted their fate, but Harry struggled to do so, especially after a few drinks. As soon as Mia was born, he fell in love with the child and doted on her when he wasn't drunk. It infuriated him that they were separated from her by Ruth, who seemed to be doing everything in her power to shut them out. More often than not, they sat on the other side of the fence and watched their granddaughter being babysat by their neighbor.

Jodie pulled her legs up onto her chair and wrapped her arms around them. She closed her sore eyes, murmuring, "There's nothing we can do."

"There must be a way to stop this nonsense." Harry waved his bottle of gin in the air as Jodie listened to the liquid sloshing inside. "Don't you see what she's doing? She's brainwashing Mia to try and take her away from us."

Jodie watched her granddaughter go in and out of the garden playhouse Ruth had purchased for her. "She already has."

A glass of water in her hand, Ruth sat on the patio, smiling and laughing as Mia climbed up the steps to her playhouse.

Jodie felt tears prickling behind her eyes, but she refused to let them fall. When Mia glanced their way and waved, she forced a smile and waved back. Then she could no longer take it; she needed her anxiety medication. Standing up, she walked through the garden into the house, took a pill from the bottle, and swallowed it with a mouthful of water. Then she stood by the open kitchen window and watched her grand-daughter.

"I decorated inside, Grandma. Come and look." Mia's voice drifted toward Jodie, her granddaughter's words shaking her to the core.

Had she just called Ruth grandma?

Jodie's pills weren't working fast enough. The dark cloud that lived in her head started to engulf her, and the blackness tried to pull her under. As her breathing became erratic and her face heated, she put her hand on the kitchen counter to steady herself. She struggled to gain control as the walls closed in on her and the tremors worked their way up from her feet, and, as the pain in her chest intensified, her heart started to beat faster and faster. She took a few deep breaths and tried to calm herself down.

Maybe if she closed the door, the sounds would be muffled and she would not be able to hear the little girl calling another woman her grandmother. But as she crossed the kitchen to close the back door, she saw Harry charge toward the fence. She wanted to call for him, to tell him to leave it alone, but it was too late. Still holding his bottle, he was already asking Ruth for a word. Ruth made him wait as she hugged Mia and kissed her on the cheek.

"Go inside now. Play with the new tea set I bought you," she said to Mia, who obeyed immediately.

As she stepped outside, Jodie braced herself for the inevitable argument that was about to ensue between her husband and Ruth. Despite her head swimming, she crossed the garden and stood next to Harry. Ruth had gone too far. Teaching their grandchild to call her grandma had never been part of the deal.

"What's with that look on your face? And on such a beautiful day?" Ruth's tone was light and airy.

As far as Jodie knew, this was the first time Mia had called her grandma, and she was obviously overjoyed.

"What do you think you're doing?" Harry's voice was loaded with so much hatred that it gave even Jodie pause.

Ruth put a hand to her lips. "Oh my. Is that any way to treat a friend? Let alone a close and friendly neighbor."

Harry shot back, "I don't see you or your twisted games as friendly."

Ruth inhaled sharply. "Now, don't be so harsh, Harry. What's the matter with you? Jodie, you need to tell your husband to watch his tone."

As Harry leant over the fence to get closer to Ruth, Jodie said nothing. Keeping his voice low but forceful, he told her his mind. "You have gone too far. How dare you make our granddaughter call you—"

"Grandma?" Ruth gloated, smiling and cocking her head to one side.

Harry stepped closer to her. "I want you to stop playing your insidious games and leave my daughter and granddaughter the hell alone before I do something I'll regret."

In an amused tone, she asked, "And what would that be? Are you going to hit me?"

He continued in a low, slurred growl, sounding more drunk than angry. "You're sick garbage, you know that? Leave my granddaughter alone. You can't replace us, her real family."

Ruth snorted then leaned in. "You are not her family. Are you too intoxicated to remember that?"

"Something's wrong with you," he said as the veins in his neck pushed through the skin. "You need help."

Ruth's smile became a little crooked. "And I think you're a disgusting drunk and you also need help."

She stepped back and crossed her arms over her chest. Her eyes never left Harry's face, and he was the first to look away from her. He started toward the house, his face red and his feet unsteady from the alcohol, but Ruth wasn't done with him yet.

"I've had it with you," she called after him, but he was already halfway across the yard and never heard her say it. She turned to Jodie then. "I think you need to remind your husband of our little agreement, don't you?"

As she walked away, Jodie remained by the fence, holding on to it for support. Through Ruth's low kitchen window, she watched her and Mia having a tea party. Ruth had opened the window as soon as she entered, so their voices were audible.

When the other woman reached for a cup, Mia giggled and said, "Grandma, do you want hot tea or hot chocolate?"

"I'd love some tea." Ruth smiled and patted the child's back. "I'd also like two ginger cookies with it, please." She lifted her head and met Jodie's eyes.

Jodie turned and walked back to the house, where Harry was watching the baseball game on TV, but she knew he was still thinking about the argument with Ruth. She crossed the room and sat next to him, but he didn't look her way. He was so upset that his face was flushed and his breathing was accelerated.

When she touched his arm, he pulled away. "Don't, Jodie. I'm not in the mood to talk about it."

She sighed heavily. "I'm going up to take a nap. I'll see you later."

Jodie lay on her bed and closed her sore eyes, trying to block out the world. She felt herself slipping away as the darkness pulled her in, until everything faded to black.

In the middle of the night, she thought she heard a noise and went to check that the front door was locked.

Then she spotted it, an envelope with Harry's name on the front. Someone must have slipped it under the door. She opened it with trembling fingers. Inside was a single sheet of paper, and a photo of Lynn, their real Lynn Avery sitting on a swing at Rodeo Park with a big smile on her face.

Only four words were written on the note.

You took a life.

Jodie knew that if there was one thing you could say about Ruth, it was that once she set her mind to something, she always got what she wanted.

She would never let Avery or Mia go, and she would not let anyone get in her way.

CHAPTER 44

RUTH: THREE DAYS BEFORE THE ACCIDENT

Ruth slipped her feet into her slippers and stepped out into the garden, stopping at the fence that separated her house from the Gregors'.

She listened.

She could clearly hear Jodie and Harry arguing and throwing accusations at each other, and a smile spread across her face. The note tucked under their door last night was a nice touch. They needed to be taught a lesson.

How dare they? Ruth thought. How dare they threaten to keep her away from her granddaughter? Mia was hers. She had a right to be a part of the child's life after raising her mother singlehandedly.

She cursed under her breath when she thought back on the years when she was a young woman, ready and willing to have a child of her own. She used to be a qualified child welfare social worker, and she would have made a great mother, but she was denied it repeatedly during her short marriage. That was until Avery came along and gave her the chance of a lifetime: a chance at motherhood. She took the job very seriously.

"You killed our daughter," Jodie screamed at her husband.

Ruth stood, her hands clenched into fists as she listened to Jodie's voice rise in volume. Normally, she would have been sympathetic toward a parent who had gone through the loss of a child, but when she found out how the real Lynn Avery had died, she felt no sympathy. She had no doubt in her mind that Harry had been working on his computer while little Lynn ate her lunch and choked on that chicken bone. Due to his obsession with his job, he did not pay attention until it was too late.

As for Jodie, well, she knew what Harry was like and should have been there, and if she couldn't, she should have asked her to babysit the child. But she didn't, and for that, she too was to blame.

From where she stood, Ruth could hear her sobs and, just for a moment, she allowed tears to fill her own eyes. Then she went back inside and put on the kettle for a fresh cup of tea, and she only came out again, an hour later, when she saw Keith riding up to the Gregor house with his bicycle.

It was a good thing he was here. He had intended to bring Mia again the following Saturday, but he'd sent her a message the night before to cancel. She wanted to know why. Ruth hated people canceling on her. She had planned on baking cookies with Mia. Instead of going over to the house, she decided to wait until he was leaving to speak to him. She was always greeted by him when he came by.

But she did hope that Harry and Jodie had pulled themselves together. The last thing they all needed was for Keith to discover their secret and ruin everything. She made her way down the garden and over to the fence again to listen, and she could not hear much at first, but then, after a while, Keith's agitated voice drifted toward her.

"Something strange is going on here," he shouted, "and if you won't tell me what that is, I need to get you help or call the police."

She trembled as her hand touched her throat, and when

Keith finally burst through the back door and into the garden, she knew from the wild look in his eyes that they had told him.

"Hello there, Keith dear," she called after watching him pace for a while. She tried hard not to reveal the panic in her voice. "Are you all right? You look unwell."

That day, Keith, who was usually a polite young man, did not respond. Ruth was shocked because he had always been respectful and well-mannered since Avery introduced him to her, and in her eyes, he was the perfect son-in-law, the kind of man she had hoped Avery would marry.

But today, he did not speak to her. He simply shook his head and turned to walk back to the house, his eyes full of anger and suspicion.

He knows about the kidnapping, Ruth thought to herself when she watched him go.

Now that the truth had been revealed, what was she going to do? She imagined the police showing up and making arrests. She couldn't bear the thought of not seeing Mia again. No, she had worked too long and too hard to let it all slip away. She needed to speak to him.

When Keith showed up again a few days later, Ruth was not about to be ignored again. When her neighbors' front door banged shut, she got up and ran to speak to him before he left.

"Keith, dear," she called as she approached.

Keith did not answer as he pushed his bike toward the street.

She again attempted to stop him by stepping in front of the bicycle. "I wanted to have a word with you about bringing Mia to visit."

Keith stared at her, his eyes cold and blank. "I know, Ruth," he said. "I know Harry and Jodie kidnapped Avery. I also know that even though you knew about it, you kept quiet all this time.

You're all sick." His lips pressed together in an angry, straight line. "Avery trusted you more than her parents. But you betrayed her. She needs to know about this."

"Keith, you can't tell her. You will break that poor girl's heart."

"Maybe, but she deserves to know the truth. So do the police."

Ruth grabbed his wrist. "You can't tell the police. You won't do it."

He pulled his hand free. "That's exactly what I will do, after telling Avery everything."

"Then please keep me out of it," Ruth begged, her voice shaking. "I'm—"

"As guilty as they are," he said. "I never want to see you near Avery or my daughter again." He hopped on his bike and cycled off and Ruth watched him go, her heart beating wildly. She couldn't let Keith destroy everything. Mia could not be raised without her watching over her to make sure she was properly cared for and wouldn't end up like little Lynn, buried under the shade of a willow tree.

Running into her house, she grabbed her car keys and followed him. In the end, she had no choice but to do what was right for her and for her granddaughter.

There was a witness, unfortunately. Jodie had heard her fighting with Keith before driving after him, and the next morning, Ruth received a visit from her.

"I know what you did," Jodie said to her, looking like someone who had just been dragged out of the grave.

But Ruth knew that Jodie would never tell anyone, since Ruth knew her own darkest secret.

The only other person who knew the truth was Keith himself, and she lived every day hoping he would never wake up to tell the world. She didn't want to have to take any other drastic measures.

CHAPTER 45

The day Mia was kidnapped, there was a loud banging on the front door and the shrill of the doorbell woke Ruth from a nap. When she went downstairs, she heard Jodie's voice. She yelled for her to open the door, accusing her of taking Mia.

Ruth wasn't about to engage in conversation with a crazy woman. It was time Jodie accepted the fact that Mia lived with her now. So Ruth went back to her room and Jodie continued her yelling for a while. Eventually, she thought she heard Avery's voice and returned downstairs.

"You're just doing everything you can to hurt me, aren't you?" Jodie snarled when she reappeared on the doorstep. "First the rabbit, then the drawing, now you're hiding my grand-daughter."

Ruth didn't know what she was talking about, but, fortunately, Avery stepped in to defend her. When Jodie changed her tone and asked to talk to Ruth, she was hesitant at first, but she could see in the other woman's eyes that it was important. She led Jodie to the living room and they sat down while Avery waited in the car outside.

"What was all that about?" she asked.

"I'm sorry." Jodie's lips trembled and her skin had no color whatsoever. "I thought it was you."

"That's absurd, and you know it."

"Now I do," she said and leaned in to whisper. "I think I know who took Mia. It must be the new teaching assistant at her school. If she's the one who gave Mia the rabbit and helped her with the drawing, she must know that I took Cassidy those many years ago."

"Oh yes, I remember seeing that rabbit on the news," Ruth said slowly.

"And the picture that Mia drew for me and Harry was of the river and the bridge." Jodie pounded at her chest with her fists and kept looking at the windows as if expecting someone to be looking in. "What if that woman is related to Cassidy?"

Ruth's forehead wrinkled. "I think you're working yourself up over nothing, Jodie. You need to pull yourself together."

Jodie grabbed her arm. "You know I told Keith what happened."

"What you did, you mean?" Ruth pulled her arm away.

Jodie nodded and buried her face in her hands. "He said he'd found the family. What if he met them and he told them who we are?"

"Jodie, you shouldn't have told him." Ruth's voice was sharp. "It was a mistake. But now we need to handle this. Where do you think Mia is?"

Jodie raised her eyes once more. "That's what I'm trying to tell you. I think the teaching assistant took her. I think the picture was a message."

"They said on the news that she had a sister. Do you think it's her?" Ruth asked, her own fear rising.

"My gut tells me she is and that she took Mia to the river, where it all started."

Ruth jumped to her feet. "Then you need to tell Avery right away."

Jodie rose as well and began pacing the room. "But I can't tell her the truth. I can't. Oh my God, what will I do? She will never forgive us."

Ruth grabbed the woman by the shoulders and forced her to look into her eyes. "If that woman is really who you think she is, everything is going to come to light." She released her again. "Avery will be upset when she finds out, but I can help because she trusts me. I will talk to her and make sure she forgives you, but you must do something for me in return."

Jodie nodded and asked, looking desperate, "What?"

"I need Harry to confess to hitting Keith with his car."

Jodie looked at Ruth as if she was crazy. "But he didn't. You did. "

"I did it to help you. Now, your husband is going to say that it was him, that it was fueled by alcohol. If he doesn't, I won't help you get Avery or Mia back. You'll lose them forever." Ruth walked to the door and opened it. "Go out there now, and tell Avery to go get her daughter. The sister will react to her better than to you or Harry, and that will give us sufficient time to sit down with Harry and get our story straight. If Mia's not where you think she is, we can call the police."

Later, as Ruth sat in the kitchen alone with a glass of brandy in her hand, she took a deep breath and thought about the mess she was in. Asking Harry to confess to the hit-and-run was the last thing she wanted to do, but it was the only way to protect herself.

More importantly, it was the only way to make sure she wasn't taken away from Mia. She would do anything to make sure that never happened.

She had a plan for every eventuality.

CHAPTER 46

AVERY

The Lobster Roll has a homey atmosphere similar to a living room. Although the tables are somewhat small, the leather couches and cushioned chairs make up for it and they even have a fireplace, which makes the space particularly cozy during the cold months, as well as a large flatscreen TV for those who want to watch sports. On the first Saturday of each month, they play a movie voted for by their loyal customers. Simply put, the place is like a home away from home.

Celeste is wearing a green silk, slim-fitting dress, and I'm wearing a red, long-sleeved shirt and a black skirt. We're finally celebrating tonight, but not just the success of Opal Touch, which Celeste has finally agreed to co-own with me.

With all the ups and downs I've experienced in the past year, there is plenty to be thankful for. Finding out who I really am and where I come from, even as it hurts, is one of them. Above all, I'm grateful for Mia's safety and Keith's life, and that my biological mother is still alive, despite her ongoing battle with cancer. Putting everything behind me will take some time, but I will do it, one step at a time.

Celeste and I are sitting at a small round table for two with a nice view of a nearby fountain. I lift my glass of water and smile at her. "*Salud* to our success and much more."

Celeste lifts her cosmo. "I'll drink to that, partner," she says over the sound of jazz music playing in hidden speakers. We clink our glasses in a toast just as the waiter sets two long platters of large fire-roasted lobster tails on the table between us. The sight of the meat slathered in chive butter sauce and herb-seasoned salt makes me salivate.

"This is so good," I say as I eat. "It reminds me of the lobsters I had in Maine when Keith and I were there for our honeymoon."

Celeste soaks up some of the melted butter sauce on her plate with a chunk of warm bread. "I'm so glad we came here. This sauce alone is incredible." She pauses and eyes me. "With so many clients walking in and out all the time, we haven't had much time to talk lately. How are you really?"

I stop eating for a moment and gaze out at the fountain, then I slowly exhale. It wasn't only that we didn't have time to sit down and talk, but I was unable for a long time to talk about what happened without going to a dark place and remaining there for days.

"To be very honest," I say, taking a sip of water, "it hasn't been easy. It's extremely depressing and traumatizing to wake up one day and find out that your life has been a lie."

Celeste nods. "Yeah, I can't even imagine, but I bet it's also a relief to finally know the truth."

"You're right. It kind of is. It's good to know why me and my mother—I mean Jodie—were never able to bond. I still can't believe she kidnapped me."

Celeste pops a piece of lobster meat into her mouth and chews. "And for that she deserves to be punished."

I nod and scrunch up my face at her. "I know it's weird, but I kind of feel a little sorry for her."

"Don't look at me like that." Celeste's expression turns serious. "The woman hid your identity, abducted you, and gave you a dead child's name. She should be imprisoned for what she did."

I shrug. "To be honest, I think she'd still be in prison even if she weren't behind bars. Living with the guilt she has for the rest of her life is punishment enough for her." I pause and look down at my food. "I wanted to go and see her."

Celeste's eyes widen. "You what? Why would you want to do that?"

"I don't know. The need for closure maybe? Last time I visited, shortly after they were arrested, I don't feel I got it."

"I understand. So did you go again?" Celeste asks, leaning forward. "And did you get the closure you need?"

"Nope. Apparently, she's not in the state of mind for visitors. She was moved to the psych ward of the prison after telling an inmate she was planning to commit suicide."

Celeste takes a sip of her drink and nods. "How about Harry?"

I dip a lobster piece into my melted butter. "He didn't want to see me."

"I don't blame him. The guilt must be eating him alive too. Anyway, how are you handling all the attention from the press? Every time I turn on the TV, I see a photo of you as a child."

"I'm too busy living my life to pay the press much attention."

"That's good. Have you heard anything about Ruth?"

"Nope. Unfortunately, she still hasn't been found. No one knows where she is. I'm not sure how she managed to disappear without a trace." I pause. "You know what? Let's not talk about those people. We're here to celebrate."

"You're right about that," Celeste says. "How about sharing a glass of champagne with me for once?"

"Not gonna happen. I'll stick with lemonade and water."

Celeste calls for a waitress and gives me a mischievous grin. "The reason for champagne is because I have something of my own to celebrate as well."

"Is that so? And what would that be?" I tilt my head to the side and give her a curious look. "Why do you have that look on your face, like you're up to something?"

"Maybe I am. Donnell and I are engaged." She lifts up her hand and wriggles her fingers to show off a diamond ring. "Isn't it beautiful?"

My eyes widen as I grab her hand and hold it up to my face to get a closer look at the ring. "It's so beautiful. When did this happen?"

"Yesterday evening." Celeste winks. "He picked me up from work, drove me to a beautiful lake and got down on one knee. It was perfect."

Glowing with joy on her behalf, I stand up to embrace her. "I'm so happy for you, and I really can't wait for the wedding."

"Thanks, darling. You do know that you're my maid of honor, right?" she asks when we pull apart.

I laugh out loud. "I didn't, but now that I know, I feel honored. Thank you."

Celeste holds her glass up to mine. "To new beginnings."

Instead of lifting my own glass, I call for the waitress and order the champagne. "I'm making an exception tonight," I say to Celeste with a smile.

When I arrive home, it's almost 11 p.m. and Keith and Mia are already in bed. Before going upstairs, I head to the kitchen for a glass of water to dilute the alcohol in my system. Sipping my water at the table, my eyes are drawn to the bundle of mail in the middle of the table. I pick it up and begin to sort through the envelopes, and there's one that catches my attention. On the front, my name is scrolled in calligraphy. There's no address, so I assume it was hand-delivered.

I go and grab a knife from the drawer to slit it open, and a folded page falls out. It's a handwritten letter on a crisp cream sheet of paper that looks a lot like the one I saw a few months ago, the one with the message: You took a life.

As my eyes scan the words on the page, my breath catches in my throat.

Dear Avery,

I hope you are in good health when you receive this letter.

Now that everything is publicly known, you are probably aware that I knew about your kidnapping. I may have kept Jodie and Harry's secret, but I'm not a monster like they are. Your childhood would have been filled with neglect and abuse if I hadn't taken care of you.

Fate is cruel and robbed me of the chance to have my own children, even if I deserved them more than most. In you, I saw a child I could love and raise as my own.

As soon as you made Mia my goddaughter, I promised to protect and care for her as I had done for you.

It troubles my heart that after everything I have done for both of you, you have robbed me of the ability to see her, especially at this time when she needs me most. You do not deserve that child, not anymore, not now that you have proven to be an unfit mother by allowing her to be kidnapped by your sister. You have fallen short, as your own mother did by failing to pay attention to you at the river, or as Jodie and Harry did by allowing their daughter to die under their care.

Rest assured that this is far from over. I will continue to take my role as a godparent seriously. Someday soon, when you least expect it, I will return to get Mia, and I will not allow anyone to stand in my way.

I write this letter with a heavy heart because I know our relationship has ended, but, despite the fact that you have abandoned me, I will never abandon Mia. She is my priority. I will not rest until she is safe with me.

Sincerely yours,

Ruth

A LETTER FROM L.G. DAVIS

Dear reader,

Thank you so much for taking the time to read *My Husband's Secret*. I hope you enjoyed the story and all the twists and turns it took you on. I'm so grateful for the opportunity to share with you Avery, Mia, and Holly Rabbit's story. I hope it kept you entertained.

If you'd like to keep up to date with all the latest news or find out what I'm working on next, please sign up at the link below. This way, you'll never miss a release. The email address you provide will never be shared, and you can unsubscribe at any time.

www.bookouture.com/l-g-davis

I would also appreciate it if you would consider posting a review. It would be wonderful to hear your thoughts about *My Husband's Secret*, and your feedback would encourage other readers to read it. Thank you in advance for your time.

It's always a pleasure to hear from my readers. If you want to get in touch with me, you can visit my Facebook page, follow me on Twitter or Instagram, or visit my website. Feel free to contact me at any time. I look forward to hearing from you.

Thank you again for turning the pages.

Much love, Liz xxx

KEEP IN TOUCH WITH L.G. DAVIS

www.author-lgdavis.com

 facebook.com/LGDavisBooks

twitter.com/lgdavisauthor

instagram.com/lgdavisauthor

ACKNOWLEDGEMENTS

This book would not have been possible without the support of many people who helped me along the way.

Let me begin by thanking my family and friends, especially my husband, Toye, and our two children, Dara and Simon. Thanks to your encouragement and passion for my writing, I've been able to keep doing what I love. Thank you for the patience, and for keeping the kisses and snacks coming when I had tight deadlines to meet.

Also, I would like to thank Bookouture's entire team who worked so hard to make this book amazing from cover to cover, as well as their help and guidance throughout the publishing process.

Rhianna Louise, my editor, deserves a special thanks. I am so fortunate to have you as my editor and cheerleader. Thanks for your hard work, your great suggestions, and for supporting me during the ups and downs of the writing process.

Lastly, I would like to thank all of the bloggers, reviewers, and readers, who picked up a copy of *My Husband's Secret*, read it, and helped spread the word. I love and appreciate you all so much and I look forward to sharing my next story with you.

Thank you, thank you, thank you.

Printed in Great Britain
by Amazon